Holly Smale is the author of *Geek Girl*, *Model Misfit* and *Picture Perfect*. She was unexpectedly spotted by a top London modelling agency at the age of fifteen and spent the following two years falling over on catwalks, going bright red and breaking things she couldn't afford to replace. By the time Holly had graduated from Bristol University with a BA in English Literature and an MA in Shakespeare she had given up modelling and set herself on the path to becoming a writer.

Geek Girl was the no.1 bestselling young-adult fiction title in the UK in 2013. It was shortlisted for several major awards including the Roald Dahl Funny Prize and the Branford Boase Award, nominated for the Queen of Teen Award and won the Teen and Young Adult category of the Waterstones Children's Book Prize. Holly is currently writing the fifth book in the *Geek Girl* series – *Head Over Heels*.

www.facebook.com/geekgirlseries

*For Mum. Who has given me
so many stories.*

GEEK GIRL

ALL THAT GLITTERS

HOLLY SMALE

HarperCollins *Children's Books*

First published in Great Britain by HarperCollins *Children's Books* 2015
This paperback edition first published in Great Britain by
HarperCollins *Children's Books* in 2015
HarperCollins *Children's Books* is a division of HarperCollins*Publishers* Ltd,
HarperCollins Publishers
1 London Bridge Street
London SE1 9GF

The HarperCollins *Children's Books* website address is: www.harpercollins.co.uk

1

ISBN 978-0-00-796818-3

Printed and bound in England by CPI Group (UK) Ltd, Croydon CR0 4YY

MIX
Paper from
responsible sources
FSC® C007454

FSC™ is a non-profit international organisation established to promote
the responsible management of the world's forests. Products carrying the
FSC label are independently certified to assure consumers that they come
from forests that are managed to meet the social, economic and
ecological needs of present and future generations,
and other controlled sources.

Find out more about HarperCollins and the environment at
www.harpercollins.co.uk/green

glitter [glit-er] verb, noun

1 To sparkle with reflected light
2 To make a brilliant show
3 To be decorated or enhanced by glamour
4 Tiny pieces of shiny ornamentation.

ORIGIN from the Old English *glitenian:* 'To shine; to be distinguished'

I

My name is Harriet Manners, and I am a genius.

I know I'm a genius because I've just looked up the symptoms on the internet and I appear to have almost all of them.

Sociological studies have shown that the hallmarks of extraordinary intelligence include enjoying pointless pursuits, an unusual memory for things nobody else finds interesting and total social ineptitude.

I don't want to sound big-headed, but last night I alphabetised every soup can in the kitchen, taught myself to pick up pencils with my toes and learnt that chickens can see daylight forty-five minutes before humans can.

And people don't tend to like me very much.

So I think I've pretty much nailed this.

Other symptoms of genius I recognise include:

1. Difficulty sleeping
2. Random temper tantrums for no reason at all

3. Messiness
4. General strangeness.

"I'm confused," my father said when I triumphantly showed him my ticked-off list. "Aren't they also the symptoms of being a sixteen-year-old girl?"

"Or a baby," my stepmother added, peering over at the list. "Your sister also appears to fit the list."

Which just goes to show why so many of the intellectual elite are misunderstood. Even our own *parents* don't recognise our brilliance.

Anyway, as the biggest sign of a high IQ is asking lots of questions and I got to the page by googling…

Am I a genius?

…I'm feeling pretty optimistic.

Which is good, because this morning is my first day back at school so I'm going to need all the extra brain-power I can get.

That's right, I am now an official sixth former.

By my calculations I have spent exactly eleven years of my life at school so far: 2,145 taught days, or approximately 17,160 hours (not including homework or the free tests I downloaded to take on holiday).

In short, I have invested *over a million minutes in education* in preparation for this precise moment. The day when all my carefully collected knowledge will be valued and appreciated, instead of just irritating people.

Finally, school is getting serious.

Gone are the homework-haters and eye-rollers, and – thanks to an influx of new students from other schools – in their place are people who really *want* to learn. People desperate to know that gerbils can smell adrenaline and a caterpillar has twelve eyes, or that there's enough carbon in your body to make 900 pencils.

People just like me.

And I couldn't be more excited.

As of today, I have five A levels to study, two universities to introduce myself to early and a bright career in palaeontology to begin pursuing in earnest. I have statistics to analyse and frogs to dissect and thigh exercises to start so I don't get cramp when I'm brushing soil away from dinosaur fossils in the not-so-distant future.

I have brand-new, like-minded friends to make.

It might be the same school with a lot of the same people, but things are about to change. After eleven years of scraping insults off my belongings and retrieving my shoes from the cisterns of toilets, this is my chance to start all over again. A new beginning.

A chance to shine.

This time, everything will be different.

Luckily, one of the really *great* things about being a genius is that it's easy to multitask.

So this morning I decide to make the most of it.

I learn that there are forty different muscles in a bird wing while I'm getting out of bed.

I discover that a sea urchin can walk on its teeth while I'm combing my hair, and that parasites make up 0.01 per cent of our body weight while I'm brushing my teeth.

Clothes, socks and shoes are all picked out and donned as I fully absorb the fact that a snake smells with its tongue and hears with its jaw. I study the names of British kings and queens as I run down the stairs, and by the time I reach the kitchen I'm on to Secret Service code names (Prince Charles is "Unicorn", which is a shame because I was hoping one day they'd use that one for me).

"Did you know," I say as I lean down to kiss Tabitha on her little round cheek, "that the average person will eat 500 chickens and 13,000 eggs in a lifetime?"

My baby sister clearly didn't, because she gurgles happily at this new and unprecedented information. Then

I reach over her fluffy head to grab a hard-boiled version of the latter listed from the table.

"Harriet," my stepmother says.

"And we'll each eat thirty-six pigs," I continue as I start peeling the egg with one hand. "And thirty-six sheep."

"Harriet."

"And eight cows."

"Harriet."

"And 10,000 chocolate bars." I pause with the egg halfway to my mouth. "I think I may have eaten my rations for that already, though. Maybe I should become a vegetarian to balance it back out."

A hand lands on my arm.

"Good morning, Annabel. How did you sleep? I'm fine, thank you. Isn't it a beautiful day today? Thanks for making me breakfast, even though I am now leaving bits of shell all over the kitchen floor for you to clean up."

I blink at my stepmother a few times, then at Dad. I've lived with Annabel since I was five, yet sometimes she is still a total mystery to me.

"Why is Annabel talking to herself?"

"She's an alien unsuccessfully trying to fit in with the rest of the human race," Dad says knowingly, dipping a bit of toast in egg yolk and then dripping it on the table. "Is there anything in your book to help us figure out what she wants with us poor earthlings before she sucks our brains out with her tentacles?"

I start flicking eagerly through the chunky tome in my hand. There are 729 pages and I'm only 13/20ths of the way through, so there's almost definitely some kind of precedent.

Or at the very least something interesting about spaceships.

"Sadly, all signs suggest that your brain is already gone, Richard," Annabel says grimly. "So I'm probably going to starve."

Then she pulls a chair out and gestures at it.

"Put your fact book down, Harriet, and have some breakfast. I start back at work tomorrow morning and none of us have heard a sensible word out of you for the last twenty-four hours."

I don't know what my stepmother is talking about. Every single sentence I've said has been scientifically and historically accurate. There's a bibliography proving it in the back.

I shove a piece of toast into my mouth.

"Can't," I say through a spray of buttered carbohydrates. "No time. Things to learn, places to go, kindred spirits to meet."

Quickly, I stomp into the hallway and grab my satchel

from the corner whilst simultaneously discovering that in 1830, King Louis XIX ruled France for just twenty minutes.

"Look how awesome she is," Dad says proudly as I open the front door. "That's my daughter, Annabel. My genetics, right there. Harriet Manners: model and style icon. Fashion legend. Sartorial maverick extraordinaire."

I stick one ear of my headphones in.

"Harriet," Annabel says. "Hang on a second. Where are you going?"

I'm not entirely sure how I'll use the Louis XIX information, by the way. Not everything I read is potentially useful or relevant, even to me.

"School!" I put the other ear in. Tchaikovsky's *Swan Lake* starts blaring out at full volume. "See you this evening!"

And my first day as a proper sixth former begins.

2

So, I've done a little studying on the art of making new friends and I'm happy to report that there appear to be a few basic rules for us all to follow.

I have boiled it down to: find things in common, smile and laugh lots (this indicates a sunny and welcoming personality), ask questions, remember details and never wear the same outfit as them without asking first.

Which sounds deceptively easy.

Over the last sixteen years I've successfully made just four friends: my stalker classmate, Toby Pilgrim; my dog, Hugo; a Japanese model called Rin (who would happily befriend a sausage); and my Best Friend Nat, who I met when I was five and literally couldn't have less in common with if I tried.

So I think it's fair to say I need all the advice I can get.

The way I see it, the fact book in my hand isn't just fascinating trivia, relevant to the trials and tribulations of daily living (which it also is). It's a *bridge* between me and

14

other people. With these scientifically proven nuggets of information, I'll be able to find things in common with *everyone*.

Oh, you like tennis? Well, did you know that the longest ever match lasted eleven hours? You're a big fan of keeping fit? The most push-ups ever performed in one day was 46,001!

Have a cat? Cats kill more than 275 million creatures a year in the UK alone!

It doesn't matter whether it's film or sport or songs or animals or a fondness for fizzy drinks (they dissolve teeth!): somehow, I'll be able to find a connection. A link between me and them. Something to pull us together.

All friendship requires is focus and dedication.

And a little bit of knowledge.

I learn all about crocodiles as I wander down the road to school and past the bench where Nat usually meets me (except now she's at fashion college on the other side of town).

Caterpillars get a brief look-over as I quickly glance around for Toby – there's no sign of him – and pull my phone out of my pocket to check for texts from my modelling agent, Stephanie (as per usual, absolutely zero – my fashion career appears to have fallen into some kind of coma).

US presidents fill in the gap as I clumsily open and walk through the school gates.

The world's largest lakes occupy my opening of the stiff front door and stroll down the silent corridor into my empty classroom.

Then I take a seat, turn to a page about the London Underground, and wait.

I've specifically chosen to get to school early today so I have plenty of time to adjust before my new form arrives. Thanks to Dad's job at the time, I was living in America for the first few weeks of term – being tortured by a tutor who turned out to be a fake, and fainting on fairground fashion shoots – so I really need the extra time. This way I can acclimatise to my new environment, cram some last-minute knowledge in and maybe stop my stomach from rolling over and over like a sick guppy while I'm at it.

Nervously, I clutch my book as tightly as I can.

Focus, Harriet.

The London Underground is the world's first underground transport system. It has a network of 402 kilometres, carries 1,265 billion people a year and is actually more overground than it is undergr—

"Harriet Manners?"

I swallow. This is it. This is where my new beginning

starts. *Be cool, Harriet. Be casual. Be as full of relevant yet breezy information as physically possible.*

With a deep breath, I plaster on my biggest and friendliest smile and put my book down.

"Good morning," I say in my brightest voice. "It's super nice to meet y—"

Then I stop.

Because standing in front of me is a group of what appear to be fully grown adults, holding clipboards and pens.

And every single one of them is staring at me.

3

For the first few seconds, I assume my classmates have just aged quite a lot over the summer holidays.

That's how weird teachers look in casual clothes.

Then – like the Magic Eye picture of a galloping horse Dad has stuck in the garage – strange colours and shapes slowly start to make sense.

Mr Collins from biology in high-waisted jeans and a green polo-neck jumper. Drama teacher Miss Hammond in a beige jumper, tie-dye pink skirt and woolly lilac socks. Receptionist Mrs O'Connor – devoured by an enormous yellow jumper that says DEFINE 'NORMAL'!!! – and my English teacher Mr Bott in his standard black suit, white shirt and thin black tie, like a magician on his way to a funeral.

I blink as the entire school staff gradually crowds in from the corridor so they can stare at me curiously, the way little children gather around a pink-bottomed rhesus monkey at the zoo.

Any minute now, somebody's going to throw me a banana and ask me to dance.

You know what?

I'm so confused right now, I might just go ahead and do it.

Finally Mr Bott takes his pen out of his mouth. "Would you like to explain what you're doing here, Miss Manners?"

"Umm." I look back at my book in bewilderment. "I'm studying, sir."

"That's as maybe. But the school is closed for teacher training today. You're not supposed to be here."

And – just like that – I suddenly see my morning all over again. The empty roads. The blank phone. The closed school gates. The wedged-shut front door, silent corridors and empty seats.

The fact that Toby wasn't following three steps behind me for the first time in known history.

Annabel's confusion as I left the house.

Oh my God.

There's a special kind of reef fish called the *Enneapterygius pusillus* that glows with a bright red light in order to communicate with the fish around it. From the heat in my cheeks right now, it feels like I'm attempting it too.

Every other student on the planet is trying to get out of school. I'm the only one who accidentally breaks *in*.

I stand up quickly. *Think, Harriet.*

"I was just, umm…" *What?* "Bringing a gift for you all. For the… errr… teachers. To wish you luck. With… the training."

Then I hold out the stupid *Big Book of Trivia for the Loo* that got me into this mess in the first place. In fairness to the authors, the warning was in the title. I probably should have left it there.

Miss Hammond beams and takes it off me. "That's so sweet of you, Harriet! How thoughtful! And *what* a spectacular outfit you've chosen for today," she adds brightly. "You've really harnessed your inner rainbow."

I look down and my cheeks promptly go supernova.

Thanks to getting dressed while reading, I'm apparently wearing a yellow T-shirt, a red jumper featuring a Christmas pudding – in October – a pair of pink pyjama bottoms with blue sheep all over them and the bright purple knee socks Nat bought me "as a joke", slouched down around my ankles.

On one foot is a green trainer.

On the other is a blue one.

My daughter. Model and style icon. Fashion legend. Sartorial maverick extraordinaire.

Maybe I'm not such a genius after all.

4

Anyway.

While I'm stuffing my mismatched shoes in my satchel and shuffling home in my not-a-whole-lot-better socks, I may as well update you on what's been happening since I returned from New York, right?

That's what you want to know.

Exactly what I've been doing with myself since I split up with Nick Hidaka – Lion Boy, ex-supermodel and love of my life – on Brooklyn Bridge just over three weeks ago, and flew home without him.

So here it is:

Nothing.

Not literally, obviously, or I'd be dead.

Over the last three weeks I have breathed approximately 466,662 times and processed 4,200 litres of blood with my kidneys. I have produced thirty-seven litres of saliva

and 9,450 litres of carbon dioxide.

I've had eighteen showers, four baths, brushed my teeth forty-two times, eaten sixty-seven meals and consumed more chocolate bars than I can be bothered to count (and that's really saying something).

But that's about it.

Other than basic survival – and packing up the house in Greenway while we waited two weeks for our flight back to England – almost the only thing I've done voluntarily is read. With my curtains shut and my bedroom door closed, I've devoured words like never before: buried myself in books and submerged myself in stories.

I've read during breakfast and lunch and dinner; until the sun's come up and gone down and come up again.

And not just fact books.

I've fought dragons, attended balls and chased a whale. I've won wars, lost court cases, travelled India, ridden broomsticks and stranded myself on numerous islands.

I've died a dozen times.

Because here's the thing about a book: when you pick up a story, you put down your own.

For a few precious moments, you become somebody else. Their memories become your memories; your thoughts turn into theirs. Until, page by page, line by line, you disappear completely.

So until today – until my new beginning – that's exactly what I've done.

Because I thought maybe if I could just bury myself deep enough, for long enough, I could shut the world out and myself out with it.

And then I wouldn't have to think about how the last time I saw Nick is the last time I'll see him, and the last time I kissed him is the last time I'll kiss him. About how life keeps going on as it always has.

Or how my heart can beat 100,000 times a day.

Even when it's broken.

5

Unfortunately, vanishing has its side effects.

And – as I quietly turn on to the path leading back up to my house – I can see two of them: standing on my front door step.

Without a sound, I quickly dive into a nearby bush.

Maybe there are advantages to walking around in your bare socks after all.

"Are you *sure*?" Nat is saying, shifting from one foot to the other. Her dark hair is curly, and hanging down her back like well-behaved snakes. "You're *certain* Harriet's not here?"

"I'm definite," Annabel confirms gently. "Unless she's scaled the outside wall and re-entered through her bedroom window, but given Harriet's inherent fear of PE it seems unlikely."

That's putting it mildly. Frankly, there's more chance of me growing wings and flying back in.

"It's actually easier than it looks," Toby says cheerfully.

Even from a few metres behind I can read the orange letters on the back of his T-shirt: VOTED MOST LIKELY TO TRAVEL BACK IN TIME, CLASS OF 2057.

"If you take the first flowerpot on the left there's a little toe-hole in the wall just above it, and then you can use the ivy trellis as leverage the rest of the way." He pauses. "You should probably reassess your exterior plant framework, Mrs Manners. It's not very security-conscious."

The corner of Annabel's mouth twitches. "Oh, I'd imagine we will now."

"If you want, next time I'm up there I'll stick a little warning note on the outside of the window telling all other stalkers to go away."

My stepmother laughs because she obviously assumes that Toby is joking.

I, however, know better.

I am literally never opening my bedroom curtains again.

"*Focus*, Pilgrim," Nat says crossly, leaning to the side and poking his arm. "What kind of rubbish stalker are you, anyway? You don't even know where Harriet *is*."

"In fairness, my concentration has been a little distracted with an exorbitant level of homework, and also the TARDIS I've been building in my garden."

Toby holds out bright blue fingers as evidence.

Nat stares at him for a few seconds in disgust. "What *is* your problem?"

"I'm glad you asked," Toby says happily. "I'm struggling to make it look as if it has truly travelled through time and space. Any suggestions?"

There's a silence, then my best friend sighs and turns back to Annabel. "I haven't seen or heard from Harriet *all weekend*. She's not picking up calls, she's not answering texts and she didn't remind me seven times about the parrot documentary on telly. I really need to talk to her."

"She's just jet-lagged, sweetheart. It takes a little while to settle back into a new time zone, that's all."

"And you don't know where I can find her?"

There's a tiny pause. "I don't, I'm sorry."

"Right." Nat's shoulders slump slightly. "Well." She looks sharply up at my bedroom window, and then kicks the front doorstep a couple of times. We've been home six days and my best friend is not an idiot: we're five hours ahead of New York, not in a different solar system. "I have to go to college. Will you tell her I called again?"

"Of course." Annabel nods and looks at Toby. "And I'll tell her you popped by too."

"You don't need to," he says proudly. "She'll know. I've left one of my new calling cards." He points to the wall and there's a little round, bright green dot stuck there. "It says TPWH™, which stands for Toby Pilgrim Was Here, Trademarked."

"I'm impressed," Annabel smiles. "Very organised and efficient."

Literally nothing fazes her. She's like Gandalf but less beardy.

Nat glances at my bedroom window again.

She kicks the doorstep a few more times.

Then, with an audible exhalation, my best friend swirls round and stomps back down the garden path in bright silver shoes.

With my stalker trailing after her.

6

I watch Nat leave with a guilty twist of my stomach.

Then I wait as long as I can.

I am invisible. I am undetectable. I am a ninja of imperceptibility, as hidden as a leafy sea dragon, elaborately constructed to blend into my surroundings, and—

"You can come out now, Harriet."

Oh. So – maybe not.

Slowly, I creep out from inside the bush and brush dried mud and dead leaves off my pyjama bottoms.

"You know," Annabel says, gently removing a small spider from my eyebrow. Apparently I'm even more camouflaged than I intended to be. "I'm not enjoying all this subterfuge very much, Harriet. It's much more your father's style."

"I know," I say awkwardly. "Thanks for lying again."

In Greek and Roman mythology there's a three-headed dog called Cerberus who guards the entrance of the

29

underworld to prevent the dead from escaping and the living from entering.

For the last few days, that's exactly what my stepmother has been doing for me.

On cue, my phone beeps three times in quick succession:

When one door of happiness closes, another one opens! :) xx

A break-up is like a broken mirror. It is better to leave it broken than to hurt yourself trying to fix it! :) xx

If you walk away and they don't follow, keep walking. :) xx

And this is exactly why I'm avoiding Nat.

Ever since I returned from America, it's been like having my own personal therapist crossed with a woodpecker. What exactly happened? *Peck.* What did Nick say? *Peck.* Do I miss him? *Peck.* Was it definitely the right decision? *Peck peck.* Can't we make it work? Has he been in contact? How do I *feel*?

Peck peck peck peck until the tree falls over.

And it doesn't matter how many times I tell her I

don't want to talk about it, Nat has decided that we are heartbroken and she's committed to working through it.

Together.

Incessantly, over and over and over again.

Without a single moment's peace, and with the help of quite a lot of fridge magnets, motivational T-shirts and quotes off the internet.

Never mind picking the lock: my best friend is trying to smash me open with a sledgehammer.

I take a deep breath and type:

Very wise! Speak soon! :) x

Then I put my phone back in my pocket and glance desperately over Annabel's shoulder at the house. I've got the works of Terry Pratchett waiting on my bedside table. If I take two stairs at a time, I can be balanced on the back of four elephants and a giant turtle within thirty-five seconds.

I love Nat.

She's my best friend: the person who knows me inside and out, who can finish my sentences when I don't even know what it is I want to say yet. But – as a magnet might tell me – I can't start the next chapter of my life if I keep re-reading the old ones.

I just want a new story, that's all.

"Harriet?" Annabel says as I start racing desperately towards my next escape.

I turn round blankly. "Hmm?"

"You don't need to shut us all out, sweetheart. Me, your dad. Natalie. You can talk to us about it."

"Sure," I say, and then start heading back to my bedroom.

Because for the first time ever, that's exactly the problem.

Maybe I don't want to.

7

So, my plan for the next morning is as follows:

1. Try not to notice Toby crouched behind a nearby pot plant outside my house.

2. Or standing behind a tree.

3. Or lying on the grass, pretending to be part of the foliage.

4. Tell Toby that he may be my self-confessed stalker turned-comrade, but now we're sixth formers he really needs to find another hobby because his obsession with me is getting a bit embarrassing.

5. Walk to school, paying close attention to any sign that may say SCHOOL CLOSED FOR TRAINING on the way.

33

6. Make brand-new friends.

7. Have a brilliant and thoroughly educational day.

Admittedly, the last point on the list is a bit vague, but I'm leaving it up to the teachers.

That is what they're paid for, after all.

The way I see it, yesterday was just a dress rehearsal: one that went spectacularly badly. Statistically, a first impression is usually cemented in seven seconds (although obviously I've disappointed people far more quickly than that).

This time, I'm not taking any chances.

At 8am, I stand on the doorstep and double-check my carefully selected outfit. A quick study of the psychology of colours has established that white clothes make strangers think you're honest, yellow clothes make them think you're friendly and orange implies that you're a whole lot of spontaneous fun.

So I'm wearing a white jumper, orange leggings and yellow pumps. Hopefully this will silently represent an excellent personality before I've said a word.

It may even be powerful enough to make me appealing *after* I've said some too.

Then I roll my eyes at the enormous rustling purple

hydrangea to my right. "Come on, Tobes. We're friends now. Why don't you just walk to school *with* me instead of hiding in bushes?"

There's another rustle and a small squeak. Then Annabel's cat, Victor, struts out from behind the pot with a piercing expression that says: *I'm not going anywhere with you, weirdo.*

Flushing slightly as a neighbour gives me the kind of glance you give to people who talk to plants, I decide to go ahead and just start walking to school on my own.

"Tobes," I say with a small smile when I reach the tree at the bottom of my road, "you're not being very subtle. I can totally see you…"

A squirrel runs out.

"Toby…" I say as a jogger runs past.

"Tob—" I start again, but it's just a leaf skittering along the ground.

With growing confusion, I continue walking: past the bench Toby isn't crouching behind, in front of the lamp-post Toby isn't pretending to fix with a small screwdriver, past the old man with a big newspaper held up to his face.

"Sorry," I say after I've pulled it down and shouted "Ha! Gotcha!"

"Girls these days," the man snorts angrily, burying

himself in it again. Which is really unfair: I'm pretty sure I'd have done that if I was a boy too.

By the time I approach the road to school and – somewhat reassuringly – spot a group of students in school uniform, I'm starting to feel a little off-centre. I hadn't realised quite how much of my day is constructed around various degrees of pretending to be irritated with Toby.

Finally, I spot him: crouched on the floor next to the front school gates in a pale brown T-shirt with little flecks all over it. He's obviously pretending to be a boulder. Or a huge tortoise. Or something else that would never, ever be found outside a British school in a million years.

"Toby," I say with a huge wave of relief. "There you are. I really don't think you need to—"

"Hello, Harriet!" he says, redoing a shoe and standing up. His pale sideburns are fluffy and sticking out, and I realise he must have grown another four centimetres over the summer: he's starting to look like a lightning bolt. "Did you know that Velcro was inspired by the tiny hooks on a burr that stuck to the inventor's dog? I prefer it to laces, even if evidence of string *does* date back 28,000 years."

I beam at him.

That is *exactly* what I needed to make me feel

grounded and secure this morning. A fascinating, shoe-based historical fact, guest-featuring dogs.

"That's interesting, becau—" I start enthusiastically, but I don't get any further because Toby sticks two thumbs up and starts powering towards the school gates, slightly-too-short trousers flapping around his ankles.

"See you later, Harriet!" he calls over his shoulder.

"But," I stutter in amazement, "w-wait, Toby. Don't we have class together? Shouldn't we… go in at the same time?"

Or – you know – with him ten paces behind me.

It's kind of a tradition.

"We're in different forms now, Harriet!" Toby says cheerfully. "Plus I have a super important project to get on with before class starts. Have a great day!"

And my stalker disappears into school.

Leaving me following ten paces behind him.

8

It's amazing what a difference a day can make.

Or – you know.

An open and functioning school you don't have to break into.

As I push through the glass sixth-form doors, I can feel a terrified, nervous hopping sensation starting at the bottom of my stomach. It takes fifty hours for a snake to fully digest a frog, and for part of that time the frog is still alive. Given the feeling in my stomach, I'm starting to wonder if I've accidentally swallowed one too.

Everything has changed.

There is now noise and chaos everywhere. Classrooms and corridors are filled with people: giggling, laughing, shouting, singing. Chair legs are being scraped on the floor, various items are flying through the air – rubbers, crumpled-up notes, packets of crisps – and there's a faint smell of board-marker and furniture polish that's halfway between a cleaning cupboard and a sofa shop.

38

People I don't recognise are stomping up and down the stairs proprietorially, and students I do know have transformed completely. Braces are off, long hair has been chopped, short hair grown and extended. Acne has erupted or disappeared. A few tentative moustaches have sprouted like shadowy upper lip infections. Everything that was banned last term is scattered defiantly: heels, short skirts, piercings, lipsticks, shaved heads. All worn with pride and triumphant chins.

It's the same school, yet – somehow – not at all.

Sixth form has been open just four weeks and it already feels like everyone has made this world their own. Now it's my turn.

With another froggy stomach hop, I reach the door of my new classroom and stand outside on one foot for a few seconds, peeking through the window.

Then I anxiously pull out my phone.

Really wish you were here. Hx

I press SEND and wait a few seconds.

There's a beep.

Me too. Raid the vending machine for me. ;) Nat x

I smile – I was obviously going to do that anyway – and take a deep breath.

You can do this, Harriet. You are a goddess of insight and possibilities; a warrior of chance and fate. A goldfish of optimism and opportunity.

Oh God. My brain is shutting down already.

Then, with all the courage I can muster, I hold my breath, square my shoulders and lift my chin high.

And push into my brand-new world.

9

The really great thing about having the head of drama as my new form teacher this year is – thanks to my role in last year's production of *Hamlet* – I already know her.

The not so great thing?

She already knows me.

"Harriet Manners!" Miss Hammond looks up from her desk so enthusiastically that the beaded fringe on her tie-dye scarf gets caught on a pencil pot. "You've returned to us for the second time! How utterly wonderful!"

Oh, *sugar cookies.* I really hope she's not going to bring out the book I gave her. I don't want my first introduction to the class to involve the word *loo.*

"*You guys*," she continues chirpily, waving a hand around. There are so many bracelets, she sounds like an enormous Slinky. "For those who haven't had the pleasure of meeting her before, Harriet Manners has veritably *boomeranged* back after a glamorous adventure in Nooooo Yaawwwk!"

41

I flush a little bit harder.

"Apparently Americans eat more bananas than any other fruit," I blurt anxiously. "And twenty-five per cent of them think the sun orbits the earth."

Oh my God. What is wrong with me?

"Which isn't why I came back," I add quickly, the back of my neck starting to prickle. "I like bananas."

I like bananas.

Yup. There are over a million words in the English language, and I chose those three in that particular order to impress a group of strangers.

I am never reading a fact book again.

The students in the class murmur "Hey, Harriet" while they try to make sense of me too.

"Why don't you plop yourself down there?" Miss Hammond says, pointing to a free seat. "We're doing a team-building exercise first thing, so it's perfect timing! You're going to fit back in like a kitten in a straw basket full of other kittens. I can tell already."

Still blushing, I walk cautiously to the corner of the class and place my satchel on the floor. Then – trying not to notice the thirty-two eyes still following me – I take out my new folders: three colours with dividers for easier organisation.

Followed by my new school diary and a set of biros.

Five pencils, an eraser, three highlighters, glue, a hole punch, ruler and Post-its. A tape-dispenser and compass. A calculator and protractor.

A full, rainbow-hued box of felt-tip pens. A traditional fountain-pen.

With little ink-pot.

Finally, I add a couple of shiny blank notepads with pictures of dinosaurs all over the front.

What? I just really like being prepared, that's all.

When it's all laid out neatly and at perfect right angles on my desk I feel much calmer again, so I fold my hands tightly on my lap and survey the slowly expanding class with a growing sense of excitement.

I vaguely know some of them already.

The two leads from the play last year are on opposite sides of the classroom: Christopher (Hamlet), sullen and still wearing a black polo-neck, and pretty Raya (Ophelia, obviously) with a glossy black ponytail, camel-like eyelashes and permanently pouted lips. I also recognise Eric, the school football captain, now slightly pirate-like with a shaved head and a gold hoop earring, and my old classmate Robert, who has apparently developed an interest in hair gel – the front of his hair looks like if he ran fast with his head down he could probably kill somebody with it.

Two of Alexa's key minions – Liv and Ananya – are seated together at the back: one with pale skin and a bleached white top-knot, the other with dark skin and a large, black high-bun. They're wearing the same floral onesies in contrasting colours and are united by identical, intensely bored expressions.

But much *more* excitingly, there are also at least a handful of faces I don't recognise at all.

Which one of these is going to be my new kindred spirit?

The girl with pink glasses? She looks like she's on first-name terms with her optometrist too. The girl with neon purple hair and a rainbow-coloured nose ring? I'm a big fan of bright colours too. How about the boy with freckles and a red bag? I, too, have freckles and a—

OK, I think I might just be clutching at similarity straws now.

Finally, almost every chair but the one next to me is taken.

"Oh, *shoot a hamster*," Miss Hammond says, slapping her head lightly with her wrist. "What a twit I am! I left the register in the staffroom." She stands up and jingles a few times. "Back in two ticks, peeps."

And – in a whirlwind of orange and pink – our form teacher disappears into the corridor.

The room immediately starts bubbling with noise again, and I cautiously start staring hard at individuals and then giving them my brightest, friendliest smile. The kind that says *I can't wait to ask you questions and then remember the details!*

A few of them actually smile back.

You know what? I like sixth form already. People are glancing at me, but it doesn't feel hostile.

It feels curious; quizzical and interested.

I can feel my entire body starting to relax.

I was so right: this was *exactly* what I needed. A fresh start. A new beginning. The closure of an old page, and the opening of a new one. The unfolding of a different story.

Except it isn't.

Because, just as I'm congratulating myself on making such an excellent – albeit fruit-enthused – first impression, the classroom door opens again. And in walks the Captain Hook to my Peter Pan; the Voldemort to my Potter.

The Cruella De Vil to my hundred spotted puppies.

Alexa.

10

II

No no no *no no no*.

12

No NO NO NO NO NO NO NO NO NONONONONONO NONONONONONONONONONONONONONONONONONO NONO.

13

If you yelled for one year, seven months and twenty-six days, you would produce enough sound energy to heat one cup of tea. Hook up my brain right now and I should be able to boil ten in three seconds flat.

This can't be happening. It *can't* be.

Alexa isn't doing any of the same subjects as me. She has a totally different schedule: English, History, Geography. I was *sure* she had a different form room. I rang and checked with Mrs O'Connor to confirm that I'd been moved to another class, just in case.

And emailed. Five times. With a supporting text.

I thought I was finally *free*.

With a flick of the grown-out blonde hair which Nat chopped off for being horrible to me nearly a year ago now, Alexa strolls into the room and looks at us through heavily lined eyes.

"*Hi,*" she says with a small cat-smile.

"How *are* you all today?"

She's the only person I know who can make a general greeting sound like a specific death threat.

"Lexi! Over here!" Ananya sits up straighter and sticks a hand in the air. "Thank God you're here: this class is *so boring.*"

"Ohwowowow," Liv squeaks, bopping up and down in her seat, "areyoukiddingLexiyoulook*amazing*todayIlove yourskirtI'vetotallygotonejustlikeitexceptit'sredanda differentlengthandshapebutit'sprettymuch*identical*."

When an elephant lies down it only needs to breathe four times a minute. Every time Liv gets excited, I can't help wondering if she has a similar lung capacity.

Alexa ignores them and swivels to look in my direction.

I'm not kidding: her entire face has just lit up. As if she's six, it's Christmas morning and I'm a solid gold bike somebody's left under the tree.

The frog in my stomach has suddenly gone very still.

"Do you mind if I take this seat?" she says, sashaying towards me in sharp-heeled black boots: the kind you can skewer somebody's soul with.

"Yes," I say as clearly as I can. "Immensely."

But apparently it's a rhetorical question, because Alexa kicks back and puts her feet on our desk, knocking my compass on to the floor.

I'm going to leave it there. I don't think drawing my bully's attention to a sharp metal object with a stabby point is the smartest possible decision at this precise moment.

"I'm *so* delighted you're finally back," she says flatly, picking one of my notepads up and staring at the T-Rex on the front with a wrinkled nose. "Overjoyed, in fact."

"Are you?" I say tightly.

"Totally." She's now fiddling with my ink pot. "School's so *dull* without somebody fun to play with."

Which would be quite sweet if we were five and she didn't mean the way a tiger plays with a three-legged goat or a cat plays with a mouse just before she rips it apart.

Skeletal muscle consists of 650 striated layers connected to bones, and I'm so cold and rigid now every one of my fibres feels like it's made out of stainless steel.

This is a disaster.

Actually, no: it's a catastrophe; a cataclysm; utter ruination. A meteorite could be about to obliterate England, and it would still be second on the Worst Things That Could Possibly Happen Today list.

There's no *way* I can make new friends and start again with Alexa snapping at my heels. She's going to make everybody hate me before I even get a chance.

Again.

"And I just love the look you're going for today," she adds in a voice so loud it could blister paint. "Ducks are so hot right now."

Ducks? I look down in confusion at my white jumper, orange leggings and yellow shoes and then flush bright red. She's right: I look exactly like a member of the Anatidae family.

That is *not* the sophisticated first impression I wanted to give at all.

"Hey, you guys," Alexa continues at the top of her voice, gesticulating with one of my pencils. Everybody in the class is now staring at us in silence. "For those of you who haven't met Harriet Manners, we've known each other a really long time, haven't we?" The frog in my stomach is now totally frozen. *No. No no no no.* "A really, really long time. Eleven years, in fact."

"Alexa—"

"Oh, they're just going to *love* our childhood memories, Harriet. They're *adorable.* Do you remember when we were five and you peed yourself on the story-time carpet and they had to buy a whole library of new books?"

"OMG!" Ananya laughs from behind me. "I remember

that, Lexi! That was *hilaire*."

"*So gross*," Liv squeaks. "Like, *ewwww*."

I feel sick. "It was *milk* and I squeezed my carton too hard."

"What about the time you took your skirt off during Year Four Cinderella and ran around the stage in your knickers?"

Oh God. Oh God oh God oh God –

"*The button fell off and I didn't notice*."

"And goodness, everybody," Alexa says, taking a nice big breath while she unsheathes her claws and gets ready to rip my metaphorical intestines out. "Just *wait* until you hear about the time that Harriet Manners—"

The door smacks open.

14

"Guys!" Miss Hammond breezes into the room, carrying roughly twenty-five toilet rolls. "I just found these and had the *best* idea for our team-building game. This is going to be so much fun and—"

She abruptly stops and peers over the top of them. As if she's protected by the world's softest, strongest, most absorbable wall.

"Alexa Roberts?"

"Hey, miss! Wow, is your tummy feeling OK? Are they all for you?"

Miss Hammond is slowly changing colour.

Six months ago, Alexa single-handedly attempted to destroy *Hamlet* before getting detention every day for a month. From the energy crackling between them now, it looks like neither of them has forgotten about it.

"What are you doing in here?" Miss Hammond says sharply, dumping all the rolls on the desk so hard that three bounce straight on to the floor. "This is Form A.

You're in Form C, with Mr White."

"*Am* I?" Alexa stands up and flicks her hair. "Oh no. I must have got lost on my way there, somehow. Or maybe I was just *drawn* here by some invisible and irrepressible force."

She smiles and I can't help thinking that if Alexa put this much obsessive compulsive behaviour into her schoolwork she'd have graduated school by now. And university. And possibly obtained some kind of PhD.

"Out," Miss Hammond snaps, pointing at the corridor. "Now."

"But miss…"

"*Now.*"

"I just think…"

"*Immediately.*"

"*Fine.*" My nemesis stalks towards the corridor, and then turns round. "But I think it's really important that you all know about the time that Harriet once—"

"Nobody cares, Alexandra," Miss Hammond snaps, slapping her hands on her desk. "And if you come near this room again, you're suspended, effective immediately. Do I make myself clear?"

"But—"

"No buts. *Scoot.*"

Miss Hammond crosses the classroom quickly, slams

the door on Alexa and pulls down the blind so we can't see her. Then she turns back to a stunned, silent class and smooths down her skirt.

Like a warrior in 100% organic cotton.

"Right," she says softly, and her voice is all sunshine and kittens in baskets again. "Grab a toilet roll each, guys, and let's get out on the playing field, build teams and really *connect.*"

I've never brought an apple in for a teacher before, but – as almost the entire class smile at me sympathetically and start grabbing their bags – I think I might just do that.

I'm getting my fresh start after all.

15

So, here are some facts about toilet roll:

1. It was invented by the Chinese in 600 AD.

2. Britons use 110 rolls each a year, which is the equivalent of six miles of tissue.

3. 72% of people hang toilet paper with the first sheet going *over* the roll.

4. The US military used toilet paper to camouflage their tanks in Saudi Arabia during the Desert Storm war.

5. Novelty paper includes: glow-in-the-dark, money, Word of the Day and Sudoku.

How do I know this?

Let's just say a few months ago I had a bad cold combined with a long car journey with Toby that I've never fully recovered from. I've sworn not to blow my nose anywhere near him again.

Miss Hammond appears to be even more excited than Toby about its possibilities.

She giddily ushers all of us outside: past the enormous tug-of-war being conducted by Mrs Baker, beyond a taciturn Mr Bott and small groups constructing tables out of newspaper, far away from Mr White and rings of students passing balloons between their knees and laughing.

(Every couple of minutes there's a loud BANG that I suspect is not unrelated to Alexa.)

"Right," Miss Hammond says cheerfully, planting a stick in the ground with a stripy pink sock taped to the end. "We had a *very* enlightening teacher training session yesterday, didn't we, Harriet?"

The whole class turns to look at me.

Excellent. Now I look like an undercover teacher trainer.

"And we were reminded of how we are all part of the *same beautiful puzzle*. Held together by the invisible *threads of harmony and happiness.*" She pauses. "Please stop hitting Robert with the roll of tissue, Eric."

"But we're just bonding, miss," Eric objects, doing it

again. "Our thread of happiness depends on it."

"Lovely! That's the spirit!" She beams at us all and then gestures at a blonde girl to take her roll off the top of her head. "So we're going to play a little game to help us form lifelong *connections*. After all, there's no *me* in team!"

"Yes, there is," Christopher objects. "It is literally right there."

"And meat."

"Mate." "Meta." "Atem."

"That's not how you spell atom, idiot."

"See how you're already working together?" Miss Hammonds claps. "So in a *burst* of inspiration, I am calling this game *The Riddle of the Mummy*."

Liv's hand goes up.

"Mine is in Vegas right now, miss. She goes there after every summer holiday to recover."

"Er, excellent, Olivia! And your eventual arrival, Mr King, is always a pleasure, however unpredictable."

A boy in a yellow T-shirt shrugs and takes a place at the back of the group.

"So," Miss Hammond continues brightly, "I'm going to ask you all riddles, and in teams of three you'll try to answer them as quickly as possible. The team that gets it right first gets to take three steps towards *The Sock of Survival*."

I can feel an excited, fizzy feeling starting to run down the back of my neck.

I *love* riddles.

They're like facts, except backwards and you can solve them and that's even better. Plus, competition really helps to sharpen my mind and bring out the best in me. Miss Hammond couldn't have picked a better way for me to make new friends if I'd sent in a handwritten request form.

Which I didn't, just to clarify.

"To make things a bit more jolly," she continues, beginning to wind the end of a loo roll round her ankle, "I'm going to turn myself into an Egyptian mummy and chase you, to help motivate you to keep moving forward! If I tap you on the shoulder, you become a mummy too and you're out of the race. And so on and so forth."

Oh my God.

This is getting better and better. I love ancient history *too* (although mummies technically originated in South America but maybe that's not super relevant to the game right now).

Miss Hammond keeps winding the tissue until it's binding her legs together like a penguin after knee surgery.

"The team that reaches The Sock of Survival first –

without all turning into mummies – wins!"

A flurry of hands immediately go up.

"What do we win, miss?"

"The satisfaction of knowing you did it together!" There's a pause while all the hands come down again, and Miss Hammond adds slightly reluctantly: "And a ten-pound voucher for the school tuck shop."

A murmur of approval goes round the class.

I'm now buzzing so hard it's as if I'm filled with bees or electric toothbrushes, and not just because the prize is sugar.

This is it. This is going to change *everything*.

From this point onwards, I will no longer be Harriet Manners, pee-er on books, skirt-dropper and irrational lover-of-bananas. I'll be the Riddle Master. Sweet Winner. Saviour of Socks. Avoider of Mummies and Destroyer of Toilet Rolls.

This is going to be *amazing*.

Miss Hammond starts grouping people together, and then hops over to me. "Harriet Manners? I've put you with India Perez and Olivia Webb."

I smile shyly as the girl with neon purple hair and Liv walk towards me. India smiles back and my insides do another excited little frog hop: *and so my new close and irreplaceable lifelong friendships start.*

Honestly, I'm kind of fascinated by her already.

Apparently Queen Elizabeth the First used to pretend that there was a piece of glass between her and the rest of the world to make her feel more royal, and it kind of seems like India has one too. Beneath My Little Pony hair and scowling eyebrows, she has dark eyes and an air of dignity and nobility. She reminds me of a powerful Egyptian princess.

We are *definitely* going to win now.

"Anya!" Liv calls as we stand behind a line made out of skipping rope. "Ans! A! Ani! Over here! We'll totally share answers, right?"

India frowns as Ananya pretends to have temporarily lost her hearing facilities.

"You will totally not," she says steadily. Then she turns to me. "Does this sort of exercise happen a lot at this school? Because it would have been extremely useful to have that in the brochure."

"Umm, I think it says *We are a school dedicated to the creative exploration of the individuality of our students*," I admit. "Page eight. Halfway down, under the photo of people making forts out of boxes."

India lifts a black eyebrow so it looks like a tick at the end of an essay. "Did you memorise the sixth form brochure?"

"N-no," I lie. "I just… umm…" *Sound more hip, Harriet.* "I used that page as kindling to build a really cool fire… for no reason, because I… err, burn stuff I don't care about, etcetera."

India puts her eyebrow back down.

"OK," she says, and I relax again.

I think I just passed my first social test.

"All right, my little intrepid puzzlers!" Miss Hammond calls, now covered head to toe in white, like an overexcited golden Labrador puppy. "Are you ready to journey back 5,000 years to a time of mystery and intrigue?"

There's a chorus of "yeah," "suppose so," "whatever," "I guess," are we going to be recycling all this tissue because this is kind of environmentally unfriendly?"

(That last one was me.)

"And…" She shakes a tiny tambourine that seems to have appeared out of nowhere. "*Go!*"

16

It starts off perfectly.

"How far," Miss Hammond says, looking up and down the line, "can a person run into the woods?"

There's a short silence while people whisper.

"We don't know how big the woods are," India murmurs as our group crowds its heads together. "There must be information missing. That can't be the whole question."

I grin at the other two while my brain clicks away happily. This is *so much fun* already. It's so intimate. So *bonding*. I really feel like part of a *team*.

"I've got this one," I whisper back conspiratorially, and then stick my hand up. "Halfway, miss. Because if you run any further, you're running back out of them again."

"Excellent, Harriet Manners! Take three steps forward!"

I high-five Liv and India like BFFs and we move towards our goal. Miss Hammond closes her eyes, shuffles

forward with a small embalmed-dead-person groaning sound and taps Robert on the shoulder.

"Ah, *man*," he says as he starts wrapping himself up in toilet tissue. "This is utter b—"

"Language, Robert." Miss Hammond claps her hands. "I am the beginning of the end, and the end of time and space. I am essential to creation, and I surround every place. What am I?"

"God!" Christopher's group yells.

"Santa Claus!"

"Taylor Swift!"

"Nope!" Miss Hammond says to all three groups. "Sorry! Take a step backwards, guys."

I wink at my group jubilantly as two more people are reluctantly ingratiated into ancient Egypt.

"You are the letter E, miss," I say loudly.

"I am indeed, Harriet!" We step forward again. "What loses its head in the morning but gets it back at night?"

My hand goes straight up, with the speed of a question-answering ninja. "A pillow!"

And – riddle by riddle, answer by answer – my group starts racing towards the goal. I know what is so fragile that saying the word breaks it (silence). I know what has many keys but can't open a door (a piano) and what gets wetter and wetter the more it dries (a towel).

Between us, we even know how many months have twenty-eight days in them. India lowers her head to whisper, although we're so far ahead by now that there's no real point.

"All of th—"

"Four!" I shout in excitement. "Twenty-eight days hath September, April, June and November!"

"I'm afraid it's all of them," Miss Hammond says gently. "All months have *at least* twenty-eight days. One step back, team."

Oops.

But luckily it doesn't matter if we make a mistake now and then, because nobody can catch up. We're too far ahead for even the mummies to grab us.

Finally, we get within touching distance of the sock.

Studies have shown that during competitive games, cortisol, prolactin, testosterone and adrenocorticotropic hormone levels increase dramatically. I'm now so rabid with excitement I'm basically floating on a fluffy cloud of my own chemical cocktail.

It's just my team, Christopher and Raya left.

"What kind of room has no doors or windows?"

My mind starts racing, jittering, turning itself inside out and back again. A prison? No, because how would you get in or out? Maybe a cellar, if a trapdoor in the floor didn't count as either…

Is it a play on words? A groom, a broom, a…

"A cupboard?" Raya suggests, but I suddenly know. *Wham.* As if my brain was in the dark and a light's just been switched on: once you see the answer, you can't *unsee* it.

I punch the air.

"I've got it!" I yell, and beam triumphantly at Liv and India. "It's a *mush-room,* miss!"

Then, with three quick hops, I reach the sock and start automatically doing my happy dance: hands punching the air, knees bent, bottom wiggling.

"We win!" I squeak jubilantly. "We win we win we win! Wooooooooooo!!!"

17

My cheeks are flushed. My knees are shaking.

All the standard responses to success, adrenaline and unexpected physical activity.

I *knew* it. Best. Day. *Ever.*

This is *exactly* like Rebecca's birthday party eleven years ago when I won all the games. We played Pass the Parcel and I explained the rules to anyone who held on to the package for too long, and Musical Chairs where I encouraged anyone who was walking too slowly to hurry up, and Musical Statues when I helpfully pointed out people who were moving and… and…

And nobody wanted to play with me ever again.

Cucumbers consist of ninety-five per cent water. Without warning, it suddenly feels as if I may have become one. Every cell in my body is rapidly turning into liquid.

No. No no no *no.*

I abruptly stop wiggling my bottom and – with infinite slowness – turn around.

68

And there it is.

Every single one of my peers is standing in silence: arms folded, faces sullen. Glaring at me with narrowed eyes and raised eyebrows. Unimpressed. Outraged. Bored stiff by a game they haven't participated in.

Precisely the same as when we were five, except they're considerably bigger now and even angrier because this time they're covered in broken up bits of toilet roll and they're not quite sure why.

Oh my God: I've done it again.

I was so desperate for my team to win, I didn't think about anything else. I was trying my hardest, but in doing so I've made the entire game about…

Well. *Me,* I guess.

With a sick lurch, I'm suddenly not so sure I need Alexa to make me unpopular after all.

Oh, who am I even kidding?

Maybe I never actually did.

Swallowing, I turn slowly to Liv and India. Their arms are folded as well. I hold up my hand to awkwardly high-five them. "We won, guys. Yay?"

They both stare at it, suspended in the air. The loneliest hand that has ever existed in the 65 million years since our primate ancestors first evolved them.

"Not really," India says finally. "*You* won, Harriet. All by yourself."

And – as she turns in silence and starts walking back to the sixth-form building, followed by every member of my class – I can't help but marvel at the irony.

Because, despite my best efforts, *all by myself* is exactly how I've ended up.

18

The poet John Donne once wrote that no man is an island. I'd like to seriously question the accuracy of that statement.

In the middle of the South Atlantic Ocean, 1,700 miles from Antarctica, lies Bouvet Island. It has an area of forty-nine kilometres squared, is covered in glaciers and ice, and nobody lives there or ever has. According to Wikipedia, it is the remotest island in the world.

Thanks to today's misadventures, it is *still* a more popular destination than me.

The rest of the morning can be summarised thus:

1. I apologise to India and Liv and give them my share of the tuck-shop voucher.
2. They tell me it's fine, honestly, and then avoid me.
3. I overhear a girl in maths say I'm "still an arrogant, weird know-it-all".

4. I briefly consider telling her that *weird* originally meant "has the power to control fate" and if that was true I wouldn't be in this mess in the first place.
5. I realise it'll prove all three points and think better of it.

News of my unsporting smugness and apparent *In Your Face* dance spreads around sixth form with the speed of a forest fire. By the time I get out of double physics with Mr Harper, it's everywhere.

I try to outrace it – attempting to start friendly conversations with strangers as fast as I can – but it's impossible. The flame hops from student to student via whispers and raised eyebrows until all I'm doing is circling the common room like a desperate squirrel with its tail combusting.

I'm smiling, trying to find things in common, asking questions and remembering details as hard as I can.

But it's too late.

My seven seconds are up. The first impression has been made, and with every attempt to undo it I just look even more pathetic. It doesn't matter what I do or what I say any more.

I am the school weirdo.

Again.

By the time I'm ejected from my sixth failed conversation attempt ("Did you know that pirates used to wear gold hoop earrings because they thought it improved their eyesight?") I've officially given up.

I haven't seen Toby all morning. I should probably focus the remainder of my efforts on the one person in the year that still wants to talk to me.

But he's not in the common room, he isn't in the dining hall and when I take my lunch to his normal spot in the bush behind the gym hall, he's not there either.

Seriously. For a stalker, Toby is becoming ridiculously difficult to track down.

By the time I eventually find him, tucked into the corner of the art studio, I've basically resigned myself to playing noughts and crosses on the floor of the playground. I've already got two chalks ready, just in case I can persuade a year seven to play with me.

Although, given how quickly my leper status is whizzing around the school, even that's looking optimistic.

"Hey, Toby!" I say, pushing through the art room door. He looks up with slightly mad eyes, like a miniature Albert Einstein except without the moustache or Nobel prize.

"Harriet Manners!" he says, pulling his earphones out and quickly flipping over a piece of paper in front of him. "What an unprecedented surprise!"

I am so, *so* happy to see him.

"Are you having lunch in here today?" I say, bouncing forward and slamming my satchel enthusiastically on the table. "Did you know that in the average lunchtime you eat 150,000 kilometres of DNA? Although I'm afraid this cheese sandwich may have a few less, judging by the state of the lettuce." I plop it on the desk in front of him.

"Want to share?"

Toby gently pushes the sandwich off his piece of paper and brushes a few crumbs away.

"That's very kind of you, Harriet. But Mum made me sushi." He prods a little Thomas the Tank Engine lunchbox on the chair next to him. "Except we didn't have any fish so it's beef and I'm not keen on wasabi so it's mustard." He opens it and peers in. "With bread instead of rice."

"So," I say slowly, "it's a beef sandwich, then?"

"Absolutely," Toby agrees, holding one up. "Except Mum cut the crusts off and rolled it up into little balls so I'd feel like I was getting an interesting cultural experience."

I grin and glance briefly around the room.

Thanks to a total lack of artistic interest and even less ability, I've spent as little time as possible in this part of the school. There are paints and brushes everywhere, bright canvases leaning against walls and a general atmosphere of creativity.

I don't like it.

Entirely subjective grades make me uncomfortable.

Toby looks, if possible, even more out of place. The front of his brown T-shirt says COME TO THE NERD SIDE – WE HAVE PI and he's wearing trousers with an electronic computer keyboard across the lap, though he isn't actually plugged into a computer. At the moment anyway.

"So what are you doing?" I say, sitting down on the edge of his desk and reaching curiously for the piece of paper.

Toby moves it away. "It's my project for the Science Fair."

"Oooh." The Fair isn't for another three months, but maybe I need to get started on mine too. "What's yours on? Can I see?"

"I'm afraid not," Toby says, shifting the paper into his satchel. "Showing you would jeopardise its top-secret status by definition of it no longer being a secret of any kind."

"That's very true." I frown. "So if it's science why are you in the art room?"

There's a tiny pause while Toby stuffs a sushi-sandwich in his mouth, and then says:

"It's quiet and private and away from… people."

"Cool." I look at the sunshine streaming through the windows. "I might do my project on the effect of music on animal behaviour using Hugo and Victor as voluntary subjects, or maybe study the Oort cloud because the edge of it is 4.6 trillion miles from the sun so I can investigate the composition of the—"

"I have a question for you," a voice interrupts from behind me. "Maybe you can add this to your investigation while you're at it."

I spin round in surprise.

Somebody is sitting in the corner near the door, almost totally hidden behind an enormous sculpture of an angel made out of plaster, clay and wire. I had no idea there was anyone else in here: that's how quiet they are and how big the sculpture is.

And how little my genuine interest in the art room has been, obviously.

"Umm," I say, blinking a few times. I *do* love a good question, after all. "Sure. Hit me with it."

"Do you ever," the voice says, "and I mean *ever*,

think about anyone other than yourself?"

And I don't even know who they are yet.

But I asked them to hit me with it, and it feels like they just did.

19

Apparently, there are over 6,000 languages in the world and by the turn of this century half of these are expected to die out. Judging by my speechlessness at this precise moment, my brain thinks English is one of them.

"S-sorry?" I finally manage.

Then I take a few steps forward until I can see a boy behind the sculpture.

He's pale and tall, with mousey hair, thick dark eyebrows and a round face, and – for some reason I can't fathom – he looks slightly magical. It's only as I get a few metres away that I realise he has two slightly different coloured irises: one pale blue, the other light brown.

Otherwise known as *heterochromia iridis* and entirely a result of melanin levels in the eyes rather than enchantment or a Harry Potter spell.

Sadly. I checked.

"Seriously," the boy growls, grabbing some clay and sticking it into the angel's leg, "I've never known anyone

so obnoxiously wrapped up in themselves. It's quite amazing."

His magical quality takes another enormous step down.

"Sorry? We haven't even met, have we? I don't think I've ever even seen you before in my entire life."

The boy looks at me steadily for a few seconds.

"I'm in your form. I was in the team next to you this morning. For a full hour."

I get a little closer, and – now I'm not distracted by the thought that he might be a wizard – I can see that, yup: he's the new boy in the yellow T-shirt who was late this morning, except now he's disguised by blue overalls.

In fact, I think when we went back to the form room at the end of team-building to do the register he was sitting at the desk directly in front of me as well.

OK. The defence isn't looking good right now. Annabel would tell me to start plea-bargaining immediately.

Instead, I automatically go on the counterattack.

"Well," I say, desperately sticking my nose in the air and crossing my arms, "you didn't say hello to me either."

"Yes, I did," he retorts bluntly. "Twice. You were too busy telling India about the essay you wrote for your English exam. Four months ago."

I flush. It was all about masculinity and gender in

Othello and I thought it might be a good way of making peace with her. I don't think it worked.

"But—"

"And now this poor guy just wants peace and quiet to work on his project, and you follow him in here, ignore his pretty obvious hints and gab away about yourself again."

Follow *him*? *Excuse* me?

"Actually Toby's *my* stalker," I snap indignantly. "*Not* the other way round." I pause slightly while I consider how that sounds. "OK, that's not exactly what I…"

The guy with the heterochromia snorts.

"Yeah, my mistake," he says, grabbing a piece of wire and bending it into a C shape. "You're lovely. I can see why you fit into glamorous New York with all the bananas."

My mouth flaps in silence a few times – he wasn't even there when I said that; I *knew* people were talking about me and my bananas – and then I turn desperately to Toby. Why isn't he protecting my honour?

Because he hasn't heard a single word, that's why.

His head is bent over the piece of paper again, his earphones are back in, and he's lost in Toby-land: scribbling away frantically, humming the theme tune from *Star Wars* under his breath.

I rush over and pull out an earphone.

"Hello again, Harriet!" he says, quickly folding his arms across the desk. "Maybe I could encourage you to wear a bell round your neck so people know you're coming? Our cat's got one. It's very handy."

"Toby." My cheeks are getting hotter and hotter. "Tell this… this *boy*…"

"Jasper. For the third time today, my name is Jasper."

I'm not sure how, but this is getting steadily worse. "Please tell Jasper I'm actually quite nice if you get to know me!"

Toby turns to Jasper with reproach in his eyes.

"Harriet Manners," he says with total sincerity, "is the sweetest girl in the entire universe. She is a sterling example of what great niceness the human race is capable of. Should we ever need an ambassador for outer space, I will be voting for her to represent us."

A little grateful knot of embarrassment forms in the base of my throat, and I turn to Jasper triumphantly.

"S—" I start, but before I can get to the "ee" Toby continues:

"Sometimes she is so kind she even lets me sit on her doorstep when it's raining and she's too busy to let me in."

Oh my God. That just made it a billion times worse.

But if I let him in *every* time I'd never be on my own again.

"Right," Jasper says flatly, picking up another piece of wire. "Sorry. She sounds utterly charming and not at all like a stuck-up princess."

I can feel myself starting to get angry.

"Toby," I say, turning back to him. "You don't really mind me being here, do you? I'm not in the way, am I?"

Then I look triumphantly at Jasper with my *ha* face at the ready.

"Actually," Toby says, "you are a bit in the way, Harriet. It would be useful if you could go away today. I really need to focus on my project. And maybe tomorrow too, actually."

"But—"

"And Thursday."

"I—"

"In fact, while we're discussing it, could you maybe leave me alone for the rest of the week? Next week would also be extremely handy as well."

It feels like something is starting to tighten inside my chest. Toby doesn't want to hang out with me either?

Then I turn back to Jasper and the corner of his mouth is turned upwards slightly in a little smirk.

That does it.

A lightning bolt is 54,000 degrees Fahrenheit, and it feels like one has just shot through me: white-hot anger is scorching and fizzling from the top of my head down to my fingertips and back again.

Swallowing, I stick my chin in the air and start heading towards the door in dignified silence.

Somehow I don't quite make it.

"You don't know me," I say, spinning round. "You don't know who I am, or how I think, or why I do the things I do. You know *nothing about me at all*."

"You're totally right," Jasper says as the bell for the end of lunchtime rings. He stands up and pulls off his blue overalls so that the yellow T-shirt is fully visible again. "And you know what?"

"What?"

"That's just fine by me."

And without another backwards glance, Jasper walks straight past me and out of the door. Leaving both the angel and me speechless, white and rigid behind him.

20

By oneself. Excluded. On your tod.

It's a good thing I brought my thesaurus with me, because I have plenty of quality *me time* to expand my vocabulary over the rest of the day.

For the next four hours, I am completely *unescorted*.

I am *solo* as I eat my sandwich in the corner of the common room and drop it down my top, *companionless* as I mess up a rat dissection in biology because nobody wants to pair with me and *lonesome* when an experiment in chemistry goes wrong because I can't hold both the test tubes at the same time.

I even try to make myself feel better by replacing these words with positive synonyms: I *independently* stare out of the window, I chew my nails *unaided* and *unassisted*.

But it doesn't matter how many different words I use, they all boil down to the same thing.

It's my first day back at school.

And I am completely alone.

*

"Anyway…" I say as I wait for the final school bell to ring. I'm now sitting on the little wall next to the playing field, kicking my duck pumps on and off at the heels.

The caretaker picks sheets of tissue off the ground and throws them in a black plastic bag.

"He doesn't even *know* me," I say quietly. "He's just so *rude*."

"*Can I borrow some toilet rolls*, she says," the caretaker mutters, picking up another few bits. "*Just a few*, she says. And next thing I know every roll in the school is all over the grass and nobody's got anything to wipe their bottoms with for the rest of the week."

"Exactly!" I say triumphantly. "Or almost exactly, anyway. That's nearly the same thing."

I kick my feet against the wall despondently.

At least I've found somebody who will talk to me. I hadn't expected my first kindred spirit in sixth form to be a fifty-seven-year-old man in dungarees and a tool belt, but beggars can't be choosers.

Plus he spends a lot of his time under tables and in cupboards, so we actually have a surprising amount in common.

Steve bends down again. "I'm supposed to be practising my spinning tonight, not cleaning up after hours. That hippy can bring in her own supplies next time."

I shake my head in empathy. Then I hop off the wall so I can pick up a few bits of tissue and pop them in the bag. I like to spin round too: maybe he has a special office twirly chair like Dad?

We work industriously together in companionable silence for a few minutes, and then I clear my throat and say: "I've got a miniature game of Scrabble in my satchel – would you like to play it with me tomorrow?"

There's a thoughtful pause while Steve considers this.

"Hang on… Chicken wire? Did you say the statue is made out of chicken wire? I *knew* I was missing a roll. That little blighter."

"Isn't he just the most horrible, unpleasant—"

"Quack quack," a familiar voice says and I immediately stop moving with my hand still clutching a bit of tissue: bent double, with my bottom firmly poking in the air.

I can't help feeling as if I'm not as well protected as I could be.

Slowly, I straighten up and turn to look at Alexa.

She's standing a few metres away with her hands on her hips. Ananya and Liv are at either side, and India is standing just behind them.

Huh. That was fast.

I guess she's picked her team already.

I look at the wad of crumpled tissue in my hand, then at the black bin bag. Then at the middle-aged man I'm chatting to. On my own. Voluntarily, when I could just go home.

There's a piece of loo roll stuck to my knee, and another attached to the toe of my shoe. Tuna is still coating my front, and I smell of a day's worth of embarrassed dry sweat.

In the meantime, Alexa is noticing exactly the same things.

"You're hanging out with the *staff* now? Like, people who are actually *paid* to be here all day?"

"Actually, Steve's…" *only part-time,* I'm about to say, and then change my mind.

"So where are your little sidekicks now, Harriet? Where's Team Geek?" Alexa elaborately looks around her. "I can't see them. Are they hiding?" She picks up a bit of loo roll and pretends to look under it. "Helloooo? Geeks? Come out, come out, wherever you are."

"Nat's gone to fashion college," I say as firmly as I can, even though Alexa already knows this. "And Toby's really, really busy with something super important."

"Oh *yes,*" she says, narrowing her eyes and putting the paper back down again. "That's *right*. You're totally on your own now, aren't you?"

Alexa has always known how to find the rusty nail and smack it straight on the head.

My eyes start prickling.

"No," I say with as much dignity as I can muster. "I'm not alone. I have…" *Steve,* I'm about to say, and then change my mind for the second time.

"This is pathetic, even for you." Alexa sounds genuinely cross. "Where's the *fun*, Harriet Manners? Where's the challenge? You've ruined everything." She clicks her fingers and turns away. "She's not worth it, guys. We've got better things to do."

As if I'm one of the fabric mice we give Victor and he's chewed all the catnip out of it, rendering it useless and of no interest any more.

The bell rings and Alexa starts marching towards the front gates with her Underlings behind her. India looks at me with disdain for a few seconds, then turns and follows them.

My eyes are smarting, my vision is starting to wobble and my throat feels like there's a sofa cushion stuck in it.

Then my phone beeps.

How was your first day?? Tell me tell me! Nat xxx

How am I supposed to answer that with any self-respect?

A-maz-ing!! SO MUCH FUN!! Couldn't have gone better!!! Can't wait for two more whole years of this!!!! Hxx

With a lie, that's how.

I put my phone away, hiding my face behind my hair so Steve can't see my chin starting to crumple.

"It's all right, love," he says, giving me an awkward pat on the back as I head towards the school gates. "Those nasty little minxes will get what's coming to them."

"Sure they will," I say over my shoulder, even though I know they obviously won't.

Because Alexa's right.

There's a big difference between not-popular and *un*popular, and I hadn't even noticed that until I was on the other side. I may have spent years struggling to make friends at school, but this is the first time since I was five that I've had *none.*

And of the two options, I can't decide which is worse:

a) being brought down a peg or two every school day
   of your life for eleven years

or

b) finally being so far at the bottom that there's nowhere left to go.

21

They say that every cloud has a silver lining.

Which is obviously untrue.

Most clouds don't: just the rain clouds with the sun directly behind them. Given the size of the sky, that makes it statistically uncommon.

However, I'd like to think that I'm the kind of person who at least *looks* for the sunshine. A positive, optimistic girl, who hopes for the best even when the signs aren't looking good.

And – let's be honest – they're really not right now.

At all.

The first schools were established in 425 AD. I'd be quite surprised if anyone has had a less successful first day in the history of formal education.

On the upside, at least I'll be able to focus on my schoolwork properly now. Without any distractions or discussions or interesting debates. All day, every day,

for the next two years.

Most of the evenings too.

And possibly quite a few weekends, if Nat gets really busy with college.

Oh my God.

Of all the planets in our solar system, we would weigh the most on Jupiter. I'm starting to wonder if I've somehow accidentally ended up there instead.

Bits of the day are beginning to rattle around inside my head like coloured balls inside a lottery machine, and every time they collide with each other, another little piece of me gets heavier.

I like bananas! My lungs. *I've got this one!* My tongue. *It's a mushroom!* My kidneys and liver. *Do you ever think about anyone but yourself? Maybe you could leave me alone?* Eyeballs, spleen, pancreas, veins, muscles.

She's not worth it: every single one of my bones.

Until, organ by organ, I weigh so much I'm surprised I don't have to drag myself down the road by my fingernails.

Finally, I manage to reach the bench on the corner of the road where Nat and I have met every morning for the last ten years, even when our parents had to come with us.

I stand and look at how empty it is.

Then I turn around again and start walking towards the only place in the world that could possibly make me feel lighter again.

The local launderette.

22

No, in case you're wondering.

I haven't been back here since Annabel and Dad broke up and then had their big romantic laundry reunion nearly a year ago. Initially, I thought it was because it had become *their* place, not mine any more. Then I thought it was because I'd just worked out how to clean my clothes for free at home, like a normal human being.

But now I'm wondering if it's simply because I haven't needed it the way I need it now.

When I don't know where else to go.

I still love this place.

I love the bright lights, the soapy smells, the soft purring of the machines. I love the heat and the shininess of the glass in the tumble driers. But most of all I love the way that nothing could ever feel alone in a place where so many things are jumbled together.

94

I rub my eyes and pull a chair over to my favourite machine. The glass is still warm, and there are baskets filled with piles of abandoned clothes everywhere. Somebody's even left a shoe behind: it's peeking out from behind a particularly large heap of jumpers and underwear.

I pull a blue sock out of my bag and a memory suddenly flashes: snow, warm cheeks, a cold hand squeezing mine.

So I swallow and put it in the drier as quickly as I can.

Then I start fumbling through my satchel for the fifty pence I need to put it on a quick spin. Followed by another fifty pence.

Then another pound in shrapnel.

And a two pound-coin.

After the day I've had I may be here some time. I am about to own the driest sock in existence.

I'm just chipping a bit of melted chocolate off a pound so that the machine recognises it as something other than a snack when something small and shiny flies through the air and lands in my lap.

I blink at the newly arrived coin, then at the empty room.

Maybe there's some kind of strange gravitational pull levitating the money out of the machines and throwing it at my head. I suppose I could do my science project on that instead.

Reaching into my bag, I pull out another ten pence and there it is again: money, soaring through the air.

Except this time it's a pound, which is even better.

I look around the empty room – still nothing – and am just quickly calculating how long I'll have to stay here before I am rich enough to buy a castle when somebody laughs.

"You actually think it's magic flying money, don't you?"

Then I see the shoe in the pile moving. A pointy, silver shoe that stormed down my driveway yesterday morning, attached to my best friend.

"Nat?"

A dark, curly head pokes out from behind an enormous pile of clean jumpers and trousers. She's obviously been lying in them, like some kind of enormous cat.

"Obviously. God, you took *ages*. I was starting to think I might actually have to do some washing." She stands up, puts *Vogue* down and picks off a pair of huge beige knickers attached by static to her jumper.

"Gross," she adds, flinging them into the corner

so they hit the wall with a *fffpp*. Then she turns to where I'm still sitting, frozen in surprise. "How's it going, Manners?"

23

Seriously.

I have *got* to start checking rooms before I walk into them. Apparently chameleons and dragonflies have 360-degree vision, and I am clearly neither. If I were a small animal, I'd definitely have been eaten by now.

"Nat, what are you doing here?"

She hops on top of one of the machines. "Finding you, obviously. I've got a selfie with Vivienne Westwood – she was nowhere *near* as difficult to pin down."

I jump with considerably less nimbleness on to the machine next to her. "I'm sorry."

"What's going on? I'm so worried, I've just spent an hour sitting in a laundry basket, covered in old-lady clothes. I may never fully recover."

I take a deep breath and decide to confront the metaphorical elephant in the room head-on. "I'm fine, Nat. Honestly. Nick quit modelling and went back to Australia, and we both decided together that a long-distance

relationship was too painful. I know we made the right decision, I just don't want to talk about it, that's all."

"Really?"

"Really really."

"Really really really?"

"All of the reallies."

"So you're OK?"

"Yes," I say as confidently as I can.

Nat studies my face carefully, then her shoulders relax very slightly. "Thank God, because I need to tell you something and if I don't I'm going to explode all over my second-best dress and then we really *will* need a launderette."

Suddenly I notice again how perfectly curly her hair is.

In fact – now I'm not hiding in a bush fifteen metres away, being attacked by spiders – I can see a general shininess about Nat, as if her insides have just been dipped in something twinkly. Her eyes are sparkling and her cheeks are pink; there are little dimples in the corners of her mouth and her skin looks like it could glow in the dark.

I look down: the varnish has been chewed off every single one of her nails.

Then I remember her on my doorstep yesterday.

I really need to talk to her.

Oh my God, why did I automatically assume it was about me? Ugh. Maybe Jasper has a point after all.

"Is it François? Are you back with him?"

"*Who*?" Nat frowns. "Oh, the French dude. Ugh: no. He won't stop sending me postcards with rabbits cuddling in front of the Eiffel Tower. This one is called Theo. He's studying photography at college, and we kissed on Friday night for the first time. He's all right, I guess. For a boy."

My best friend is playing it cool, but her entire face is luminous as if something has been set on fire behind it.

I stare at Nat in confusion. She has left literally fifty-six messages on my phone over the last few days, and not a single one of them mentioned this.

"But… why didn't you just tell me?"

"Because you're my best friend and you've just had your heart broken and this is terrible timing and I didn't want to make you sadder."

I suddenly love my Best Friend so much it's hard to swallow.

"Nat," I say finally, "do you know what happens to metal when it touches another piece of metal in outer space?"

"It makes a really loud screeching sound and the universe goes *aaaaaargggh stop it*?"

I grin at her. "There's no sound in space, so no. What

happens is that those two bits of metal weld together permanently. Nothing that makes you happy could possibly make me sad, Nat. We're *welded*."

She considers this briefly and then pulls a face. "Remind me never to go into space with Toby, in that case."

We both laugh, then sit in comfortable silence for a few seconds with one shoulder touching.

"So how did you know I'd be here, anyway?"

Nat stretches and yawns. "I tagged you with an electronic chipping device while you were sleeping. Like a cat."

My hand automatically goes up to my neck.

"Plonker. As soon as I got that last text I knew where you'd be, Harriet. You never use exclamation marks in a text unless you're lying. So I figured your first day back had blown, and you'd be heading straight here."

I blink at her in amazement.

See what I mean? Nat had known I was coming to the launderette before I even knew it myself.

Now, *that's* a best friend.

"Well," I start, ready to tell her everything: about Toby and Alexa and Jasper, and how nobody likes me. About how lonely I am without her already, and how I want her to come back to school so it can be just us again, the way it always has been.

Then I stop.

If we're welded, it works both ways, right? My sadness will make her sad too, and I don't want that. It's her turn to be happy now. I've had my big, amazing romance. My best friend deserves to have the world light up for her too.

"*Au contraire*, Natalie," I say as airily as I can, with a quick hand flourish. "In fact, I'll have you know I won the class quiz in my very first hour."

This doesn't have the impact I'm hoping for.

"Oh my God," Nat sighs, putting her hand over her eyes. "How bad? Post-it on the back of T-shirt bad or head-down-the-toilet bad?"

Just *once* I'd like Nat not to see straight through me.

"The former," I admit. There was a Post-it saying *I AM A KNOW-IT-ALL* on my satchel at breaktime. "But don't worry: it's just a brief hiccup. I'm sure they'll forget about it eventually."

"Of *course* they will." Nat puts her arm round me and leans her head against mine. "Lots of people make a slightly bumpy first impression and nobody ever remembers."

We're both lying, by the way: scientists have found that first impressions are very difficult to undo and can often be permanent.

"Exactly!" I drop off the machine with as much enthusiasm as I can muster. "And a school year is only 190 days, right? 1,330 hours will be over before I know it."

There's a short silence.

"That's a really long time, Harriet."

"Actually, it's only three days on Mercury. Plus I've got you and Toby – as soon as his project is over, anyway – so what else does a sensible girl really need?"

"But Harriet, I'm not—"

"So do you want to come to mine tonight? I've designed a game of fashion Monopoly for us to play and it has a doll's house sewing machine you can use as your little placer."

Let's just say that last free period was *really* boring.

There's another short, uncomfortable silence.

Then Nat frowns and hops off the machine, landing on a half-open detergent box with a little puff of white powder like a dragon.

She stares at the floor for a few seconds.

"I... can't tonight. I mean, it sounds great. But if you... If we... Some other time?"

"Oh." I feel slightly popped. "I guess you're busy with Theo tonight, right?"

"Huh? Oh. Mm-hmm."

I nod as another memory flashes: a seagull, a swing, a fur hat.

A kiss.

Then I swallow and push it away as fast as I can.

"Excellent!" I try and grin. "Can't wait to meet him! Have fun!"

Nat gets to the door then bites her lip, runs back and abruptly throws her arms around me so hard she almost knocks me over.

"Don't give up, Harriet. They'll love you as much as I do, I promise. Just give them a bit of time, OK?"

She kisses my cheek, hard.

Then my best friend bursts back out of the laundry doors into the dark, leaving a white fog of soap behind her.

24

I wait until Nat has definitely gone.

Then I sit back down in the chair, lean my cheek against the warm tumble dryer and watch the sock going round and round and round in never-ending circles.

Just like my stupid little life.

My phone beeps.

My little chunky-chip! Is this the face that launched a thousand lips?! Sparkle monkey everywhere! Fairy wins again! Gravy

I stare at it for a few seconds, then turn my phone upside down in case it reads better the other way up.

It does not.

It's midday on a Tuesday in New York right now. My bonkers ex-agent has clearly had *way* too many cups of coffee.

Although at least Wilbur's still in contact: we may not

105

be working together any more, but he still talks to me more than my current modelling agent.

The last three times I rang Infinity Models I never even got past the receptionist.

Still bemused, I type:

Wilbur, have you been eating sequins again? xxx

I wait a few minutes – he's obviously peaked and passed out – pop my phone back in my bag and make a mental note to ring him tomorrow when he's slept through the caffeine spike.

Then I close my eyes and try not to notice how, despite coming to my happy place, there's an organ in the middle of my chest that still belongs on Jupiter.

25

According to scientists, it takes sixty-six days to form a new habit.

I'm obviously going to need every single one of them.

As I walk slowly home, every bush is stared at, every flowerpot glanced behind, every tree trunk checked. At one point I find myself making a little detour around a rubbish bin, just in case there's somebody lurking there. Honestly, I haven't behaved this weirdly since I went on a rampaging Flower Fairy hunt, aged six.

Or had so little success.

Because it doesn't matter how hard I look, or how slowly I walk, or how many times I whisper *I believe in you*: it's no good.

There's nobody following.

Nobody listening, nobody watching.

For the first time in five years, Toby isn't there.

"Dad?" I say as I push open the front door. "Tabitha? Did

you have a nice d—"

I freeze.

Newspapers are strewn around the hallway. The sofa has been dismantled; blankets and clothes are scattered down the stairs. One living-room curtain is closed, every drawer is out, every cupboard is open. The rubbish bin is lying on its side: contents splurged all over the floor.

There are approximately 35,000 robberies reported every month in the UK, and it looks like we've just become one of them.

"Dad!" I shout in a panic, dropping my satchel. "Tabitha! Are you OK?"

What if they've taken my laptop?

Nobody will ever see the presentation I was making about pandas doing handstands.

"Dad!" I yell as I race into the bathroom. The medicine cupboard has been pulled apart. "Dad!" I yell in the kitchen where the fridge door is still open. "Dad!" I shout in the totally ransacked cupboard under the stairs. "Da—"

Dad walks in through the back door with Tabitha, snuggled up in his arms. "Daughter Number One! The conquering heroine returns!"

I fling myself at them so hard I may have crushed my little sister irreversibly. "Oh my goodness, you poor things. Did they hurt you? Did they threaten you? You could have been *kidnapped*!"

Actually, they *may* have been kidnapped and then returned. If I was a robber, I'd have brought my dad back pretty quickly too.

"Did the who which what now?"

"The burglars!"

"We've been *burgled*?" Dad says in alarm. "When did that happen? I was only in the garden for thirty seconds. Blimey, they move fast, don't they?"

I look at him, and then at the chaos around us.

Now I come to think of it, nothing seems to be *missing*. It just appears to be... heavily rearranged. There isn't a single cup left in the cupboard: they're all sitting next to the sink, half full of cold tea. The plates aren't gone: they're just randomly distributed around the living room, covered in ketchup.

"*You* made all this mess?"

"What mess?" Dad glances around. "Looks fine to me. I tell you what, I don't know what Annabel was going on about. This stay-at-home-parent malarkey is a *doddle*. I even wrote a poem after lunch. Do you want to hear it?"

"You wrote a *poem*?"

"I did indeed. I rhymed artisan with marzipan. And Tarzan." Dad looks at my sister smugly. "We're just trying to work out how to get *partisan* in there too, aren't we, Tabs. *I am partisan to a little marzipan while watching Tarzan.*" He thinks about it. "If only it was *Tarzipan*. Such a shame."

Oh my God. The only thing missing in this house is the thing between my father's ears.

"But—"

"I feel a bit cooped up now, though," he continues cheerfully. "I might take Hugo for a walk, stretch the legs, get the air moving around the brain again. You can take care of Tabitha, right?"

He plonks her in my arms before I can tell him there's clearly enough air moving around his brain already.

"But Dad—"

"Oooh, *medicine-man*!" he says as he grabs his jacket, whistles at my dog and marches out of the door I left hanging open in panic behind me. Hugo bounds after him, giddy with excitement. "That rhymes too! God, I'm a creative genius. See you in a bit, kiddos!"

And the door swings shut behind them.

My sister and I look at each other in disbelief for a few seconds. Not for the first time, we are entirely on the same page. *You think that's bad?* her round blue eyes are saying. *I've had eleven hours of this and I'm only four months old. I can't even physically crawl away yet.*

I glance at the clock on the kitchen wall.

It's five-thirty and Annabel will be home from her first day back at work in an hour. Exhausted, drained and desperate to spend time with her tiny baby. I could be wrong, but I don't think washing up, re-folding towels in a cupboard and reading Dad's inaccurate attempts to rhyme *marzipan* are on that list.

Which gives me no other choice.

With a quick sigh, I give my sister a kiss on the cheek and put her back in her little bouncy chair so that she can keep me company.

Then, like all the King's soldiers and all the King's men, I roll my sleeves up.

And start putting the house back together again.

26

Here are my top three days in history:

1. The day in 1877 when S. W. Williston discovered the first diplodocus fossil.

2. March 12th, 1610, which marked the publication of The Starry Messenger by Galileo, thus proving that the solar system didn't revolve round the earth.

3. My birthday. Obviously.

Suffice to say, today is not on this list.

Frankly, it wouldn't even make it into the top 5,000.

I had so many brilliant plans for my first day back at school. Facts and stats and equations and carefully controlled explosions; laughter and soul-searching and conversations about life and death and what our favourite

trees are (mine – the Socotra dragon blood, followed closely by the rainbow eucalyptus).

I was prepared for everything and anything on my first day as a sixth former.

I just never thought I'd spend quite so much of it *cleaning*.

By the time I've finished vacuuming the hallway, all I want to do is crawl to my bedroom, bury myself under a pile of books like a hedgehog and never come out again. I can be one of those people who says *reading is to the mind what exercise is to the body* while never moving another muscle.

"Harriet!" Annabel says in surprise, coming in through the front door as I'm halfway up the stairs with Tabby in my arms: she's earlier than I thought she'd be. "How was school? I thought you might still be at some kind of extra-curriculum or social activity."

Then she pauses, rubs her eyes and looks round the spotless house. "Crikey," she adds with a grimace. "Now I feel terrible. I'd assumed your father would spend the day trashing the place and writing terrible poetry. I clearly don't know my husband at all."

I really don't have the heart to break it to her.

"School was great," I say brightly, clipping a smile on

like Lego. "How was work?"

"Amazing. Frankly, I'd forgotten how much I enjoy telling people I'm going to sue them."

Annabel grins at me – attired once more in her fitted suit and black heels and obviously feeling completely herself again – and I smile back.

Then I pull my phone out of my pocket and stare at the empty screen. "Oooh, six missed phone calls and seven text messages from like-minded people with similar interests who want to spend quality time with me. Better go reply to them all."

Annabel takes Tabitha off me with a gentle, "I missed you, squirrel." Then she looks up with dark eyes. "I'm so glad your first day back went well, sweetheart. I was worried it would be tricky to fit back in so late into term."

I nod. For once, I'm glad my stepmother is too exhausted for her mind-reading superpowers to kick in properly.

"Not at all! It was ace!!!!" *Fake quadruple exclamation marks.* "I just have a little extra reading to do before tomorrow!! So I shall say goodnight!!!"

There go five more.

Then I do a weird little royal wave all the way up the stairs until I'm locked safely inside my bedroom.

Where I fling myself face down on my bed.

And promptly start to hyperventilate.

Apparently if you hyperventilate before you go underwater, you can hold your breath for much longer because CO_2 levels in your bloodstream are lower.

Frankly, I'm breathing so fast now I'm basically a mermaid.

What's the expression? *Be careful what you wish for.*

I wished for everything to be different; I thought that way it would change for me too. I'm not sure it was such a smart ambition after all.

Everybody else has moved on already.

Nat has college and Theo. Toby has a brand-new, top-secret project that doesn't involve me. Annabel has work, Dad has "poetry" and Tabby has the imminent hurdle of solid foods to attend to. My grandmother Bunty is painting murals in a beach hut in Rio, Wilbur's still creating fashion havoc in New York, Rin's moved to South Japan.

My modelling agency has forgotten who I am.

Nick's still gone.

Even Alexa and her minions have found something better to do.

And in the meantime, I'm just the same old me, doing the same old things, over and over again. Carrying the past around with me, exactly as I always have.

There's a humpback whale in the ocean that sings at fifty-two hertz: too low for any other whale to hear. Scientists aren't sure if it's a genetic anomaly, or a sole survivor of an extinct species, or just a whale who accidentally learnt the wrong song. They just know that it's probably the loneliest mammal on earth.

I know exactly how it feels.

As if I'm swimming desperately round and round in repeating circles, singing as hard as I can, but nobody can hear me.

For the first time since I left America, I put my pillow over my head.

And burst straight into tears.

27

According to a recent study, the average teenager cries for two hours and thirteen minutes a week. Thanks to saving it all up, I'm very close to hitting that target in just one session.

I cry until my face hurts and my pillow's wet.

I cry until my chest aches and there are no tears any more: just an exhausted *ng ng ng* sound.

Never mind Jupiter: my heart is now on the sun. It's on a white dwarf. It's somewhere on a neutron star, weighing millions of tonnes and about to rip a channel to the bottom of my toes.

Because there's the massive lie I told Nat: one with a gaping, obvious hole in it.

I am not *OK* at all.

Finally, I stop crying.

I wipe my nose on my duvet and sit up. I grab a piece of paper and a pen from my bedside table.

And I start writing.

Dear Nick,

Here are some things I know about you.

From the moment you were born, there have been 276 major earthquakes and 87 volcano eruptions; 39 solar eclipses and 85 super-moons. The seas have risen by 5 centimetres, and the average temperature of the earth has increased by 0.2 degrees centigrade.

Over the last seventeen years, the planet you are on has travelled 138,253,139,000 kilometres around the Milky Way, 22,673,602,167 kilometres away from the Voyager Probe and 16,590,377,250 kilometres around the sun, taking you with it.

You have had 70 birthdays on Mercury, 27 on Venus, 9 on Mars, 1 on Jupiter (and you will be 29 years old before you have your first birthday on Saturn).

Your heart has beaten 654 million times.

But none of these things are going to stay the same. With every day, you're going to travel a little further, get a little older: the sea will rise, volcanoes will erupt. And all these things I know about you won't be true any more.

Just one thing will.

I miss you, and that's never going to change.

Harriet xxx

28

Quickly, I cram the letter into an envelope.

I scribble an address on the front and stick three rare stamps on it that will carry the letter far, far away: to a strange, foreign place I've never been before. Then I shove my trainers on and run down the stairs before pride or shame or hope can stop me.

"Harriet?" Annabel says as I run through the hallway and fling open the front door. "I thought I could hear crying. Is everything OK?"

"Yes," I say as I close the door softly behind me. "At least, I think it will be now."

I run all the way to the postbox. Which isn't saying much: it's only at the bottom of the road.

But still.

And as I run, Nick runs with me.

*

120

Home, Hertfordshire – January (10 months ago)

"Did you know that snow isn't actually white? It's translucent. It just reflects light uniformly, which makes it *look* white."

"Jump," he instructed, hopping over a large slushy ice puddle and squeezing my hand with his warm, dry fingers. I'd taken my left glove off, claiming it was because I had one randomly hot hand.

This was a small white lie.

Or possibly a translucent one, reflecting light.

My stomach flipped over, and I jumped too late to avoid a totally wet and icy sock.

"Like polar bears, right?" Nick continued as we kept running towards the train station. "They're not actually white either, are they?"

I was impressed: I told him that *months* ago. His ability to retain useless but fascinating information was getting nearly as good as mine.

"Exactly," I said, slipping slightly so that his arm went temporarily round my waist. "We – I mean *they* – aren't what they look like at all."

Then I cleared my throat in embarrassment.

Oops. It was one thing comparing myself to a misfit polar bear in a rainforest in my head occasionally: quite another to do it out loud to my boyfriend.

"I was twelve the first time I saw snow," Nick grinned as we started running down the stairs to the train platform. "I was so excited I got out of bed at 3am and tried to make a snow angel in shorts and a T-shirt."

I rolled my eyes.

"Half of the world's population has never seen snow, Nicholas. Considerably fewer would be that stupid."

He shouted with laughter and my heart squeezed shut for a few seconds, just as it had the first time he did it in Moscow.

"Luckily, I've now got the world's biggest smarty-pants to balance me back out again."

With a quick spin, Nick stopped, wrapped his arms round me and pulled me so close I could feel his breath warming the end of my cold nose. I had just a second to notice that everything was white and still and calm, like a snowglobe just before it gets shaken.

Then he kissed me and it all disappeared: the snow, my wet sock and both my feet with it.

When we finally stopped kissing, we'd missed the train.

"I think I need to balance you faster, in that case," I laughed, cheeks ridiculously warm. "It's an hour to the next train and now you're going to miss your Hilfiger casting."

"Totally worth it. Tell me something else about snow."

"Umm." I rummaged through my brain for a few seconds while Nick opened his big grey coat and pulled me inside it so I wouldn't get cold. "Anything?"

"Tell me anything, Polar Bear Girl," he said, wrapping his arms round me. "Anything at all."

"OK." I found my best snow fact and smoothed it out for a few seconds until it was all neat and clean. "If you had a million snow crystals and compared two of them every second, you'd be there for nearly a hundred thousand years before you found two that matched."

Nick wiped a snowflake off my cheek and pulled me a bit closer. "Funny," he said as it started snowing again. "I must be smarter than we thought. It only took me seventeen years."

And he kissed me again.

I run until I reach the bright red postbox.

For a disorientating second, I can almost believe Nick's here and not on the other side of the world. That it's snowing again and I have one cold sock and two hot cheeks. That he's still with me.

That I'm not on my own.

"I miss you," I whisper, kissing the envelope and posting it through the hole.

And it's like magic: I immediately feel lighter.

As if I've pulled out all the heavy words and sent them far, far away, where they can't weigh me down any more. *I miss you* is gone and – just like that – my heart lifts to a white dwarf, then to the sun, then to Jupiter. Then Neptune and Saturn.

Until, finally, I'm on earth again.

Back where I belong.

29

You know what?

People can say what they like about my hippy grandmother – and judging by my parents they often do – but Bunty told me once that sometimes all you need is a good cry and an even better pen.

I think she might have been right.

By 7am the next morning, I'm feeling infinitely brighter and more positive. In fact, I've even found the massive flaw in my First Day Back plan.

I didn't have one.

After years of careful strategising, I can't believe I tried to fit back into a new life with nothing but a toilet book and an apparently pathological interest in bananas to win people over.

I will never be winging anything again.

Luckily my new plan – aka Harriet's Win People Over And Make Them Like Me Again Plan (HWPOAMTLMAP, for short) – is *so* well designed it starts working before I'm

even through the school gates.

That's how powerful it is.

"Hey," a girl in a yellow dress says, tapping me on the arm. "Do I know you from somewhere? We played volleyball last year, right? Or were you at Meg's party in February, dancing on a table?"

Volleyball. Party. Dancing on a table.

"That doesn't sound like me," I say doubtfully. "If I'd been there I'd have definitely been under it."

She laughs, even though I wasn't actually joking.

"No worries – I'll work it out. Catch you around!"

The girl wanders off and I stare in amazement at the enormous bag I'm carrying with the plan inside it.

Goodness. It's not even *open* yet.

Another two students smile as I wander through the corridors, a girl I vanquished in debate club two years ago nods at me and a group of three boys abruptly stop talking as I walk past.

And no: I'm not dressed as a bumblebee or a duck, my trainers are matching and my clothes are seasonally appropriate.

For the first time ever, I've actually checked.

"Yo, Harriet," Robert says as I reach the classroom. I open my bag and pull a pink plastic Tupperware box out. "It *is* Harriet, isn't it? You look really… nice today."

I blink at him. "Sorry?"

"Yeah. You look really... Err. Cute."

Robert has been in my form for five years, and he once sat on my foot: that's how utterly invisible I usually am to him. I stare at him in shock, then at the box I'm holding, and it all promptly makes sense again.

Oh my goodness: the poor, poor boy.

His parents clearly aren't feeding him properly. His blood sugar levels must be dangerously low.

"Thanks, Robert," I say gently. "You look nice too."

"Do I?" He grins and leans forward until I'm at risk of being stabbed in the eye by one of his gel-points. "Maybe we could look nice together at lunch sometime?"

"Sure," I say sympathetically, awkwardly patting his arm. "I'll save some sugar for you."

"That's what *I'm* talking about," he says, wiggling his eyebrows. "I reckon there's a bit of sugar with my name all over it."

Huh? How does he know that?

"There is, actually," I say in surprise, pushing the classroom door open. "And chocolate chips too, and quite a lot of peanut butt—"

But before I can get any further, every person in the room swivels round.

And the room explodes around me.

30

All I can hear now is a chorus of my name.

"Good morning, Harriet!" "Hey, Harriet!" "How was your evening, Harriet?" "What did you get up to, Harriet?" "Over here, Harriet!"

As if my class has been replaced by a flock of twittering, excited birds.

"Harriet!" Ananya says as I take a bewildered seat. "Or can I call you Ret?"

Ret? That makes me sound like a man with a big moustache and a Panama hat.

"Umm, of course," I mumble in surprise, putting the box on the desk in front of me and getting an even bigger one out. "Ret. Retty. Or… you know. Harriet is also fine."

"I'm so sorry we didn't get a chance to catch up properly yesterday. Sixth-form homework is *mad*, right? I mean, where do they think we get the time from? Does it grow on *trees*?"

"Actually, thyme is a flowering herb," I say distractedly,

still blinking at the rest of the class. "It grows best in pots."

Ananya stares at me blankly, and then explodes in a fit of giggles. "Oh my God, that's so funny! How do you think that quickly?"

I don't know what she's talking about. One neuron in the brain fires 200 times a second, but none of mine have done a single thing since I walked into the room.

I knew my plan was good, but this is ridiculous.

"Oh wow-wow-wow," Liv breathes, pointing at me. "IsthatChanell*love*itit'sso*retro*IreallywishIhadonetoo wheredidyougetitfrom?!"

I glance down in confusion at my bright jumper. I don't know much about designers, but I don't think Coco Chanel was a big fan of badgers wearing top hats and bow ties.

"My grandmother embroidered it for me."

I mean Granny Manners: not Bunty, obviously. The latter would rather poke her own eyes out with a biro than get caught appliquéing knitwear.

"OMGthatis*so*unfair. My nan died *years* before badgers became cool. That is literally so *typical*."

I'm not quite sure how to respond to that.

Then I glance cautiously around the room. Everyone's still staring: Robert keeps winking at me, five girls are whispering and even India gives me a brief nod.

This lot must be *starving*.

I can't help but notice that Jasper is still facing the front, utterly unmoved.

We'll just see about that.

With a sense of triumph, I open my Tupperware box and the comforting smell of freshly baked butter and sugar rises into the air. Inspiration hit me last night, at some point around the fiftieth mumbled *sugar cookie.*

All I needed was something simple and traditional. Something that would show the class that I care about them and want to be their friend: that I'm not as stuck-up as I made them think.

So – in a flash of positivity – I rushed down to a late-night supermarket.

Then I spent the entire night making, icing and decorating three hundred dinosaur-shaped sugar cookies. Pink *Isisauruses* and green *Tangvayosauruses*; purple *Argentinosauruses* and orange *Camarasauruses*. Each one personalised so that everyone in my class had their very own biscuit: name written in silver balls and jelly sweets perched on top.

With enough to win over the rest of the year too.

Maybe a few extra for the teachers.

Three for Steve, obviously: he looks like he has a sweet tooth.

And I might be exhausted, and I may still have flour in my eyebrows, but I don't care. The word *mate* comes from the Middle Low German word *gemate,* which literally means *to eat together.* So maybe this is my best shot at making friends.

Because as people start smiling, chattering to me and munching their way through the biscuits, I think I've actually done it.

I am finally part of a team again.

31

News of my awesome dinosaur biscuits spreads far and wide.

In fact, I don't want to sound smug but I may need to rethink my career objectives. Had I known my baking talents were this prodigious, I'd have taken home economics instead of woodwork.

Unless you intend to be an undertaker, there are only so many wooden boxes a girl needs to make.

During double maths, Raya sits next to me and asks "how I did it" because "it's the sort of thing she's *always* wanted to do but never had the confidence."

"Well," I say. "It's actually surprisingly easy."

Then I explain all about the importance of making sure the room is cool and how it's essential to really focus on the dough. "Although you don't want to work it too hard," I add helpfully. "It'll make it tough."

Raya shakes her head in amazement. "I've *heard* that it can be tough," she says with wide eyes. "Is there… you

132

know. A *lot* of dough involved?"

"It depends," I say, thinking about it honestly. "On this particular occasion, huge amounts. Like, ridiculous quantities. Masses."

I mean, it was 300 cookies, after all.

During breaktime, the girls from the netball team tell me how "lucky" I am because they're "so amazing".

"Thank you, but it's not really luck," I say as modestly as I can. "There's an awful lot of hard work involved and a lot of horrible ones get thrown out in the process. I have to stop my dog eating them."

"Your *dog*? How does that work?"

"I lock him in the laundry room for an hour or so."

"Huh."

By lunchtime, I've been asked to go ice-skating, offered an "ironic" pen with a plastic, fluff-coated unicorn coming out of the top, and gifted a bracelet made out of pink and yellow rubber bands.

I obviously make the best biscuits in the world.

Seriously.

Recent studies have shown that a combination of fat and refined sugar can reduce levels of neurofactors produced by the hippocampus, thus slowing brain capabilities. I'm slightly concerned I may have chemically damaged my classmates permanently.

Let's put it this way: I may postpone trying any until I've at least finished my AS levels and maybe graduated university.

Plus I offered Toby one and he didn't take it.

I think enough said.

By the final period, I've basically set up my own market stall in the corner of the common room. There's a flurry of people lounging around it: chatting and eating and laughing merrily, covered in a fine layer of icing sugar like plastic snowmen.

"Harriet! Want to go shopping this evening?"

"Or down to the local park?"

"Hey, Harriet! How about we go to the cinema and watch something with…" Robert looks me up and down. "Talking cartoon penguins in it?"

I beam at him. I do *love* a good cartoon penguin.

"That's hilarious," Ananya says flatly, taking his sixth biscuit off him. "Are you actually kidding? I think Ret's got slightly higher standards than a sixteen-year-old schoolboy with a face she could buy in Pizza Hut, thanks very much."

Liv appears from behind her.

"I mean, as *if* you could ever compete. Make a wish, fall asleep and dream on." She starts giggling. "OMG, that's brilliant. I'm so funny."

India looks up from the sofa and stares at Robert levelly in silence for a few seconds. "Don't be so creepy," she says coolly. "Also, consider holding back on the hair gel. It's not a dangerous weapon."

Robert glances at all three girls, and then shrugs.

"Oooh, I'm so *intimidated*," he says, taking another biscuit. "Hubble bubble. Laters, witches."

He wanders out of the door, winking at me and still munching away, and I blink at the girls now flanking me: one in front, and one to either side.

Quietly, the rest of the group around the table is dispersing: four girls make an impromptu trip to the vending machine, Christopher decides he has a monologue to learn somewhere far away and Raya apparently needs to redo her make-up in a different room.

Why does it suddenly feel like I've got another three-headed Cerberus? And – much more importantly – what on earth are they talking about and what is going on?

"Umm…" I say awkwardly. "I'm not sure you had to be that…"

Unkind, I'm about to say when I spot two different-coloured eyes in the corner of the room, fixed firmly on mine. There's a plant called the *Mimosa Pudica* that curls up abruptly when touched: folding in on itself to protect itself. It suddenly feels like that's what my stomach is doing too.

Jasper and I stare at each other for a few seconds as my insides retract sharply.

Then he looks away with a scowl, picks up his bag and starts pounding with a rigid back towards the door of the common room. At which point it flings open and Alexa storms in, staring at her phone.

"Hey," he says, dodging to the side. "Be careful where you're—"

But it's too late.

Alexa keeps walking and – with an enormous crash – the two people who like me least in the world collide.

Straight into each other.

32

There's a very good reason why anacondas and crocodiles aren't kept in the same zoo enclosure.

The same logic should probably extend to these two.

Jasper's art bag has fallen open and paints have gone everywhere: smashing into little pieces all over the floor. Reds and blues and greens and yellows are spread in a powdery, wet rainbow across the carpet. A couple of sheets of white paper have fallen out, and they're soaking it all up like soggy rectangular butterflies.

"Brilliant," he sighs, bending down. "Just… brilliant."

He holds the paper up, and for a few seconds I catch an incredibly beautiful pencil sketch of a large orange leaf with an autumn forest drawn inside it: browns and oranges and reds, now ruined by a thick splodge of black and purple.

In the meantime, Alexa is still finishing her text.

"Watch where you're going," she says without looking up. "Freakazoid."

"Oh, I'm so sorry." Jasper throws his paints back in his bag. "I hadn't realised I was the invisible man. Huge apologies for your inability to walk straight through me. I'll look into a way of rectifying that as soon as possible."

Then he flings his bag back over his shoulder, crumples up the ruined pages, throws them into a nearby bin and thunders out of the door. Honestly, there's some comfort to be taken from seeing that Jasper seems to dislike Alexa nearly as much as he dislikes me.

Some comfort. Not lots.

He's still not calling her names or refusing to eat any of her home-made peanut butter biscuits. Despite my best efforts, he hasn't touched a single one.

"Whatever," Alexa snaps absently, still staring at the screen of her phone. "Bye bye, mutant eyes."

Then she presses a final button and looks up.

Slowly, she scans the common room with a bored expression until her eyes finally alight on my corner.

"Oooh," she says, stalking over to me and wrinkling her nose. "Are you selling upside-down ferret biscuits, geek? How adorable."

Excuse me? Upside-down ferret biscuits?

I indignantly draw myself up to my biggest possible

size and make my voice as confident as possible.

"They're Sauropods, actually, Alexa. It means *lizard-footed*, and they were dinosaurs originating in the Triassic period with long tails and long necks. *Diplodocus* and *Brontosaurus* are the most famous versions, although technically the latter was a mistaken *Apatosaurus* and so has never actually existed. It is a dinosaur *myth*."

"Still looks like an upside-down ferret," she says, putting one in her mouth. "Tastes a bit like one too."

Actually, now I'm looking at them again I suppose they kind of do. *Bat poop.* I might need to invest in some proper cookie cutters.

Alexa turns to her minions.

"What are you all doing in here? I told you to meet me on the tennis courts. There's a year ten and she's totally losing it with her boyfriend. It's hilarious. I want to go heckle."

She spins and starts sauntering out of the room again.

"And I thought I told you not to bother with *her* any more," she calls over her shoulder as Ananya and Liv stand up to follow her. "Let's go. As in, *now*."

Except – as she pushes open the sixth-form door – for the second time in two days my nemesis doesn't get quite the exit she was hoping for.

139

"No," a sharp voice says from behind me. "Actually, Alexa, we're not going anywhere."

33

Crayfish warn each other by emptying their bladders at the first sign of danger. As the scariest person I've ever met slowly turns to face us, I'm a bit concerned I'm about to do the same thing.

I've known Alexa Roberts for eleven years, and I've never seen this expression before. Her face is very still and calm, but I'm pretty sure something is about to burst through the surface.

Like, maybe an alien or a great white shark.

"Excuse me? Would you like to repeat that, new girl?"

"Which of those seven words are you struggling with?" India says coolly, picking a little silver ball off a biscuit and sticking it in her mouth. "I'd imagine it's *no*, so I'll give you a few more pointers. We are going to stay here with Harriet today. All three of us. Is that any clearer, or would you like me to draw you a picture?"

Ananya and Liv are now frozen in the space between us mid-step, like enchanted forest fawns turned to stone.

141

They glance at Alexa, then India, then Alexa again.

Then at me.

Until it looks like they're watching a really confusing and awkward game of ping-pong.

Finally Ananya clears her throat.

"Actually," she says slowly, unfreezing and taking a small step back, "Indy's right, Lexi. It's a bit cold outside today. Maybe we should stay here. What do you think, Olivia?"

"Like, *totally.*" Liv folds her arms and takes a step towards me as well. "Also, I think you might be a bit over right now, Lexi. Sorry."

For the first time in history, my nemesis and I now have exactly the same facial expression. A mirrored series of Os: two for eyes, one for a mouth and two tiny ones for shocked, flared nostrils.

She turns slowly towards me, and I'm just about to leave a terrified, Harriet-Manners-shaped hole in the wall when her face abruptly changes.

Muscle by muscle, Alexa relaxes.

Her shoulders lower, her eyes normalise, her nose wiggles, her mouth twitches and a small bubble of sound pops out of her mouth. My entire stomach twists into the shape of a fresh pretzel.

Worse than anger, more dangerous than vengeance.

Is Alexa actually... *laughing*?

"*Oh*," she says, putting a hand over her eyes. "Oh, of *course*. I *get* it now. This is brilliant. How stupid *are* you? You actually think a bus stop is going to *change* things? That everything will be *different* now?"

"A bus stop?" I echo in confusion. "I'm not a bus stop."

At least, I don't *think* I am. I'm so discombobulated right now, though, I wouldn't put any money on it.

But Alexa's not even looking at me any more: she's focused intently on Ananya and Liv. "She's still *Harriet Manners*. The geek who once brought a woodlouse to school and tried to make us hold it."

OK: I was six, his name was Malcolm and I thought he was cute.

"That was a really long time ago," Ananya says, taking another step towards me. "People change."

"*Yeah*," Liv adds. "Maybe we actually *like* her."

"Nobody actually *likes* Harriet," Alexa laughs. "Even her creepy little stalker is nowhere to be seen any more. She's on her own for a *reason.*"

My stomach pretzels a little bit further.

"That's your opinion," India says firmly. "We don't agree."

"Exactly." Ananya takes another few steps until she's

right next to me. "And this is getting a bit boring, Lexi. It's the same old thing, over and over again."

"*Yeah,*" Liv says, standing on my other side. "Also, hanging out on the tennis courts is *so* Year Eleven. Move on, babe. Let it go."

I'm staring at this exchange in bewildered silence.

I'd always seen the Underlings as faceless, voiceless henchmen: existing purely to provide background and visual support, but without identities of their own.

I was obviously very, very wrong.

I'm kind of expecting Alexa to break now the way I would – going red, possibly crying and hiding under a table – but she still looks intensely amused. I can't help being slightly impressed, in spite of myself.

That is pretty majestic self-confidence.

"You're right," she says finally, shrugging. "Things *were* getting a bit boring, weren't they? This way is *so* much more fun. Let's shake it up a bit."

I blink at her. What? What are we shaking?

Oh, God. I bet it's me, isn't it.

"See you around, Harriet Manners," she continues as I stare at her in amazement. "*Enjoy.*"

And the girl who likes me least in the world blows a kiss in my direction and exits the room.

Leaving her three closest friends with me.

34

Here are some things I know:

1. The average human eye can distinguish between 500 shades of grey.

2. Greenland is the coldest country on earth.

3. We all have muscles in our ears that could once be used to move them.

4. A comet's tail always points away from the sun.

Unfortunately, *what the hell is going on* is not on that list.

Call me deeply intuitive – although nobody ever does – but something is starting to tell me that this isn't all about biscuits.

I wait until the bell for the end of school rings and the girls leave in a wave of enthusiastic kisses and hugs. Then

I reach forward and break the tail off a *Camarasaurus*. Or it could be a *Giraffatitan:* honestly, they all just look like upside-down ferrets now.

It's not great.

In fact, I'm going to be honest with you: on a scale of biscuits I've ever eaten (which is a lot) it's pretty near the bottom. Plans to bolster my future palaeontology earnings with a bakery probably won't be materialising.

Frowning, I pull my phone out of my satchel and my ears suddenly go numb with shock. There are ten missed calls from Nat and eight from Stephanie at Infinity Models.

RING ME NOW THIS IS INSANELY URGENT. Nat x

Hands starting to sweat, I hit 1 on Speed Dial. Nat picks up on the first ring, and that's when I know it's serious.

"Meet me in town," she says. "Now."

"But—"

"Seriously, Harriet. You need to see this."

35

I don't even make it to the fountain.

Next to where a large proportion of my year hangs out after school, eating crisps, throwing the packets into the water and then being forced by passers-by to pick them back out again, is a bus stop.

It's where most of the buses pass through on their way to school, on their way home from school, on their way to the shops, to the hospital, to rollerskating, to... anywhere, actually.

In other words: it's right in the middle of everything.

As I slowly approach it, I see a girl I recognise.

Her face is very white and freckled, her eyes are wide and bright green, her nose and chin are slightly too pointy for comfort and her hair is pale red and unbrushed: hanging in a fluffy, knotted mass around her shoulders.

She's sitting in a lake, surrounded by glitter.

Her white dress is sparkling with a thousand tiny flashes of light, the water is glowing and shimmering

around her, and a purple sky is starred above. Behind her is an enormous, pointed mountain with a white tip and a few glowing clouds spiked on top of it. Her eyes are shining, and she's enormous: at least fifteen foot tall, if she stood up.

And next to the sparkling girl is another, much smaller one I also recognise. This one is leaning against the bus stop, against the poster. Her brown eyes are narrowed and her eyebrows are drawn together in consternation.

I reach them both in silence.

"That's not even everything," Nat says after a few seconds, grabbing my hand. "Just wait 'til you see the rest of it."

I am literally *everywhere*.

There's a huge poster of me in the designer section of the local department store: this time floating in Lake Motosu, hair and lights swirling round me as if I'm the Lady of Shalott, except set on fire.

In the make-up department is another photo: me, locked in a glass box in Akihabara, with pale pink hair, gigantic green manga-eyes and bright pink, glossy lips.

The bus-stop photo where I'm crouched in front of Mount Fuji has been turned into shiny flyers and is now being distributed outside the shopping centre to anyone who walks past.

In the window of the local chemist's is an extreme close-up of my face: eyes bright and burning and fixed slightly to the left, as if I'm staring at somebody important that the camera can't see.

Which – obviously – I was.

Nick was standing slightly behind the photographer, and he had just kissed me in the middle of a lake at sunset: I was finding it quite hard to concentrate properly.

With a shake of her head, Nat clicks on Facebook and holds her phone up in silence. I'm running in long adverts down the side of the page, wearing a gold tutu with gold paint all over my face (and tiny physics revision stickers – which I had all over my arms at the time – presumably Photoshopped out).

This doesn't make any sense. At all.

The majority of these are shots I did for designer Yuka Ito's new fashion line – clothes, accessories, make-up, the lot – in Tokyo last summer. Except that was cancelled: the whole campaign was shut down after fashion-house Baylee found out Yuka had broken her contract with them to set up her own label.

So what am I now doing all over everything?

With a sudden brain-click, yesterday's text abruptly makes sense: as if I've just plugged it into Wilbur-Translate on Google.

Wilbur	Every other human in the world
My little chunky-chip!	Hello!
Is this the face that launched a thousand lips?!	Your face is now selling lip gloss on a lot of posters.
Sparkle monkey everywhere!	Seriously, a lot of posters.
Fairy wins again!	Look how great I did!
Gravy	OXO = hug, kiss, hug

The *Alvinella Pompejana*, commonly known as the Pompeii worm, grows a layer of bacteria around it that protects it from high temperatures, allowing it to survive at 80°c. It is the most heat-tolerant animal on earth. Judging from the state of my cheeks right now, I may need to turn into one before I burst into flames completely.

Today's conversations are starting to replay in my head, except now they suddenly sound slightly different.

Or – you know. A lot.

Oh, there are huge amounts of dough involved. Ridiculous quantities. Masses. You really need to focus on making the dough. That's the important part.

You just need to stay as cool as possible.

I am sometimes very hot, yes. Baking, in fact. [I snort with laughter.]

Oh my God. We weren't talking about biscuits *at all*.

I stare at Nat in silence with my cheeks flaming. Why isn't there some kind of magic potion I can drink to stop me being such an idiot? Or at least make me very tiny so I can climb under a toadstool where nobody will hear me say things.

"Hey!" a girl exclaims as she walks past and double-glances at the enormous poster directly behind me. "Oh wow! Is that you?"

She points at the girl in the lake: Photoshopped and glossed and de-flawed, but – thanks to the bright orange hair, pointy nose and lack of make-up – still recognisably me.

That and the blank expression, obviously.

"Umm," I say, swallowing anxiously. "I guess so. Yes?"

"That is so cool! You're, like, famous!"

And before I can stop her, the girl snaps a photo of me with her phone and walks off.

Panic is starting to rise up like an icy tidal wave.

What is she going to do with that? American Indians used to believe that every photograph stole a part of your soul, and it suddenly feels like I've just given an irreplaceable bit of mine to a total stranger with a crystal heart stuck on the front of her bag.

Oh God. Oh God oh God oh God oh—

"Harriet?" Nat says, grabbing my arm. "Are you OK?"

"Uh-uh," I say blankly as the panic keeps rising: to my ankles, to my knees, to my stomach and my shoulders. "Mmmm. Brilliant. Superbo."

"Totally not a word," Nat says gently, patting me as if I'm a small puppy on firework night. "This is *freaking awesome*, H. I'm *so* proud of you." She strokes my arm a few more times – eyes shiny and far away – and then adds in a burst of triumph: "I *knew* you'd be a megastar eventually."

And that does it.

Panic washes up from my shoulders, into my throat and over my head until I can't breathe. Leaving me with no other option but to abruptly crouch down on the floor outside the chemist's, put my head between my knees.

And have a very un-awesome panic attack.

36

Experts say that the best way to stop a panic attack is to find something else to think about.

Unfortunately, there's a massive flaw in this logic.

I'm now so anxious about finding something else to think about I can't inhale at all.

In desperation, I close my eyes and begin reciting the periodic table loudly: starting at the alkali metals and working to the right until I can feel myself beginning to calm down again. *Lithium. Sodium. Potassium. Rubidium.* Then Alkaline earth metals. *Beryllium, Magnesium, Calcium, Strontium.* Then Transition metals: *Scandium, Yttrium, Titanium.*

I'm all the way into the noble gases before I'm stable enough to look up again.

The irony of which does not escape me.

"You know…" Nat says, sitting on her coat next to me. She hands me half a chocolate-chip biscuit she must have found at the bottom of my satchel. "You may be the only supermodel in the world who repeats the entire periodic table when stressed."

"It wasn't the entire thing," I admit sheepishly. "I still had lanthanoids and actinoids to go. And ununoctium." Then I stuff the entire cookie in my mouth and anxiously spray: "And I'm not a supermodel, Nat."

Except it comes out *nmnaspamdlnatttt*.

"Maybe not quite," Nat agrees, grinning with excitement. "But you're *definitely* about a million steps closer."

A few more waves of terror ripple through me.

You know what's utterly ridiculous?

I've been modelling for nearly a year now – since I was unintentionally spotted at a fashion event that Nat dragged me to. Ten full months of getting paid to stand in front of a camera and wear beautiful clothes in foreign countries – first Russia, then Japan, then New York – and this is the first time it's actually felt *real*. All this time, I've used modelling to run away, to run towards – to escape, find myself, lose myself, transform – but never as an end in and of itself. I've been so focused on the verb – *modelling* – that it never once occurred to me that I'm also the noun.

Harriet Manners: *model*.

Or that my face might actually one day be used in

public to, you know: sell things.

Because apparently I'm an intelligent girl with no grasp of cause and effect, who thought she could have all these great fashion adventures and then the evidence would just up and vanish as soon as she was done.

Poof! Like the magical fairytales they were.

Seriously. I'm supposed to be getting smarter as I get older. Nobody told me it would be the other way round.

"What is this dress even made of?" Nat continues, staring at the leaflet. "How does it light up like that?"

"It's thin woven optical fibres," I say distantly. "They're hollow, which allows photons of light to bounce down the centre of them and—"

A sudden memory flashes.

Nick, looking like the world's most beautiful banana in yellow wellies and a yellow waterproof coat. I can remember the exact coldness of the water, the precise warmth of my stomach and fingers and toes. The position of the stars and the lights; the shape of the mountain and the lake. The happy glow in his eyes.

The happy glow in mine.

Now immortalised and stuck all over town to remind me of exactly what I don't have any more every time I need to buy deodorant.

Without equal.

Oh my God: of all the shoots I've ever done, why did they have to stick *this* one in the window of the chemist? I'm going to smell for the rest of the year.

Wobbling slightly, I get to my feet.

Abruptly, I need to get as far away from both the shopping precinct and this particular photo as fast as physically possible.

"Harriet," Nat says, jumping up too, "I know you're freaking out right now, but I honestly think you just need a little time to process how amazing this is. This is *huge*, H. It's *epic*. You've really made it."

I stare at my best friend blankly.

"Here," she adds, thrusting a leaflet into my hand. "I'm so sorry, but I need to run back to college for a late class on evening gowns. I only popped out to pick up some extra material."

Nat pulls a bit of black satin out of her bag to show me, gives me a tight hug, then starts trotting towards the bus stop. "Call me when it's sunk in, OK?" she yells over her shoulder.

I nod, but honestly: she may be waiting some time.

According to the Oxford English Dictionary, the word *epic* can mean *impressive or remarkable*.

It can also mean *heroic or grand in scale*.

Since I was five years old, I've thought about all the

ways I might eventually make my mark on the world. Dragons I could fight and winged horses I could fly and elements I could magic into being with my bare hands. Then – when I got a little older – I dreamed about diseases I could cure, dinosaur fossils I could unearth and stars I could discover and then name.

I've spent eleven *years* of my life studying as hard as I can in the hope that one day – with enough knowledge, enough commitment and enough dedication – I might eventually achieve something worthwhile.

Something heroic. Something grand.

Something *epic*.

I just never thought for a single second that my most tangible achievement would come at sixteen years old for sitting in a lake, wearing somebody else's clothes and staring at a camera.

Doing absolutely *nothing*.

37

On the upside, somebody else knows what I look like too now. As soon as Nat's gone, I somehow stumble to the bench near my house, plonk myself down and make the obligatory call-back.

My hands are shaking, my head is spinning.

My fingers are so sweaty it takes four attempts before I can get my phone to stop taking accidental selfies up my nostrils.

"Lovely *girl*! How *are* you, darling? We haven't *spoken* for simply *ages*!"

I pull my phone away from my face and stare at Stephanie's voice for a few seconds. We haven't spoken for simply ages because last time I rang Infinity Models I heard her say:

"Who? Tell her I'm out."

"But I can hear her," I observed, and the receptionist passed the message on.

"Then tell her I'm dead. Freak polo accident."

158

"I can still hear her," I said sadly. "But thanks for trying."

I've rung Infinity Models thirteen times over the four months since my return from Tokyo, and this is the first time Wilbur's replacement has ever picked up. It's quite difficult to really get to know someone properly when they're pretending to fall off horses.

"I'm fine, thank you." I'm slightly tempted to point out she sounds pretty buoyant for a recently deceased person.

"That's 'triffic!" she trills. "And *how's* your…" There's a pause while she tries to remember anything about me. "*Anyway*, I was just calling to say that my phone has been on *fire* this morning with *love* for my best model. Those photos are *just scrummy*. What a *seuw-per* time you must have *had* in China!"

"Japan."

"Exactly! I just *adore* Mount Kilimanjaro!"

"Fuji."

"Yah! I have some *very* big designers who want to see you, ey ess ey pee. Gucci, Prada, Versace, you name it. Pop in on Monday and I'll set up some meetings."

I blink. "I'm sorry, Stephanie, but I'm at school."

"*Are* you, darling? How *delightful*! What *for*?"

"Umm." I've never had to explain the concept of education before. "Knowledge. Learning. Books and my future and so on."

"Ri-iiiiight. And that can't be cancelled?"

I haven't actually met Stephanie before, but I suddenly remember that Wilbur isn't exactly a fan, to say the least.

"Not really, because… you know. It's *school*."

"That's terribly inconvenient. Perhaps we should consider phasing it out. You know, gradually doing less of it." There are a few loud taps on a keyboard. "Yah, no, yah. I'll work something out. In the meantime, how does first thing tomorrow sound?"

"Sorry, sound for what?"

"Three days in Marrakech. Lovely job for Levaire, just come through today."

We each blink an average of 6.25 million times a year, but if I'm not careful this phone call is going to use up the rest of my year's rations and I'll have to walk round until Christmas with my eyes shut.

"Levaire? As in Jacques Levaire, the jeweller?" Even *I've* heard of him. Nat's unsuccessfully had a Levaire necklace on her Christmas list ever since she realised Santa was actually her mother. "Marrakech as in… *Marrakech*?"

"Yah, darling. Spain, Europe. Vah hot. Sand and so forth."

"Morocco," I say automatically. "North Africa." I'm starting to wonder if Stephanie needs me to send her a world map.

160

"Exactly, darling. That's what I said."

I stare at my phone.

An hour ago, I assumed my fashion career was completely done. Now my face is all over town and I'm being invited to *Africa* to shoot for *Jacques Levaire*.

With an abrupt lurch, my heart does a familiar, excited humpback whale leap: into the sky, twisting around.

I'd *love* to go to Morocco.

I know quite a lot about it already: it's the westernmost country in the Arab world, and some say Hercules himself forced apart Europe and Africa with his bare hands, thus forming the Straits of Gibraltar. It's also considered by many as one of the most dramatic, exotic and compelling destinations there is, and I've studied all the guidebooks already.

Just – you know – in case.

It would mean modelling again, and I've actually kind of missed it.

It would be an adventure.

Plus, most importantly, it'll give me something to do other than sitting on my doorstep, staring at the sky and *waiting*.

"I'll—" I start, then stop.

The whale crashes back into the water again with an enormous splash.

I can't *keep* using modelling to run away, can I? I have polynomials and factor/remainder theorem to learn at school tomorrow.

My parents will go *mad*.

Not to mention the fact that I've just discovered I don't really like seeing my face on posters very much. It gives me anxiety attacks on the floors of shopping malls.

But… *Morocco.*

"Stephanie, may I have a couple of minutes to think about it?"

"Absolutely. And Hannah, dahling?"

"It's Harriet."

"Yah. This one is fifteen."

I blink a few more times. Fifteen years? Fifteen carrots? Fifteen bottles, hanging on the wall?

"Pounds?" That's not a *huge* amount of money, but I'm really not super experienced, I haven't worked in a month, the flights must cost quite a lot and then there's hotels to think about and…

"Fifteen grand, darling. Think about it."

And the phone goes dead.

Stephanie may be gone – although probably not to the Other Side just yet – but I'm still staring at the phone.

Fifteen *thousand* pounds? Somebody wants to give

me fifteen *thousand* pounds for something I'd happily do for free?

That is an *awful* lot of money.

Not just for a sixteen-year-old, either. It's three years' income for a single man in possession of a good fortune, according to *Pride and Prejudice*. It's 911 times what Jo March sold her hair for in *Little Women* and nearly two months of James Bond's salary. It's – perhaps slightly more relevantly – one and a half whole years at Cambridge University.

My head is starting to spin; my hands are shaking.

So I take an enormous breath and decide to ring the only person left in the world who might actually have some answers.

And that is really saying something.

Wilbur.

38

It takes eighteen attempts to finally reach him, but I just keep staunchly going until I do.

Frankly, I have never played it cool in my entire life.

I don't think now is the time to start.

"Squirrel-hips!" he squeaks finally. "Hold your Shetland ponies, this boy has written the wrong name on my pumpkin-spiced latte." Wilbur's voice gets a little more distant. "It's with a *bur*, not an *iam*. Yes, like the pig in *Charlotte's Web*…. *Excuse* me?"

"My little sugar-lump," he says, coming back to the phone. "I don't care how adorable this American barista is, if he oinks at me again I *will* report him to the RSPCA."

It suddenly feels like there's a piece of apple lodged in my throat. I hadn't realised when Wilbur left England for a new fashion job in New York quite how big the hole he'd left in my life would be.

"Wilbur, what outfit are you wearing?" I really need to visualise him. "At this precise moment, what have

164

you got on?"

He takes this very creepy question completely in his stride. "A fake fur panda poncho with sticky-up ears and fluoro pink trousers that just *scream* I'm All That And A Bag of Kale Chips, darling. I look fabulous. Everybody wants to be me, or date me, or dehydrate me and keep me *forever.* Like a fig or maybe a raisin."

I smile in satisfaction. I could be in New York right now, trying hard not to cuddle him like a massive rainbow kitten.

"So what's cookin', my little pookin'? Did you get my text?"

"Umm. Yes." I swallow and to my horror, there's a slight wobble in my voice. "That's actually why I'm ringing. Wilbur, I don't understand. What's happening? Why is my face everywhere? I thought Yuka's campaign wasn't going ahead any more."

Wilbur snorts loudly with laughter.

"Oh, *dilly*-dandelion," he giggles. "That was *never* going to happen. Yuka obviously took Baylee to court immediately, like the rabid Rottweiler of fashion she is. After she won she decided to go *hugeungous* with her new label to make a point. *Shoe-fungous, moo-gungous, boo-gungous.*"

One day – when we've got less to discuss – I'm going

to ask Wilbur why he doesn't just say *big*.

"But why with me?"

"I thought that was obvious, monster-munch. You've always been her favourite ginger-frog. So much love in the room."

Over the course of my modelling career, Yuka Ito has shouted at me, turned lights off and on over my head, locked me in glass boxes, thrown me into cold water, surrounded me with dead things and fired me. She must put models she's *not* fond of in the oven and then eat them.

"But what about the gold-painted photo?" I ask in confusion. "That was for Baylee, wasn't it?"

"Indeed it was," Wilbur laughs. "Yuka poached you off them too: I think this is their way of fighting witch with fire. Oooh, that reminds me. She had a message for you and I'll remember it just as soon as this caffeine hits my bloodstream. It's a triple shot so it won't take long."

I can hear him blowing on his coffee 3,459 miles away: bright blue sky above him, yellow and orange leafy Central Park behind him, Empire State Building looming over. Brooklyn Bridge is suddenly so close I can almost see it.

I feel a homesick pang in my chest. Which is weird because I'm sitting right next to the house I actually live in.

"Boom," Wilbur continues jubilantly. "She says: *done*."

"*Done?* What does that mean?"

"Sugar-munch, if I understood what Yuka Ito was talking about I'd be the only person in the world and would have an entirely different and very lucrative career as a Yuka-whisperer."

I frown. She probably means *done*, as in *cooked*: marinated and ready for frying, quite possibly.

And then it hits me.

Last December, I stood in Infinity Models with a spotlight over my head and told Yuka I wanted to model so that *things would change*.

More specifically: me.

That's what she's done: she's given me exactly what I asked for. It just didn't happen according to the schedule I originally laid out for it, that's all.

I'm starting to realise maybe nothing ever does.

"So…" I'm ripping at the skin around my fingernails with my teeth. "What happens next, Wilbur? What do I do?"

"Chipmunk," he laughs. "I'm your fairy godmother, not your fortune cookie. Tell me, is Stephanie still wearing scrunchies without any kind of irony? She should *not* be allowed in fashion. The woman is single-handedly preventing velvet from coming back in again."

It's only now starting to hit me that I've never done this before without him and I'm not sure I know how to.

"Wilbur, if I take the job in Morocco, will you come with me? Please?"

"I'd love to, munchkin," he sighs. "I am so over New York I could hurdle it in eight-inch heels. But fairy godmothers don't go to the ball, as much as we might want to. We simply get you ready and send you on your way."

I stare at the pavement, because maybe that's the problem. "But what if I'm *not* ready?"

"Then don't go," Wilbur says more gently. "Fame, fortune, success: you can take them or leave them, baby-baby-panda. We've given you the fairytale. What you do with it now is up to you."

39

Head still spinning, I say goodbye to Wilbur.

Then, slowly, I open the sweaty, crumpled photo I have scrunched in my hands.

I stare at the glittering girl in the lake.

Underneath **YUKA ITO** in small, gold letters is a picture of a glass perfume bottle that looks like a flame: frosted white glass that starts dark gold at the bottom and gets clearer and lighter towards a tip that curves upwards. There's a tiny light built into the base, so the entire bottle looks like it's glowing from the inside.

Beneath that is one large, silver word:

SHINE

And I suddenly feel like I'm splitting down the middle: torn into two pieces.

On one side is Harriet Manners, *geek*.

Shy, clumsy, anxious and unpopular. Awkward and constantly apologetic. Collector of stick insects, inventor of personalised Monopoly games, dryer of socks. Dressed like a duck, hyperventilating on floors and hiding under tables.

Embracer of other people's stories instead of her own.

Heartbroken, lonely and left behind.

On the other side is Harriet Manners, *model*.

Traveller through exotic foreign countries, grabber of opportunities, chaser of adventures. Successful and interesting. Wearer of designer clothes, desired employee of the fashion industry, explorer of strange cities and adored girlfriend of Nicholas Hidaka.

Loved, wanted and remembered.

Today at school suddenly flashes in front of me.

That's what has changed, isn't it?

Thanks to these impossibly beautiful and glossy photos, everybody has seen another side to me. The geek they've known for years has evaporated overnight, and in her place is the seemingly confident, successful version of me. Fearless and mysterious; intrepid and brave.

They've seen this glittering girl and they like her.

And you know what?

I think I do too.

I stare at the photo for a few more seconds, and – with an abrupt *crack* – I suddenly know which one of these two girls I want to be. And clue: it's not the one who hides under her duvet, crying and wishing life was different.

"Stephanie?" I say when she picks up on the second ring. "I'm taking the job. In fact, from this point onwards I'll be taking all of them."

"*Seuwper*," she says, tapping on a few keys. "I've just put the phone down on Gucci, Wang and McQueen so we'll sort something out for when you're back. This is just the start, darling. You're going to be *huge*. Deets on the way."

As I hang up, a tidal wave rushes over me again, except this time it's not cold or panicky.

It's warm and hopeful, and it leaves me glowing.

Everything in my life has already changed, and this is my only chance to change with it. To pick up my own story and turn the pages.

To start moving forward again.

Because whether I wanted to or not, nearly a year

ago I split in half. There are now two Harriets, two lives, two people I can be.

Wilbur was right: it's up to me which one I want.

And I choose the one that shines.

40

So, here are some interesting facts about lying:

- By the age of four, ninety per cent of children understand the concept of telling falsehoods.
- Sixty per cent of adults can't make it through a ten-minute conversation without saying something that isn't true.
- Compulsive lying makes you scientifically smarter.
- We're much likelier to lie to the people we love than to strangers.
- I do it a lot.

Like, a *lot* a lot.

I don't *mean* to, obviously. It's just that I've worked out over a period of sixteen years that the chances of upsetting people, not getting what you want and finding yourself in trouble tend to be *considerably* higher if you tell the truth.

However, I have *also* learnt that building an intricate web of deceit almost always results in me getting caught in the middle of it, like a really stupid spider.

So I sit on the bench for a few minutes and think really hard. I do a little internet research. I make a couple of important decisions.

Then I decide to try something brand new.

Something unprecedented; something nobody would ever expect me to do in a million, billion years.

For the first time in known history, I resolve not to wear a thematically brilliant costume or make a fiercely relevant PowerPoint presentation. I won't be typing out any clever arguments about insects or writing pie charts or flow charts or area graphs and then forcing them on my parents.

I'm not going to run away, or cry, or cover myself in dots of lipstick and coat myself in a fine layer of talcum powder to feign sickness, and I won't pretend to fall down the stairs or break an arm or fake my own death with a very noisy vacuum cleaner.

Nope.

This time really matters, so I need to bring out the big guns. I need to concentrate all my persuasive powers and give it everything I've got.

So I do something I've never, ever done before.

I walk calmly home. I walk calmly into the living room. I sit down calmly with my parents.

And I tell them everything.

Or nearly everything, anyway.

I give them the leaflet and explain in detail about the impact of this campaign on my fashion career, and how Jacques Levaire now wants me to go to Morocco for a shoot.

But I keep my new mission to myself.

The truth can be a powerful thing; it's not sensible to overdo it.

"I'm confused," Annabel says when I've finally finished, still staring at the glittering girl clutched in her hand. "Where's the PowerPoint presentation? What's happening?"

"It's a trick," Dad says, narrowing his eyes at the corners of the room. "Mark my words, there's a camcorder here somewhere, humiliating us on telly as we speak."

He winks and blows the DVD player a kiss.

"It's not a trick," I say even more calmly. "Parents are statistically the most lied-to section of society, and I think I speak for all of us when I say I am normally at the very forefront of this movement. I just thought I'd experiment with a different approach this time, that's all."

There's a silence while Dad checks under the coffee table.

Then he explodes into the air.

"OH MY GOD my daughter is a SUPERMODEL and I'm going TO *MOROCCO*!" he shouts, running into the hallway and tugging his suitcase out from under the stairs. "Finally! Casinos, Formula One and Grace Kelly! This is the life to which I've intended to become accustomed for *ages.*"

"That's Monaco, Richard," Annabel says, still looking at the flyer. "You're thinking of Monaco."

"Oh." He pauses. "Does Morocco have private jets? Because if so I think I could be equally happy there."

Finally my stepmother looks up and stares steadily at me, as if I'm a foreign film she's trying to translate and it's much, much harder than she expected.

My hands are starting to sweat again. I've had an entire lifetime of trying to fool my parents. This was an *extremely* risky moment to stop doing it.

I grip my hands together a little more tightly.

Frankly, I know exactly who I have to convince, and it is not my father. I could have won him over with half a packet of crisps and a chocolate digestive.

"Please, Annabel. I miss modelling, it's an amazing opportunity, a *lot* of money and I will make up the two days I miss from school. I'm even prepared to take Dad with me."

Prepared. Which is not the same as *willing*.

"WOOOOOOOO!" my father yells from the corridor. "Yachts! Helicopters! A tax haven full of parties and glitz and—"

"Still Monaco, Richard." Annabel hands the leaflet back to me. "That's a lovely photo, Harriet. You look absolutely beautiful. The answer's yes."

I nod slowly.

"I understand. Thank you for your time and considera— Sorry, what?"

"You can go. Absolutely. Yes."

"But…" My calmness has now evaporated. "*What* would you – *why* would you… *Why*?"

"Why not? You've just proved to me that you're not a little girl any more. You've explained things logically, you've been honest and it makes total sense. It's entirely our fault that you missed the first four weeks of term, so I don't think two more days are going to make a vast amount of difference. In fact, I think a bit of an adventure in Morocco is just what you need right now given… everything. I'm wholeheartedly behind it."

I stare at Annabel in amazement.

What? She has got to be kidding me. I can't believe

I've spent so many years slamming doors: I could have saved *so* many hinges if I'd just tried this approach earlier.

I close my eyes tightly for a few seconds – relief rushing through me – then impulsively throw myself on the sofa and bury my nose in my stepmother's pinstripe shoulder-pad.

"*Thank you*," I whisper, lobbing my arms round her. "I'm going to be *so good,* Annabel. I'll do everything I'm told, I won't break anything, I won't get into any trouble, and I'll…"

Somehow lose Dad.

Maybe exchange him for a camel, or a really useful leather footrest.

"Oh, I know," Annabel says calmly, folding up her crossword and kissing the top of my head. "Because this time, I'm coming with you."

41

Dad sulks for the rest of the evening.

"You went to Russia with Harriet," Annabel explains as she retrieves our summer clothes from under her bed. "It's my turn, isn't it?"

"Well, if I'd known it was a *choice*, I'd have picked this trip," Dad complains. "It was *really* cold out there, and there was nothing but cabbage to eat. Plus none of the Russian supermodels would talk to me. This is *so unfair.*"

This is so unfair is then repeated for the rest of the evening.

It's so unfair as we pack our suitcases, and so unfair as we fold up our maps and get out our guidebooks. It's unfair as we pull the suncream out of the cupboard, and *really really really* unfair when we look at the temperatures and discover it's twenty-six degrees in Morocco and climbing. It's unfair as we put our suitcases in the car the next morning, and unfair as Dad drives us to the airport.

But by the time my father leaves us at the security gates, he appears to have finally made peace with the decision.

"On the bright side," he says cheerfully, kissing us both goodbye, "when Harriet goes to the Maldives, I'm first in line, right?"

"Absolutely," Annabel says, kissing him back and snuggling the top of Tabitha's head. I give my sister a little kiss as well and she squeaks so adorably I'm temporarily tempted to put her in my bag and take her with us.

"Take care of my baby, OK?"

Although – frankly – by this point it's not really clear which one of the two she's referring to.

In the meantime, my excitement levels are rising rapidly and exponentially. With the help of my guidebooks, my fact books, my translation books and my detailed maps of Marrakech, I've spent pretty much the entire last fifteen hours studying.

I know about the prehistoric rock engravings of the Figuig region. I know about the 50,000-year-old remains of a sixteen-year-old Neanderthal boy discovered in a cave near Rabat, and the magical city of Chefchaouen: painted entirely blue to symbolise the skies and the heavens.

I also know that nobody else wants to know these things: the old man next to me pretends to fall asleep halfway through me reading him the Moroccan Political History Chart on page four of my chunkiest guidebook.

But as the plane climbs through the grey clouds over London and pops into a bright blue, shiny sky, it feels like the excited bubbles inside me are multiplying by the second: not unlike the experiment we did in biology last year with micro-organisms in a Petri dish.

Except hopefully slightly more glamorously.

And with slightly less fuzzy green mould.

"Ssalamu lekum," I say experimentally to the air hostess as she brings us round peanuts. (This means *hello* in Arabic.) "Sbah el kheyr," I say cheerfully as she gives me a wet towel. (*Good morning.*) "Me ssalami," I chirp as she offers us breakfast.

"We don't have salami," she frowns. "It's a cheese or beef sandwich."

"I was trying to say *goodbye* in Arabic," I explain.

"Then that's m'a ssalama."

I quickly scan my translation book for *thank you*. "*Shukrun bezzef*," I attempt.

"Beef it is," she says, plonking it in front of me.

By the time large, dusty expanses of land outside the plane window start to speckle with exotic peach and orange buildings, I'm so high on adrenaline I'm tempted to run up and down the aisles of the plane, clapping my hands together and screaming.

Except there's already a four-year-old doing that, and it's not making her very popular.

So I probably won't.

Finally, the plane makes a smooth landing and the two of us – both child and I – break into uproarious applause. Then Annabel and I tug our suitcases through a white, delicately carved airport that looks exactly like an ornate wedding cake, towards a man holding a sign that says **HANNAH MANNERS**.

I'm way too thrilled to correct him.

According to my research, there are three Harriet Manners in the world, and for the next half-hour I am more than happy to no longer be one of them.

The driver leads us in silence out of enormous, glass airport doors into hot, dense, fragrant air. Then I hesitate for a few seconds and fiddle anxiously with a piece of paper in my pocket.

Annabel looks at me steadily.

She's let me chatter in excitement the entire way here: for six solid hours. In fact, when the lady sitting in front of us turned round and glared at me with a loud, pointed sigh, Annabel took her glasses off and stared until the lady went pink and disappeared again.

Now it feels like my stepmother's reading me as

carefully as I've been reading any of my guidebooks. I just don't know quite what she's looking for, that's all.

"Umm." I clear my throat. "Annabel, will you give me a few seconds? There's just something quick I have to do before we get there."

My stepmother studies my face a little longer.

Then she puts her sunglasses on.

"Absolutely. Take your time. I'll be in the car, making sure your father hasn't already exchanged our youngest for a PlayStation."

She winks at me and I wink back.

Then I walk across a bright, sunlit pavement into the shade of an enormous palm tree, feeling more full of hope than I have in weeks.

Maybe this time I don't need Wilbur after all.

42

Cautiously, I move around the side of the tree until Annabel can't see me. Then I open the scrumpled piece of paper that has been clutched tightly in my hand ever since I printed it out this morning: the online research I did while sitting on the bench last night.

The bit of truth I kept from my parents.

How To Find Your Inner Star!!!

1. *Be Confident!* You are a creature unlike any other!
2. *Take Risks, Be Brave!* There is no limit to what you can do!
3. *Be Stylish!* Shake it up and try something new!
4. *Inspire!* Lead, never follow!
5. *Don't try too hard!* It just looks desperate!!!!
6. *Believe in yourself!* Soon everyone else will to!

I've been surreptitiously reading and memorising it since I found it.

184

I didn't write it, obviously.

If I *had*, I'd have corrected *to* to *too* and held back on quite a few of the exclamation marks. That much punctuation is basically the grammatical equivalent of grabbing somebody by the collar and shaking them while screaming right into their face.

Which is exactly why I screenshot the list directly off the internet and left them all there. This is incredibly important, and I don't want to get anything wrong because I've gone and corrected some grammar.

Also, maybe this kind of aggressive positive energy is *exactly* what I need in my life right now. Something to get me moving in the right direction, when I'm not sure quite how to do it by myself. It's like having my very own perky, bouncy life coach in my pocket, or maybe some kind of tiny sergeant major.

Jubilantly, I kiss the list that's going to alter my life.

I put the paper in my pocket, walk to the car and climb into the back with the most confident swish of my head I can possibly manage.

Then – just for added impact – I put my sunglasses on.

They're bright red and they've got glitter all over them. I got them in the airport and they remind me of Dorothy's magic slippers.

Except I didn't have to kill anyone to get them.

Obviously.

"Ready?" Annabel says as the car pulls away from the airport and begins its dusty, winding journey into the centre of Marrakech.

"I am." I smile brightly at her. "I'm ready."

Because if you do the same thing over and over again, you can't expect different results.

If I really want *things to change*…

They have to start with me.

43

When I was ten years old, I had my tonsils out.

And I *still* managed to tell the entire hospital ward that for thirty minutes after they've been removed, human tonsils can bounce higher than a rubber ball if dropped on the floor.

What I'm trying to say is: it takes an awful lot to shut me up. Within three minutes, Morocco has somehow achieved it.

As we drive slowly into the ancient medina, the world outside the car windows begins to unravel into a carnival of colour and noise. Narrow, dusty streets are crammed with people in long turquoise robes, pink scarves, blue and red and green hats, embroidery in white and grey and purple. Cars are everywhere – beeping at each other and parked willy-nilly in streets while drivers talk to each other, yell, laugh and shout – and scooters weave nonchalantly in and out of the traffic.

Dotted here and there are animals: horses, trotting

187

along the road drawing little green carriages; wild-eyed ginger cats, streaking down alleyways; brown donkeys laden with brightly woven bags and camels chewing patiently in little huddles.

And as we get out of the car and start wheeling our bags through narrow, cobbled streets, it intensifies yet further.

From uneven peach and yellow walls hang fabrics in every colour of the rainbow; red and yellow bags, silver jewellery, rows of sparkling slippers in greens and oranges, glass lanterns, carved wood and painted ceramics.

Sunshine stripes the walls and floors with lines of yellow, and the smell changes every few seconds: from fruit to incense to flowers to a faint scent of urine mixed with leather.

Sounds are blended – French, Arabic, English, American, laughter, music, shouts – and piles of food lie glistening on tables: pointed mounds of musky spices, trays of figs, mountains of oranges in carefully constructed pyramids.

Every time I turn my head, there's something else to see, something else to smell.

Finally, the driver stops outside a small, heavy wooden blue door and knocks on it.

With a loud squeak, it swings open.

And the world transforms yet again.

The chaos has abruptly disappeared.

A long turquoise pool stretches across the floor, lit from below. Lanterns line pale, marble floors with arched doorways, tinkling flute music plays, columns and ornate iron balconies stretch upwards in a mass of stone carvings.

Enormous stained-glass lights hang from the ceiling, and flowers, mirrors, incense sticks, elaborately painted furniture and silk cushions are scattered everywhere like a carnage of tired butterflies.

It feels as if we've climbed inside the lamp of a particularly house-proud genie.

"Right," Annabel says after a few minutes of totally awestruck silence. She sinks into one of the velvet sofas with a little sigh. "This is my new house, Harriet. If your father wants me, tell him I will be in this exact position for the next three years."

"That's what I like to hear." A gentleman walks towards us in white trousers and a white tunic. He has two tiny glasses of steaming honey-coloured liquid, which he places calmly in front of us. "I'm so glad you like it. Alan wa Salan. Mint tea?"

"Make that five years," Annabel says, gratefully taking her glass. "Six if there's a ginger biscuit."

"Hello, Alan," I say, sticking my hand out *confidently* and plonking my suitcase down. "It's nice to meet you, and also super cool that your first name rhymes with your last name. You must have very poetic parents."

Alan laughs.

"*Alhan wa salhan* means *welcome* in Arabic. My name is Ali, and I'm the manager of this riad. There is a Berber proverb that says you have to calm the surface of the lake to see to the bottom." He waves a hand gracefully around. "That is what I try to achieve here. Anything you wish, it is my pleasure to grant."

I beam at him. Looks like we found the genie.

"Eight years," Annabel whispers, standing up and looking at the carved stone ceiling. "Nine if there's a garden."

"I'm afraid you only have a couple of minutes to freshen up," Ali continues, gently pivoting both our suitcases and leading us quietly through a little marble hallway into a powder-blue room, full of flowers and lilac silks and bright paintings. "The crew is setting up in Jemaa el-Fnaa at the moment."

There's a four-poster bed, which I immediately sit on and start happily bouncing up and down.

"Ali, did you know that Morocco contains one of the most ancient civilisations in the entire world? The oldest ever child's skull was found here. It dates back a hundred and eight *thousand* years, which means it's all the way from the early Pleistocene period. Isn't that cool?"

"Very cool," Ali says with a small smile. "The director and stylist are in the lounge now. When you're ready, I'll take you down."

"Thank you so much." I bounce a few more times. "Also, did you know that in Morocco you have *forty* different ecosystems of animals, which used to include lions and bears and—"

I abruptly stop. Hang on a minute.

"Sorry, *director*? Do you mean… photographer?"

"Apologies," Ali says, bowing slightly. "I'm not totally up to speed with fashion terminology. What do you call a man who directs a television commercial?"

A man named Ashrita Furman holds the current world record for the most forward rolls ever done in one hour (1,330). He also holds the record for the fastest somersaults, longest top spinning, quickest leapfrogging and most star jumps, and is arguably a very twisty and flippy kind of man.

I think my stomach just beat him at all of them.

Oh my God.

I'm here to shoot a television commercial?

"I think th-there's been some kind of mistake," I eventually stutter, jumping up and grabbing Ali's hand.

"I'm not an actress, I'm a model and I'm here to shoot a campaign for Jacques Levaire and—"

"I'm afraid there's no time," Ali says brightly, handing me three sheets of A4 paper covered in very small writing. "See you in a few minutes, Hannah Manners."

44

Here are just a few occasions when I have failed to move as expected in public:

- The time I sat down on a catwalk in Moscow in front of three hundred of the fashion elite
- The moment I smashed my way out of a glass arcade game in Akihabara
- The destruction of a couture dress as a result of irritating an octopus until it squirted me with ink
- Every single time I try to put a straw in my mouth without concentrating properly
- Approximately a billion other occasions.

Frankly, my clumsiness has already been pretty well documented.

I'm not entirely sure we need any more evidence.

Especially not on film.

With my brain making small, desperate clicking sounds,

I stare in confusion at the paper I've just been given. It appears to be some kind of brief, with JACQUES LEVAIRE INTERNATIONAL TIMEPIECE ADVERTISING CAMPAIGN typed at the top. With a CV and photo stapled to the front.

It's definitely me – I recognise the freckles, the too-far-apart eyes, the pointy nose and vacant expression – but underneath it in neatly italicised letters is written:

HANNAH MANNERS
model-artist-performer-dancer-actress

I've been hyphenated *five* times?

Even in my panic I can't help feeling quite impressed: pushy American model Kenderall would be so jealous of me right now.

"Trained at RADA?" Annabel frowns over my shoulder. "Graduated from a dance programme with the Royal Academy of Arts? A summer with the Royal Shakespeare Company? Harriet, do you have a Nobel peace prize knocking around somewhere that I don't know about?"

The entire document is packed with achievements.

Short films I've starred in, awards I've won, songs I'm capable of singing entirely *a cappella*. There's a brief summary of the time I triumphed in *The Phantom of The Opera*, and a paragraph all about just how wide my splits are and how fast I can backflip. My emotional *range*, apparently, is quite outstanding.

Except none of it was me, obviously.

Having known me for a year now, I'd imagine you've already worked that out for yourself.

"Stephanie's sent them the wrong details," I say in a blank voice. "She actually, literally thinks I'm Hannah Manners."

Yah, Hannah, darling. That's what I said.

I look at Annabel with wide eyes.

I can't do this. I can't film an *international television commercial* as if I'm somebody who knows exactly what they're doing. I struggle to behave like a normal human being in private, let alone when it's being recorded for posterity and shown to millions.

I glance at the brief again.

Like, literally millions. This is being shown in England. France. Italy. America. South America. Spain. Portugal. Russia. Australi—

Oh my God. Ohmygodohmygodohmygodohmy—

Hydrogen. Lithium. Sodium. Potassium…

"Harriet, sweetheart." Annabel sits down next to me on the bed and gently pulls my hands away from my face. "This is exactly why I'm here: to sort out misunderstandings like this. Just give me a few minutes, and I'll go and explain everything."

She stands up and grabs her briefcase: always ready to fight some kind of legal battle, even on holiday.

Except... then what?

Annabel tells them I have the *emotional range* of a peanut, and then what happens? It's too late to get sent home now. I'll have to model anyway: they'll just know I'm not good enough before I've even started.

Plus... isn't this what I wanted? The opportunity to be someone better? Someone... starrier? Even if it means – temporarily – being someone *else*? Maybe Hannah can teach me a few things on my list while I'm at it.

And that does it.

"Don't tell them," I say firmly, standing up and forcing my breathing to slow back down again. "Annabel, if this is the girl they want, then *this* is the girl they're going to get."

I wave the paper in the air.

I can be risky. I can be confident. I can be *brave.*

Annabel frowns and looks at me steadily for a few seconds. "Are you sure? Because, sweetheart, you really don't have to do this."

"I know," I say, putting the paper on the table. "This time I want to."

45

In the forests of central Africa grows a plant called the *Pollia condensata*. It produces tiny iridescent fruit that reflect pinpricks of light, and biologists claim that it is officially the shiniest living organism in the world.

It used to be, anyway.

Ali politely takes Annabel to the riad *hammam* for a complimentary massage while I 'get ready'. ("Fifteen years," she says, grinning at me. "Tell your father to drag me out by my toenails.") Then he leads me into the atrium and introduces me to a small, blonde, spiky-looking stylist called Helena.

Over the following hour, I am transformed from a human being into something that could be attached to the side of a car and used as a wing-view mirror.

With little dobs of glue, Helena gradually covers me head to toe in sequins and tiny bits of glass, beads, silver and gold, necklaces and bangles and hair clips and fake purple lashes. My dress is sparkly: red and pink and gold

and silver. Even my face and hands have been sprayed so heavily with twinkle that every time I look down my vision glints, as if I've got a temporary case of glaucoma.

Seriously: *National Geographic* may want to send someone over. I am definitely breaking some kind of light-reflective record.

Finally, Helena daubs me with sticky red lip gloss, blue eyeshadow and three inches of very pale foundation, and then secures an enormous, heavy gold watch round my wrist. It looks like something that could be used to locate a submarine underwater.

"Try not to lose it," she whispers to me under her breath. "If that's even possible. It looks like it has a tracking device inbuilt."

"It doesn't," a voice says from the doorway. "Sadly, because that would be *super* useful. Oh, you're just a veritable *phantasmagoria*, Hannah! *Exactly* as I dreamt it. Well done, lady whose name I can't remember."

"I just followed your directions," Helena says, holding up a stick-figure picture she's been glancing at the entire time. I'd assumed it was a nostalgic keepsake from her five-year-old daughter. "The credit is *all* yours, Kevin. Please. Take all of it."

"It just *came* to me, you know? I wanted Bollywood crossed with Strictly Come Dancing and I think we've achieved it. Or *I've* achieved it, really. You just did the sticking."

A young, thin, slightly goat-like man hops into the room and holds his hand out to me. He's wearing little brown furry boots, a white T-shirt, brown skinny jeans, a tartan scarf and a small curly beard, and for a few seconds he reminds me so much of Mr Tumnus, I'm tempted to check him for horns and warn him about the perils of fraternising with humans.

"I'm Kevin Holland, the director. But of course, you already know that."

I shake his hand carefully.

How would I already know that? Is he wearing a name badge I haven't spotted?

Be *confident,* err… Hannah.

"Oh yes. Kevin Holland. Of *course.*"

"Constantly being recognised everywhere I go is *such* a nuisance," he continues, rubbing a hand over his beard. "I wasn't prepared for this level of fame, you know. All the awards. All the attention. Just this time last year, I had thirty Twitter followers. *Thirty.* Can you believe that?"

He looks at me with shock and indignation.

Studies have shown that we like people more when they mirror our own actions back at us, so I rub my chin too: inadvertently scratching myself with a sequin in the process.

"No, Kevin, because that is unbelievable."

"Now I have a blue tick and thirty-five thousand followers, and who are they all? Who knows? Who cares?"

I'm tempted to say: thirty-five thousand people probably know and care, but I bite my tongue.

"Then I meet Jacques Levaire at a big Hollywood party in Hackney and he's all, '*Hey, Kev, Kevin, Kevin Holland. I know you normally do profound art films that really mean something, but I would like to pay you an OBSCENE wad of money to bring that astonishing creative vision to my new line of expensive watches.*'"

I stare at Kev-Kevin-KevinHolland in surprise.

Huh. Maybe that's just how people talk in Hackney.

"I totes see what normal people miss, you know?" he continues cheerfully. "Like a superhero with x-ray vision, except I can view straight into the *human heart,* which is even more useful."

It really isn't.

Unless you're a surgeon, and judging by the state of his nails, this seems unlikely. But that sounds like a *very* geeky and Harriet Manners response, so instead of sharing this thought I toss my head back with a little laugh.

You can do this, Harriet. You are star-like.

"Absolutely!" I laugh loudly. "And what is your…

modus operandi for this particular direction? I'd really like to *channel* the right *creative vision.* Are we thinking *Marlowian*? *Millerian*? A touch of *Stoppardian* with an air of *Wildean*?"

Kevin blinks a few times, as well he might.

I have literally no idea what I just said: I'm just naming playwrights I know and making long words out of them.

"*Modus operandi?*" he says faintly. "Creative vision? Stoppardian? Millerian?"

I flush. "Umm, by which I meant…"

"Oh, I know what you *meant*," he says, grabbing my hands and kissing both of them. "*Finally*, they send me a professional I can actually *work* with."

He drags me over to the door of the riad, bangs it open with a flourish and spreads his arms out wide in the sunshine.

"Now, Hannah, let's *make some art*, shall we?"

46

*J*emaa *el-Fnaa* is an ancient marketplace in the centre of the walled city of Marrakech. It's an enormous open square used by both locals and tourists, and the origin of its name is unclear.

It means either 'courtyard in front of a mosque', 'the mosque of death' or 'assembly at the end of the world'.

I'm going to vote for the latter.

It's dusk by the time we get to the square and it feels exactly like walking into an exotic fairyland, or maybe Christina Rossetti's enchanted goblin market.

During the day the square is filled with orange-juice stalls, ladies painting hands with intricate patterns of henna, medicine men selling cures and potions, tooth-pullers with teeth laid out in front of them and people selling little glasses with MOROCCO painted on them just in case anyone has forgotten what country they're in.

But at night, everything changes.

The sun sets and the city shifts: music starts and spaces

are filled with acrobats, dancers and musicians. Storytellers sit on the ground, fortune-tellers under umbrellas, snakes fight, monkeys dance and drums thump.

Lights are everywhere: scattered on the floor on tablecloths covered with candles and night-lights, and every now and then a whizzing blue light launches into the air: thrown by an enthusiastic child.

Marrakech during the day is wonderful, but Marrakech at night-time?

Totally magic.

"Gosh," Annabel says as Ali leads us quietly between stalls. She's now glowing and relaxed, and also sneaking quite a lot of little confused glances at my make-up and costume. "Harriet, you look very…"

Then she pauses for at least thirty seconds while she considers her internal thesaurus.

"Dazzling," she finally settles for.

I pull a face, because I know exactly what she means. Held at the right angle, I could be used to create a small fire.

Ali smiles slightly and walks us past a vulture perched on the floor with a chain round its neck, beyond a group of backflipping dancers, to a corner that's been sectioned off.

In the middle of it are enormous bright white lights

and a team of people, holding cameras and looking in little screens.

And around *them* is an even larger circle of tourists.

Chatting, laughing, taking photos. Waiting patiently for the performance to begin.

I abruptly feel a bit nauseous.

There are a lot of fascinating attractions in Jemaa El-Fnaa, and it looks like I just became one of them.

"*Sooooo* sorry," Kevin says, barging forward and dragging me through the crowd. "They must have heard I was here. There's just no *privacy* for the famous, is there? No respect for the integrity of artists."

"Is that Steven Spielberg?" somebody whispers. "Is this the new Indiana Jones film?"

"Is that the blonde girl from *Twilight?* She's not as pretty in real life, is she?"

"OK," Kevin continues as he pushes me quite aggressively into an open space and leaves me there while he runs next to the camera and picks up a blackboard. "I really want this to be *fresh* and *unstilted.* Feel *the moment,* you know? So I'm going to start rolling immediately, see how the two of you *interact.* See what the chemistry is like."

I blink and stare in concern at the growing crowd.

The two of us? Oh my God. Not *again.*

Over the last ten months, I have modelled with a beautiful Australian boy, a white kitten called Barry, a strident New Yorker, a cockroach, a sad girl called Fleur and an octopus with very little patience for my shenanigans.

I fell in love with one, knocked the other over and made the rest of them hate me. As far as *chemistry* goes, it's not a brilliant start.

"*Bring out Richard,*" Kevin shouts, clicking his blackboard together. "*ACTION.*"

I turn in astonishment – half expecting to see my father – and out of the crowd walks a little brown furry creature on all fours: round brown eyes, tail straight upwards.

They have got to be kidding me.

Because I've said this before, obviously, but I've never meant it literally.

Richard is a monkey.

47

Now, I *love* monkeys.

Monkeys share ninety-three per cent of their DNA with humans. They communicate with accents, play games, recognise photos of their friends and express affection by cuddling each other. They have even been known to lie to each other: yelling *tiger* so that the others retreat to the trees and they can keep a special food treat for themselves.

Monkeys are one of the sweetest, most curious and most fascinating species on the planet, and they're third on my list of all-time favourites (under 1. elephant and 2. panda).

But I *don't* love seeing them with a chain round their neck. I *don't* love seeing them dragged across the ground of a paved market square.

And I definitely do *not* love having one shoved into my arms while the chain is secured tightly round my wrist and a little man with a beard is yelling: *"Go on then,*

206

Manners! DO something!"

Richard wraps his little furry arms round my neck and stares into my face with huge, sad eyes and a little leathery nose.

And I suddenly want to cry.

"This is a macaque," I say, disentangling his tiny hands gently. "A Barbary macaque."

"Stop shooting!" Kevin shouts as Richard starts curiously picking at a bit of shiny plastic on my dress. "No, it's not. It's a monkey."

"You don't understand." My throat is starting to tighten. "A Barbary macaque *is* a monkey. It's the only macaque not found in Asia, and it's an endangered species. There are fewer than six thousand of these left in the wild."

Kevin frowns. "Well it's not in the wild now so what are you complaining about? *Action.*"

I make the chain looser, and Richard – monkey, not father – clambers up on to my shoulder, then sits firmly on top of my head.

"You're upsetting him," I say fiercely as I feel his little furry tail curl down the back of my neck. "He shouldn't be here. He should be out in the mountains with his mum and dad. Or his girlfriend."

"CUT," Kevin yells. "I thought you were used to

working with animals? What about all that time at the circus?" He clacks his board again. "I'm not paying you to whine. *Action.*"

The crowd is starting to murmur unhappily.

"I don't think he's famous *at all*," somebody whispers.

"And I'm not sure she is either. She's *definitely* not pretty enough to be in *Twilight*. Or Indiana Jones, for that matter."

Richard clambers back down into my arms and stares at me again, hand carefully placed on my chin, and I look up in a panic to where Annabel is standing at the front of the crowd in a sharp white shirt and grey trousers, arms folded.

She looks exactly as furious as I feel and is clearly just waiting for some kind of sign from me to leap into action.

Help, I communicate silently, and with a quick motion my stepmother stands directly in front of the camera so that it's totally blocked.

"Stop filming," she says coldly. "I'm a lawyer, and if this shot isn't cut immediately, animal rights organisations will be contacted. Your client does not need that kind of publicity. Do I make myself perfectly clear?"

Kevin glares at her like an irritated seven-year-old.

Any second now, he's going to stamp his feet, tell her he hates her and wishes he'd never been born before stomping to his bedroom. I can't believe I ever thought Yuka Ito was insensitive. By comparison, she was an angora rabbit.

"*Fine*," Kevin finally sighs angrily, flinging his scarf on to the ground. "Take the flaming monkey away. He was rubbish on camera anyway."

A man comes and grabs Richard from me. He clings for a few seconds, little chocolate-coloured eyes still fixed on mine, then lets go.

I watch him leave with a lump in my throat.

Then I give myself a little shake and try to snap back into a slightly less antagonistic, fierce kind of mood. I'm here to do a job, after all. "I'm really sorry if I ruined your advert, Kevin. Would you like me to… umm." What can I offer him instead? "Handstand? Cartwheel? Make a long string of origami cranes?"

I can only do one of those things, so I may have to learn the others pretty quickly.

"No, thank you. I've got a *much* better idea."

Kevin looks around at the still mesmerised crowd and gives the first broad smile I've seen since I met him.

"Ladies and gentlemen, bring out the snakes."

48

I'm not a *lot* happier, draped in four poor snakes.

But I'm supposed to be a professional, so I try my absolute hardest to look like I might be.

With the cameras rolling, I start swaying as gracefully as I can – waving my arms assertively – so that the film crew can capture me "at one with nature". Despite the fact that nature doesn't look like it really wants to be at one with me.

The large green one keeps trying to tie itself round my neck, and I'm not entirely sure I blame it.

"Kiss it," Kevin hisses as the smaller brown one slides over my shoulder and peers with a tickling tongue into my ear.

"Excuse me?"

"Kiss the snake. Just a quick peck. And make sure the watch is on show the whole time."

I glance at the gold still weighing down my wrist. I don't think there's an alternative, frankly: you could see

this thing through a dark pair of curtains.

Then I look at the snake doubtfully.

There are 3,000 species of snake in the world, and 600 of them are venomous. If I had any poison, a random redhead trying to kiss me would be my very first target.

I swallow, take a deep breath and give it a quick peck.

"Yes!" Kevin shouts. "Again!"

I peck it again.

"Again!"

I kiss the snake again. I think in some countries we are now married.

"AND CUT!" Kevin claps his board so sharply somebody in the audience gives a little squeak. "Now, let's see what else we can do that won't get us *sued*, shall we?"

I spend the rest of the evening wandering aimlessly through the winding, narrow souks of Marrakech with a film crew trailing four metres behind me.

And every few steps, somebody yells at me.

Occasionally, it's a stall owner who thinks I have an eye for a bargain. "Hey, lady!" one shouts, trying to grab my hand. "Hey, Rihanna! You want to buy a scarf? Lovely scarf for you and your family! I give you super good price!"

"Hey, Beckham! You like nice carpet?? I have so many nice carpets!"

"You are a pretty lady! Come and have a butcher and a wag of the chin!"

But mostly, I'm just yelled at by Kevin.

Every time I reply to the stall owners, or laugh, or walk the wrong way, or say thank you very much but I already have a carpet at home, my director explodes at me.

"I said *no*, Hannah! No talking! Laughing is not fashion! Do it again! Take a left! A right! No, a *right*! Look at the watch! Faster! Slow down! And make sure you look at the *watch*! This isn't an advert for orienteering!"

Until I'm starting to feel very confused, very lost and very late for something important: I'm just not entirely sure what, exactly. Like a particularly rubbish version of the rabbit from *Alice in Wonderland*.

I'm so disorientated that during an especially enthusiastic head-toss one of my enormous dangly earrings gets caught in a long yellow scarf hanging from a pole and renders me abruptly immobile.

"What are you *doing*?" Kevin yells at me as I lurch backwards with a wince and cover my ear with my hand. "What is *this*?"

"I'm…" I pretend to rub the scarf on my face while I try to surreptitiously unhook myself. "I'm just… Really getting *into* it, you know? Into the *vibe*. Of this... uh, summer accessorising."

Into it, on to it, attached to it: pretty much the same thing.

Kevin scowls at me as I start pretending to sniff the scarf instead. "Well can you *stop*? It does not look sophisticated and expensive *at all*."

The cameras keep filming as an outraged stall owner charges forward and unhooks my earring while muttering loudly. In the meantime, all the other stallholders are now filming me on their mobile phones.

"Americans!" one says cheerfully, shaking his head. "Always making my day."

You know what?

If I can find a hole through to another universe, it might be best for everyone if I just jump straight down it.

Once released I wander a bit more – stumbling into a gutter full of dirty water – and then I accidentally venture into a one-way street at which point I have to confidently put my hand on my hip and pretend it was entirely intentional.

Finally, Kevin decides he's probably got enough footage for the day.

That or he's given up on me entirely.

It's hard to tell.

"Done!" he shouts as his phone starts ringing, grabbing it out of his pocket. "I can just pay somebody to edit all the rubbish out. Get an early night, peeps. It's a long way to Erg Chebbi, so we'll precede at four."

Then he disappears down a dark little path that presumably leads back to the riad, still yelling into his phone.

There's a short silence.

"It's *midnight*," Helena finally sighs. "How exactly are we going to get an early night? Time travel?"

"He means four *am*?" Joe the cameraman moans. "In *four hours*?"

"No *wonder* the money for this was so good."

Annabel and I wait until the entire crew has stumbled off to bed – still grumbling and rubbing their eyes – then we look at each other.

"Are you sure you still want to do this?" she says calmly. "Because this is a man that doesn't know the difference between *proceed* and *precede,* and our life is in his hands."

I nod sleepily and grin.

Despite being shouted at so much – and despite getting so much wrong – I'm actually having a surprising amount of fun, living life so far on the edge I'm basically tipping over.

Maybe I'm more like my dad than I hoped I was.

"All right, then," Annabel says with a swift nod. She gets a guidebook out. "In that case, the good news is that Erg Chebbi consists of fifty-kilometre dunes of sands blown by the wind, and it's part of the Sahara desert."

I open my eyes, suddenly very alert.

I've had a Sahara desert poster in my bedroom since I was seven, and I may or may not have cut a photo of myself out and stuck it on top to look like I'd already been there.

"And the bad news?"

Annabel puts the guidebook back in her bag and rubs a hand over her eyes. "It's an eleven-hour drive away and we're taking a bus."

49

Eleven hours on a bus is a long time.

Eleven hours on a bus with Kevin sitting behind you is an infinity.

Before sunrise the next morning, we're piled in the back of a tiny white van, driven out of the city… and into the Atlas Mountains.

As the sky slowly begins to lighten, we see the outline of dark peaks speckled with snow. Sweeping valleys and gorges are dotted with trees and rivers and here and there small turreted, castle-like *kasbahs* are perched randomly on the hillside.

We drive past goats and sheep, market stalls and little villages, including the incredible Ouarzazate: a red-walled Berber city made of mud, and the setting for *Lawrence of Arabia* and *Gladiator.*

And Kevin doesn't see any of it.

"I just came from *nowhere*," he says as we all watch

216

a man walking a donkey with a little bell along the road. "BOOM. Nobody knows how I did it.

"I suppose I've always been creative," he ponders as we stop for some traditional Moroccan *tagine* for lunch: stewed chicken with vegetables and currants in a clay pot. "Some of us are just born to really *see* the world, you know?

"Oooh!" he says as we pull over to take photos of a pretty village with peach walls and yellow flowers. "Seventeen retweets! Eighteen! Twenty!"

By the time the land starts to get dustier and the mountains flatten into brown plains, scattered with little piles of sand, the only thing stopping everyone on the bus from literally killing Kevin is the knowledge that we must be nearly there now. That, and the fact that Morocco still officially has the death penalty for murder.

Finally we pull into a small, crunchy car park and stop.

Helena and I wobble quickly off the bus into the sweltering heat, then dive into a small cement building so I can get changed again before the sun sets: this time into a long yellow, blue and orange silk dress covered in gold sequins, as dictated by an even more elaborate stick figure.

She covers my face in yet another thick layer of gunk

and secures the watch with the same horrified face as yesterday.

Then she leads me to a long line of camels, grunting and chewing with the laconic, disinterested expressions of old men with grudges. Every now and then one opens its mouth and makes a loud, grumbling sound: halfway between an angry dinosaur roar and a really acidic belch.

Annabel is standing cautiously next to them.

"Apparently the Arabic language has 160 words for *camel*," she says, grimacing slightly. "I can probably think of a couple more. However, if this is what's next on the list then…"

"Oh, there isn't a camel for you," Kevin says brightly, ambling past on an enormous brown one, with a blue scarf tied elaborately round his head. "You weren't on the crew list, lady. Frankly, you're lucky there was even room in the bus. I was all for leaving you in Marrakech."

Annabel's jaw clenches. "You're so kind."

"My charity work is well documented," he agrees. "Hannah? I'm not paying you to stand and stare gormlessly at the transport. Get on Zahara immediately, please."

He points at an enormous, white fluffy, curly camel, who turns and gives me a slow, long-lashed blink, like

218

a flirty film star from the 1920s.

Take risks, Harriet.

I clamber nervously on and squeak slightly as Zahara slowly stands up with her back legs first – tipping me terrifyingly forward – then with her front legs, so I'm flung backwards again like a rag doll.

Annabel writes something in the little notepad she's started carrying around with her. I'm not sure what it is, exactly, but from her expression I'm guessing it's not a love poem.

"Are you sure you don't need me, Harriet?" she says, holding a flat hand up and squinting against the sunshine. "Because if you do, I'll steal one of these furry old man animals. But if you don't… I suppose I could stay here and make a few phone calls."

Her fingers twitch unconsciously towards her briefcase.

It's only *just* occurring to me now that this must be the longest Annabel's ever been away from Tabitha. Plus she's just started back at work after maternity leave, and it's a Friday afternoon: she must have work coming out of her ears. This isn't a fun sunny holiday for Annabel at all.

The *only* reason she's here is to look after me.

"I'll be absolutely fine," I say as confidently as I can

while Zahara experimentally licks my left ankle. "Give Dad and Tabby my love. See you when I get back, OK?"

I blow her an affectionate kiss.

Then I ride off alone into the orange sands.

50

I should probably have said: *if* I get back.

Camels aren't known as 'ships of the desert' for nothing, and it turns out I'm not a very good sailor. As we start walking across little heaps of sand towards the dunes, Zahara begins to sway dramatically from side to side, up and down, round and round: staggering, belching, shuffling, clambering up the first of the dunes, twitching her tail and sliding back down again.

Which is a bit of a problem.

The film crew has been set up fifteen metres away so they can film me, wobbling precariously past with my head jiggling loosely like one of those little plastic dogs that go on the dashboard of a car.

I lurch one way, then the other.

I swerve and dip and squeak, and at one point slip so violently I'm hanging off the side of the camel and one of the Moroccan camel-men has to grab me as I close my eyes and hang on to the poor animal's neck for dear life.

"*Stop. Strangling. The. Camel*," Kevin hisses from his position to my right. "You are so *not* good with animals."

Finally, I find a kind of awkward rhythm.

Together, Zahara and I climb slowly up a particularly enormous and powdery dune to the very top. At which point every bit of remaining breath leaves my body in one big *whoosh*.

Annabel has disappeared. The bus has disappeared. The gravel car park has disappeared.

All that's left is sand.

Approximately eight octillion grains of sand, to be precise: spread across three and a half million square miles in tiny, sea-like ripples and enormous soft, cascading mountains, all in golds and oranges.

To my left, the shadows of the camels are stretched to the horizon, perfectly outlined in black with long, thin legs like the elephants in the famous Dali painting.

The sky is bright pink, and little yellow and tangerine clouds are scattered above us; below us the ground keeps shifting like magic from rust to orange to crimson. Little stars are beginning to pop out and the air is utterly silent. Not a bird, not a plane.

Just perfect stillness.

Modelling has opened the world up for me.

I've seen the bright lights of New York and the

candy-like turrets of Moscow in the snow. I've watched Mount Fuji as the sun goes down, and the neon colours of Tokyo as it comes back up again. I've walked the streets of Marrakech and navigated empty warehouses in London.

But of all the places I've ever been, this is by far my favourite.

It's just a shame I have to share it with Kevin.

"*Remember*," he yells from several metres away, cupping his hands round his mouth. "You are *a queen*! You are *an empress*! You are the monarch of everything you survey! Now *look at the flaming watch*!"

But as we pause on top of the dune and the crew films me for a few minutes, staring at the horizon with my dress floating in the wind, I suddenly feel every single muscle in my body start to relax. Kevin can shout at me as much as he likes: I am the luckiest girl in the entire world.

And for a brief fragment of time, I don't need to act.

As I sit on the camel and stare at the calm, empty, limitless sands spreading millions of miles around me, that's exactly how I feel: like a queen.

Brave, confident and capable of anything.

Because after a childhood of dreaming and imagining, I am finally here.

I am in the Sahara desert.

51

Things that live in the Sahara desert include:

- 500 species of plant

- 70 species of mammal

- 90 species of bird

- 100 species of reptile

- 200 million people.

Kevin appears to think he's the only one.

"Does anybody have reception?" he yells as we roll carefully back down the dune again and are brought to a juddering halt. "I need to upload this selfie, and I've got *jack.*"

Carefully, I'm helped off the camel.

I give Zahara a little pat and a thank-you.

Then I'm led to a flat piece of sand between two dunes while the crew starts setting up lights in a semicircle. I glance around expectantly: so far I've been buddied up with a camel, a monkey and four snakes.

My next task will no doubt involve subduing a fire-breathing dragon with my bare hands while simultaneously attempting some kind of whimsical recorder playing.

"Right," Kevin says, leaning nonchalantly against his camel. "This is my final shot, Hannah, and will be my *Pièce de Résistance*. Do you know what that means?"

I nod in relief: finally, something I can answer properly. "Yes. It's French for *piece of resistance*, and it traditionally refers to the most substantial dish in a meal."

"Wrong. It means this is the bit that will make me famous. *More* famous. So I need you to really dig deep and bring out your best stuff. You know. Do your thing."

I stare at Kevin for a few seconds in bewilderment.

"Sorry, my thing?"

Does he want me to do complex algebra for the cameras? Analyse a bit of metaphysical poetry? Experiment with the migration of manganite ions?

Kevin bends down and pulls two little yellow boxes out of his bag.

Then he wedges them in the sand.

"I'm thinking *nomadic*. I'm thinking *free spirit*. I'm thinking *my classic timepiece by Jacques Levaire is so glorious I can't control my happiness.* Pretend there's a campfire and sparklers if you need them. We can always CGI that in later. ACTION."

Then he waves his hand at the cameras and clicks a button on his iPod.

Oh my God. What is happening?

Except as huge white lights switch on with a bang and the cameras start whirring, I think I already know. Sure enough: a loud, tinny beat begins to thump across the sand. *Thud. Thud. Thud thud thud thud.* Then a little voice starts screeching *ooooooooh babyyyyyy hiiiighhhh iin theeee skkyyyyyyy yeahhh baby*. An electronic keyboard joins in, followed by what appears to be a random fake owl sound.

The kangaroo rat has wide toes that turn its feet into sand shoes, allowing it to run across sand really fast in the opposite direction to danger without sinking in.

I may need to quickly grow some too.

"Now," my director confirms as he leans back on the camel again and throws his hands out widely. "*Dance.*"

*

So I dance.

Or – more specifically – Hannah does.

With the skills she learnt during a short stint with the Bolshoi Ballet Academy, she swirls and spins, pirouettes and squats, jumps and curtsies. She rolls around a bit on the floor, getting sand in her eyes and mouth and hair and trying to surreptitiously spit it back out again in the most glamorous way possible.

She fake-drowns and jives, shuffles and wiggles.

She even attempts a little break-dancing. And you know what? Harriet Manners can't do any of this. But Hannah Manners?

Apparently she's not that bad at it.

I must have harnessed her powers more accurately than I ever dared dream could be possible, because for the first time Kevin hasn't got a single word of criticism.

"*Superb!*" he yells as I attempt to moonwalk across the sand. "*Marvellous!*" he shouts as I huff and puff through three extremely low star jumps. "*Genius!*" he exclaims as – in a panic – I steal a few of Dad's key moves and start doing 'wobbly-knees' and making big boxes with little boxes inside them with my hands. "This is *precisely* what I wanted! It's fresh, it's unorthodox! It's visionary! Could you, perchance, try a little *krumping*?"

Which I assume is dancing like a crumpet.

So I obediently roll myself on to the sand and try to look as bread-like as possible.

Finally, the music stops and I crash in exhaustion to the ground and end with tired jazz hands. I'm sweating all over and breathing so hard I sound like a tree being cut down.

"AND THAT…" Kevin yells, clacking his little board for the final time, "…IS. A. WRAP! Could you take a photo of me jumping?" He hands his phone to Helena. "I need one for my Facebook profile."

I sit for a few seconds in the sand, trying to get my breath back.

Then I look upwards at the sky.

The light is fading, pink has deepened to a purple-blue and stars are popping out and multiplying by the second like freckles in the sun. I give a little sigh and try to quickly take as many mental photos as I can. I'm only sixteen, after all. I can always come back and enjoy my first ever night in the desert without somebody yelling I CAN JUMP HIGHER! DO IT AGAIN! another time, right?

Right?

"You know," Joe the cameraman says, helping me up. "After careful consideration, I think I might need a couple of extra shots of the dunes. A long, long way over there."

He points far away in the distance.

"I'll come with you," Kevin says, reappearing as if by magic. "I know *exactly* the shot you're thinking of and you can't do it without me because I'm the *director.*" He holds his fingers up in a square. "Oh yes, I *see* it already. I see it *all.*"

Joe winks at me as Kevin begins sliding through the sand in the direction Joe indicated and – as if by some strange, wonderful enchantment – the air gets quieter and quieter until it's completely silent.

I can almost hear the desert heaving a sigh of relief.

Then I quickly whip my shoes off while mouthing a grateful *thank you.*

"You've got fifteen minutes," Joe says with a small grin as I start heading towards the biggest dune I can find. "Get as far away as you possibly can."

And it looks like the desert is finally mine.

52

Scientists estimate that there are 70,000 million million million stars in the known universe and at least 170 billion galaxies stretching 13.8 billion light years away from us in all directions.

Our galaxy alone contains 400 billion stars.

With all the energy I have left, I scramble on all fours up the dune. It takes a surprisingly long time: for every two scrabbles forward I slide back one, as if I'm trying to climb a mound of warm, soft sugar.

Finally, I reach the top and lie down. I spread my arms out wide with my fingers buried in the sand.

And I look upwards, at a sky now coated in glitter.

Hertfordshire/Sydney – February (9 months ago)

"I know you miss me but try and be cool, Manners. There's no need to lick the computer."

I laughed and pulled Hugo off the webcam.

He got a bit overexcited every time he saw my boyfriend, but I couldn't exactly blame him.

In fairness, so did I.

"Saliva is antibacterial," I told Nick airily. "We just like keeping things clean." Then I poked my face round my dog's little white fluffy head. Hugo immediately started licking my ear instead. "Is it nice being home?"

Nick was making the most of shooting a huge campaign in Australia by spending the weekend with his parents.

"It's great, but I keep getting this niggling feeling I've left something behind."

"You did," I said, holding up a blue sock. "I found this under my bed yesterday. It doesn't smell great. In fact, I have considerable doubts about your laundry skills."

Nick threw his head back and laughed, and every one of my two billion heart-muscle cells stood up silently and did a little invisible dance of triumph. "I gave that to you when you jumped in the snow puddle, plonker. So technically you were the last one to wear it."

"Oh." I flushed with happiness. "Of course. In that case, it smells of sunshine and roses and I've never inhaled anything so delightful in my life and shall sleep with it forever under my pillow."

We both laughed, and then the screen flickered.

"Hello?" I clicked a few buttons. "Are you still there? Nick?"

It flickered a few more times: his face appearing and disappearing again. "Harri—"

"Nick?"

"*Shoot,*" a disembodied voice said. "Why is this connection so bad?"

"It's OK, we'll just…"

Then the sound cut out too.

Over the two and a half months we'd been dating, I had grown to hate video calls with a passion. They gave me a pixelated picture of Nick – like he had been drawn or painted – but I couldn't curl up with my head on his shoulder or smell his lime-green smell or kiss him.

And there were these little unexpected awkward bits: the moments where we talked over each other, or the sound lagged, or the screen froze and we were suddenly disjointed and pulled apart.

The screen went bright again and I could see his beautiful face: fuzzy and frozen in the middle of expressing a *U* shape.

"Are you…" we both said at the same time.

"…Here."

"…There. What?"

"Huh?"

There was an awkward silence again while I flushed. My face was now frozen in the corner of the screen, like a constipated goblin. I felt strangely shy, as if we were back at the beginning.

My boyfriend was 10,552 miles away, and I could suddenly feel every single one of them.

"What were you—"

"I was just—"

"You go—"

"No, I was just saying—"

Another long silence while we both fiddled with our laptops and I tried my hardest not to throw it on the floor and stamp on it.

"Take me to the window," Nick said finally.

"Oh God, it's not *that* bad, is it? I mean, you're not going to virtually jump, are you?"

"Maybe," he laughed. "Let's see how I feel when I get there."

I clambered off my bed and took my laptop to the windowsill. Our neighbour was trimming his lawn with a dark blue fleece on. Not even vaguely romantically: I could hear him swearing and kicking the machine through the glass.

"Now turn me round so I can see the sky."

"But you can't see anything, Nick. It's just grey."

"Obviously. You're in England so that goes without saying. Now I'll do it." Nick held his computer up and I peered forward. "What can you see?"

"Black."

"Because I'm currently in the southern hemisphere, and you're in the northern hemisphere. We have two almost totally different skies, so it's dark here while it's light there."

I turned the camera round so I could blink at him incredulously. Maybe this was what happened when you became a model: people tried to explain the notion of a spinning earth to you.

"Thanks for that, Nick. That is fascinating geological knowledge that I didn't learn when I was six years old at all. Please, tell me more about the basic concept of night and day."

"I wasn't finished," he laughed. "May I continue?"

"Yes. Unless you're about to tell me that rain comes out of clouds and gravity makes things, like, fall down. In which case, no."

He growled at me so I stuck my tongue out.

"I said we have *almost* two totally different skies, smarty-pants. But there's still a crossover point and it's always there. Three—"

Nick's face suddenly went very quiet and stationary.

Oh my God, I thought, *you have to be kidding me*.

"Nick?" I shook my laptop desperately. "Three what? Three squirrels? Three blind mice?"

But there was nothing: just emptiness and silence.

"Nick?" I said in a smaller voice, shaking it again. "Come back."

And the screen went black.

Thanks to almost no light pollution, I can now see more stars than I've ever been able to before: thousands and thousands of lights slowly scattering themselves across the sky like the blue sparkle Nat used to throw all over everything when she was seven.

But I'm only looking at three of them.

After five minutes of cursing my laptop, I'd finally worked it out: Orion's Belt, also known as The Three Kings.

Alnitak, Alnilam and Mintaka.

Three of the brightest stars in the sky, and – because of their position near the equator – visible in both the northern and southern hemisphere: Morocco and Australia.

Last week I read that the heart has its own electrical pulse, which means it can function even when it has been separated from its body.

Which I thought was pretty handy.

Given that mine has been on the other side of the world now for quite some time.

But as I dig myself into the warm sand and look upwards, it suddenly feels a tiny bit closer again: beating and hopeful, as if I'm not quite as empty any more. And as I think about my letter, I feel a little closer to being whole again: more than I have in a long time. Since I walked off Brooklyn Bridge and left the boy I love still standing there without me.

Because tonight, these stars are mine.

But in a few hours, they'll belong to Nick again.

No matter where we are, no matter how dark it gets, no matter which of us can't see them, this is one connection that is never going to break.

The part of the sky we share.

53

Luckily, the return journey is a lot easier.

This is mainly because I borrow earplugs, curl up with my head on Annabel's lap and sleep the entire way back to Marrakech.

By the time the crew staggers off the bus at 7am and figuratively crawls back into the riad, Kevin and I are the only upbeat people in the party. I'd like to pretend it has nothing to do with my fifteen minutes with the stars, but that would be lying.

I honestly feel happier than I have in weeks.

My brighter mood is enhanced yet further when my director calls me a "triumph of casting" and air-kisses my hand – albeit from a considerable distance.

"I am about to have a very happy client," he chirps, grabbing his enormous suitcase and heading straight back towards the riad door. "*Kev,* Jacques Levaire is going to say, *Kev, Kevin, Kevin Holland. If only they gave Oscars for adverts, you would win them all.*"

I beam at him: I think that means it went well.

"Now I'm off to the South of France to restock my fragile, butterfly-like creative juices on a yacht," he continues. "Catch you on the fame train, Hannah."

"Kevin?" I say as he pulls on a little black felt hat and pushes the door open. I clear my throat anxiously. "I'm not actually Hannah Manners. My name is Harriet."

He's given me two of the most amazing days and an entire desert: the least I owe him is the truth.

"Whatevs," he says, shrugging.

And he closes the door behind him.

"We have a Berber proverb in Morocco," Ali says thoughtfully, appearing as if out of thin air with two more steaming glasses of mint tea. "*Every dog thinks of its own fleas as gazelles.* I think Kevin assumes his are unicorns."

Annabel opens her eyes from where she's been propped up with a straight back against the reception desk.

"Unicorns?" she says sleepily, glancing around the room. "Where? I like bees."

I smile and gently remove the phone still gripped tightly in her hand. My stepmother was sending emails when I fell asleep on the bus and still sending emails when I woke up: there's a small but real chance she may have been suing people in her sleep.

I kiss her cheek as she puts her sunglasses on over her

glasses. "I think it's time to go home now, Annabel."

"Sadly, you would be right," Ali says, forcing a tea into her hand. "But you have one hour left in Morocco before I must take you to the airport. Is there anything special you'd like to do?"

He really is our magic genie.

There's just one wish I haven't had granted yet.

"Actually, Ali," I say, glancing at sleeping-again Annabel. I don't need to check it with her: I know we're on the same page. Or we will be when she wakes up, anyway. "We have a little favour we'd like to ask before we go, if you don't mind?"

"Harriet Manners," he says, grinning and bowing slightly. "Nothing would delight me more."

By the time we get home, everything on my list has been ticked off neatly.

Everything that matters, anyway.

"You're back!" a voice shouts as we at last push through the front door. "Finally! You were gone for *years and years.*"

Annabel and I stand in the hallway and stare in amazement at the living room. I'm pretty sure we were gone three days, but for a few seconds I'm convinced Dad might actually be right.

There's fabric everywhere. My spare bedding has been spread over a couple of bits of string, Annabel's best embroidered white cotton throw is forming a vast canopy in the middle, and inside the world's worst home-made tent is every pillow in the house.

My sister is lying in a furry cocoon of fleece jumpers in the entrance, patiently tugging on one of Hugo's ears.

"I built a fort!" Dad cries, still hidden. "We have everything you could possibly need. Biscuits, and movies, and milk, and a wooden donkey I found in the loft and—"

He pokes his head out of the sheets and then stops in amazement.

We both turn slowly to look at Annabel.

Her face is bright scarlet and peeling, the normally perfect blonde fringe is fuzzy and sticking upwards, there's orange juice down her front and ink on her face from where she fell asleep on her crossword on the flight home.

Yup.

My stepmother is one of the country's top barristers.

She has gone through twenty years of education, two postgraduate degrees, one teenage stepdaughter, one baby, nine years of marriage to my father, hundreds of court cases and thirteen hours of labour without ruffling a single eyelash.

Three days of fashion have broken her.

"Harriet Manners," Dad says sternly, looking at me, "what did you do to my wife?"

Annabel gives me a long, sleepy look and then nods in satisfaction. "It was exactly what we needed," she yawns, crawling into the tent. "But it's nice to be home."

With a happy little sigh, she picks Tabs up, kisses her face and tummy enthusiastically then lays her gently on her own stomach. My sister immediately makes a delighted squeaking sound and attempts to stick a whole hand up Annabel's nose.

Then Dad gives my stepmother the kind of kiss that makes me look awkwardly at the ceiling for a few seconds.

I crawl in next to them and for a while the four of us lie quietly under the white canopy.

"You know what I'm thinking?" Annabel says eventually.

"Yes," Dad nods with his eyes shut. "You're thinking: why isn't there mouse-flavoured cat food?"

"Nope."

"You're thinking why doesn't Tarzan have a beard when there are no razors in the jungle?"

"Well, I'm thinking that now, yes. But no."

Dad sighs sadly. "I have to take the awesome fort down, don't I?"

"Nope," Annabel says, closing her eyes. "Right now, it's perfect. I'm thinking Bahamas, Maldives, Hawaii, wherever Harriet goes next, Richard. They're all yours."

54

We have a little family nap for half an hour.

Then Tabitha and Hugo start clamouring simultaneously for something to eat, so I leave them to my disorientated parents and climb out of the fort as fast as I possibly can.

I carefully inspect the post next to the front door for a few minutes to see if anything has arrived for me over the last few days. Then I check under the indoor mat, because something important might have slipped into the wrong place.

And under the outdoor mat.

Tentatively, I wave my hand around inside the letter box a few times, in case a bulky, romantic gift was simply too huge to get all the way through.

But there's nothing there.

Not today anyway.

Still standing in the open doorway, I send Nat a quick text to check if she wants to hang out this weekend,

now I'm back from Marrakech earlier than I thought.

A few seconds later my phone beeps:

Wish I could, but I already have plans. ☹ **Can't wait to hear about your trip! Nat xxx**

I send a quick reply – **OK! Have fun! X** – put my phone back in my pocket, tug my suitcase up to my bedroom and sit on the floor with my back against the wall.

Then I pull my crumpled Inner Star list out of my pocket, retrieve a pen from my desk and hover over it in deep concentration for a few minutes.

Over the last three days, I have: been on two aeroplanes, skipped school, bussed through winding mountain roads, break-danced, ridden a camel in the desert, been vigorously draped in snakes and monkeys and held quite a few conversations with a man called Kevin.

I don't want to sound smug, but I think the anonymous author on the internet would be incredibly proud of me right now. I've never taken so many potentially lethal risks in my entire life.

With a smile, I draw a neat little tick next to the two entries I've been primarily concentrating on.

1. *Be Confident!* You are a creature unlike any other!
2. *Take Risks, Be Brave!* There is no limit to what you can do!

Then I focus my attention on my next targets.

3. *Be Stylish!* Shake it up and try something new!
4. *Inspire!* Lead, never follow!

With a deep breath, I fling my suitcase open wide and energetically start pulling out the contents like some kind of magician.

Bright yellow scarves and white sequin wraps. Turquoise and purple shawls with tassels; embroidered green waistcoats; orange and blue trousers, red leather shoes and enormous silver spangly earrings. Sparkles and sequins and things with beads all over them.

Until it's all in a rainbow heap around me.

As of Monday morning, things are going to change.

The geek is gone, and in her place is a much better version of Harriet Manners. Somebody strong and brave, cool and confident. A girl who can inspire others; who believes in herself so that everybody else will too.

Or – you know. *To*.

Because if there's a star inside everybody, it's only logical that there must be one inside me as well.

Now I just need to find a way to coax the rest of her out, that's all.

55

Unfortunately, the Inner Star list's author hasn't given any more details on exactly how to do that.

Which is a shame.

Because, as of 8:30am on Monday morning, I could really do with a little more guidance.

By the time I reach the end of my road, there are four first years following me with huge eyes, like barn owls in too-big dark green blazers and little white ankle socks.

Every time I speed up, they speed up.

Every time I stop, they stop.

Until my only options appear to be: a) run b) crawl inside a bush or c) curl up on the floor in a ball like a hedgehog until they either lose interest or accidentally stand on one of my fingers.

Except that's exactly what the old Harriet Manners would do, so instead I take a deep breath and spin round.

"Yes?" I say as brightly as I can. "Is there something I

can help you with, ladies?"

Brilliant.

Now I sound like a Gap assistant after somebody has just tangled up my jumpers.

"Umm." The little redhead has started hopping from one foot to the other, glancing at her friends. "Is your name *Harriet Manners*? Are you really a *supermodel*? Because my sister's in your year and she says you're famous but Fee thinks you're not pretty enough so we're not sure."

She points at a blonde girl, who immediately goes red.

"I didn't say that! Oh my God, Lydia, you're *so embarrassing*!" Fee looks at the floor. "I just said you're quite normal-looking for a model, that's all."

Normal-looking. Honestly, that's probably the nicest thing anybody at school has ever said about me.

"Yes, my name is Harriet," I say as we start walking again. "The rest, I'm afraid, is massively inflated."

"*Massively inflated*," they breathe to each other. "*Cooooool.*"

Then they start skipping down the road next to me.

"Do you live in a *castle*?" "Does it have turrets?" "Have you ever been to Jamaica?" "My aunty's been to Jamaica and it rained." "I'd rather go to Barbados. It *never* rains there." "Don't be stupid, Lydia, it rains *everywhere*."

"Not in Antarctica it doesn't," I interrupt automatically. "The Dry Valleys are the driest spot in the world as winds of speeds up to 200 miles per hour blow there and evaporate all surface water, snow and ice."

They stop skipping and stare at me with round eyes until I can feel myself flushing bright red.

Then they explode again.

"Ooooooh." "200 miles per hour is *so fast*." "That's faster than a *car*." "That's faster than a *speedboat*." "What else do you know, Harriet Manners? Do you know *everything*?"

To my surprise, I can feel my chest puffing out like a little pigeon. I'm not used to strangers enjoying my facts quite so enthusiastically. "Not at all. But I have a lot of books like this one which really help."

I reach into my satchel and pull out *Wise Up In The Bathroom*. I really wish publishing companies would stop assuming the only place to learn trivia is on the toilet.

"*Ooooooh*." They crowd around it. "This is *so awesome*." "This is, like, the *awesomest thing* I've ever seen." "My mum says fact books are only for nerds but she's so *wrong*."

I study their faces carefully, but there isn't a trace of sarcasm or facetiousness. They're not mocking me or being ironic. They honestly think my fact book is super cool.

Even weirder, they appear to think *I* am too.

We're outside the lower building now, and for a few crazy seconds I'm tempted to go in with them so we can discuss interesting facts about bridges. They might actually be my kindred spirits.

Or – at the very least – my spirit animals.

Instead I say: "Would you like to borrow my book for the day? There's a *really* interesting section about sharks on page 143."

They take it as if it's some kind of holy grail.

"When I'm grown up, I want to be *just like you*," Lydia says, staring at it reverently.

There's suddenly a little lump in my throat. I've never been considered a goal before.

Or – who are we kidding – a grown-up.

"If you like it there's *plenty* more where that came from," I beam at them. "And if you want to meet me before school tomorrow at the bottom of the road I can give you some more."

They're going to *adore* my humorous potted history about the Tudors.

"Yay!" they squeak, jumping up and down. "We love you, Harriet Manners!" "You're the best, Harriet

Manners!" "See you tomorrow, Harriet Manners!"

And – waving shyly – the four girls run through the lower school doors.

Leaving me lit up with pleasure behind them.

56

I wait a few minutes until they've gone.

Mainly so I can wipe the stupid grin off my face and compose myself into a more sophisticated sixth form kind of mentality.

Then I glance down at my outfit.

Bright purple linen trousers, turquoise kaftan, a yellow shawl, enormous silver earrings with orange stones, three scarves – pink, green and blue – and little red leather slippers. There are sequins on at least four of those items, and tinkling bells on three.

Yup: *nailed it.*

With a satisfied sigh, I get my list out of my pocket and draw little ticks beside the next two items.

Be Stylish! Shake it up and try something new!
Inspire! Lead, never follow!

Then I anxiously contemplate the next goal:

Don't try too hard! **It just looks desperate!!!!**

Hmm.

Of everything on this list I've attempted over the last few days, this is going to be my biggest challenge yet. In Year Seven, I leapfrogged so hard I flung myself into a wall and dislocated my shoulder; in Year Eight I debated colonialism in history so enthusiastically I started crying; in Year Two I played Mary with such conviction I stole baby Jesus and...

Well. You get the picture.

Whichever part of the brain allows you to participate in anything half-heartedly, I just don't have it.

I try too hard at *everything*.

But there are four exclamation marks, which means this must be pretty important. So I stick my nose in the air as high and nonchalantly as I can physically get it.

Be confident, Harriet! You are a creature unlike any other! Unique! As special as a snowflake! As exceptional and rare as a...

A...

Northern Hairy-nosed Wombat, of which there are only 115 left in the wild.

Yup: that should do it.

And I push boldly and carelessly back into my classroom.

57

Or try to, anyway.

I'm so careless one of my three scarves gets caught on the classroom door handle and Miss Hammond has to untangle me patiently before I accidentally strangle myself.

So far not trying hard has nearly killed me.

"Harriet!" my form teacher says cheerfully, releasing me from the furniture. "You've returned yet again! It's very exciting, wondering if you'll be at school or not. A veritable Russian roulette of attendance."

In the meantime, the entire class has stopped talking and spun round to face me.

"Harriet! There you are!" "How was your weekend?" "Your earrings are *lush*!" "*Loving* this look, Harriet! It's so *quirky*!"

"Retty, you're back!" Liv squeaks as I blink at them all. She elbows Ananya sharply. "Yay! We were so worried you'd moved back to New York!"

255

"Where *were* you?" Ananya says, politely moving her feet so I don't have to step over them. "Did you do something exciting, Ret?"

I make my way shakily to my seat.

The urge to tell them every single thing I have ever learnt about camels and snakes and how the mortality rate if bitten by a black mamba is over ninety-five per cent is *immense*.

But I can't.

Don't be desperate, Harriet.

"Um." I sit down as airily as I can. "I was actually in Morocco for a few days, filming a television advertisement for Jacques Levaire."

Television advertisement?

Why couldn't I say *TV ad*? I sound like somebody who has never seen a telly before.

A few of my classmates start dragging their seats closer to me. "Morocco?" "You're really going to be on telly? No way!" "When does it come out?" "Did you get paid loads?" "What was it like?" "I bet you hung out with *loads* of stars, right?"

They're all talking at once, which makes it really hard to focus. It's normally me interrogating people relentlessly, not the other way round.

I'm not really trained for this.

"*Loads* of stars," I agree anxiously. "I've actually never seen so many stars in my entire life. Some of them were *huge*. It was pretty cool."

A few more people gravitate towards my desk.

"Which ones were they?" "Would we know them?" "I bet Harry was there, wasn't he?" "Do you have *lots* of celeb mates?" "Do you know any really hot models?"

As fast as I can, I count them up on my fingers.

Rin, obviously. Poppy from my flatshare in Tokyo. Fleur and Kenderall from New York. Shola and Rose in Moscow. The two girls who locked me in a cupboard last year just before my audition for *Hamlet*. An entire room full of models backstage at a fashion show who said I looked like an egg.

"Maybe eight or nine?" I say, still staring at my hand. "Plus twenty or so Russian supermodels in their underwear."

"Oh *sweet mother of all that is good and holy*," Eric whimpers, staring at the sky and putting his hands together. "*Thank you*, Universe."

"Everybody!" Miss Hammond calls sweetly, clapping her hands. "Everybody! We're in the middle of taking the register, remember! Let's do this thing *together*!"

Everybody ignores her and inches a little closer to me instead. I stare at them in amazement.

Is this… Is this *still* working?

"What was Tokyo like?" "Did you really live in a penthouse in *Manhattan*?" "Is it true you were spotted on a school trip?" "Are there *loads* of glam parties?"

I gawp at the chaos.

"There are parties pretty much every night, I reckon," I tell them. "Poppy went to all of them."

"*Poppy?* As in Poppy Page? Oh my God – she's *huge*." "You are so *lucky*." "Is there champagne?" "Is it true that Yuka Ito has named a handbag after you?"

"If she has I don't want to know what it's called," I admit doubtfully. "The last word Yuka had for me was *pus-filled*."

To my total astonishment, there's a loud burst of laughter.

Real, genuine laughter.

And – with a *whoosh* – a warm rush of happiness spreads over me: from my cheeks down into my chest and straight into my arms until I feel like light is about to shoot out of my fingertips, like Beast just after his enchantment was broken.

I sit for a few blissful seconds, basking in the warm glow of friendly faces. It feels as if I'm bathed in sunshine, steeped in rainbows, cuddled by a billion furry teddies, covered all over in sparkle and—

A copy of *Vogue* is pulled out of a bag and opened on the desk in front of me.

"Do you know *him*? Because if you do, I officially want to climb into your skin so I can be you *forever.*"

And my happiness rushes straight back out again.

58

The glittering girl in the photo is back again.

Except this time, she's not sitting in a lake. She's standing in the middle of a huge sumo stage with a sea of bright lights behind her.

Tiny white lights are flashing from the cameras in the audience, yellow lights are hanging in spots above her head and little cream orbs are reflected from the wooden floor under her bare feet.

Her head is tilted back, her eyes are painted dark and her bright red hair has been pulled into a tight bun. Her dress is long and dark blue, with slits up the sides and little holes cut in the bottom so that the lights shine through like stars.

It's a different kind of sparkling this time – harder, brighter, angrier – but it's still there: shot through the photo like fine gold thread woven through dense fabric.

At the bottom of the page is a glass bottle shaped

like a light bulb, lit internally from the bottom, and the large silver word:

LUMINATE

And below it are the words

BY YUKA ITO

It's a beautiful photo, a beautiful dress and it's a two-page spread in *Vogue*. But, frankly, I couldn't care less.

Because next to the girl is a boy.

He's tall and dark: all angles and points. Hips, cheekbones, eyes are slanted in parallel directions like identical flicks of the same God-like pen. His hand is resting gently on her waist, his head is lowered, and his nose is centimetres from the nape of her neck. As if nobody else is watching and it's just the two of them.

As if he's trying to tell her something.

According to my science books, the atoms that make up human bodies consist of almost entirely empty space. If you took it all out you could compress each of us into a cube 1/500th of a centimetre across.

Staring at the boy in the photo, it suddenly feels like

that's what somebody's trying to do to me too.

I wasn't prepared to see him again.

At least, not like this.

Nick.

59

Tokyo – June (4 months ago)

"Exactly how long do we have?"

"An hour, darling," Bunty said, inexplicably looking at the sun even though she had a watch on. "Or sixty-five minutes max, if I pack the lining of my clothes with coins and try to break the airport metal detector. Let's just say it won't be my first attempt."

I looked at Nick doubtfully as my maverick grandmother started rummaging through her multicoloured woven handbag.

His skin was darker than normal – deepened by the sun – and his hair was still all ruffled from where we'd kissed each other for twenty straight minutes, sitting on the pavement by an enormous zebra crossing in Shibuya.

"Make that seventy," Bunty added triumphantly, pulling out a large bottle of shampoo. "Seventy-five minutes if I can sneak in the bottle opener."

"That still isn't much time," I said anxiously, peering into my satchel. "We don't have a proper map. Or a guide. I've lost my guidebook and—"

"It's long enough," Lion Boy laughed, putting his arm round me so I was tucked into the ridge of his collarbone. "And you don't need one any more. You've got me."

A shock of electricity ran all the way from the back of my shoulders up my neck and into my head, as if I'd accidentally covered myself in warm water and stuck my finger in a socket.

Except in a beautiful kind of way.

I did. *I had him*.

"So what do you want to do?" he continued, kissing the top of my head. "For the next seventy-five minutes I am utterly at your disposal."

"Umm."

I pulled out my To Do list and stared at it blankly, brain now pleasantly fried. What did one do with just seventy- five minutes left in Tokyo?

We could go to the robot restaurant, and watch giant mechazoid robots fight dinosaurs to the bitter death. We could try to find a (very short) tea ceremony, or wander through a Zen garden hand in hand, or visit the Bunny Cafe (like a Cat Cafe but better, because – obviously – no cats).

We could attempt an hour of karaoke, or eat an hour's worth of sushi, or visit the Shitamachi Museum to look at miniature reconstructions of buildings from the late Meiji period.

There were still so many things left in Tokyo I had always wanted to do. So many things I still wanted to cross off my list.

But – for the first time ever – none of them seemed to matter much any more.

Because it wasn't just about me.

"You used to live here, right?" I said, looking up at him. "In Tokyo?"

"I did," Nick grinned. "When I was eleven my parents split up and I came here with my mum and spent three somewhat confusing years not understanding anyone."

"Then I want to see your favourite bit." I put my list back in my bag and flicked a switch that magically turned my watch into a stopwatch. "Show me the bit of Tokyo you love the most."

"Are you sure?" he frowned. "That list isn't going to tick off itself."

I loved that Lion Boy knew how much I needed to tick things off, and how important my lists were to me.

But I loved him more than any of them.

"I'm sure," I said, clicking on the timer button. "You

have 4,500 seconds, Nicholas Hidaka. Think you can manage it?"

He wiggled his eyebrows.

"Oh," he said. "I think I probably can."

"Ready?"

"Never readier."

"Steady?"

He laughed. "In my entire life, Harriet Manners, I have literally never been steadier. Especially by comparison."

"Show-off." I stuck my tongue out at him: I hadn't fallen over in *hours*. "Now… GO."

"Gone," Nick said, and he grabbed my hand.

60

"Harriet?"

"Hmm?" The entire class is still staring at me. "Sorry, what was the question again?" I suddenly miss Nick so much it's like an enormous hand is squeezing me shut.

Raya taps the photo again and I flinch and focus on a bit of desk slightly to the left.

"Oh," I say slowly. "Yes, I know him."

"Is he single?" "Is he as hot as he looks in pictures?" "I can't believe he's *touching* you. You actually got to *touch* him."

Quick, Harriet. Change the subject.

"Umm," I say faintly, clearing my throat. "Did you know that when you speak your throat's vocal folds vibrate inside your own skull, which means the voice you hear sounds nothing like you actually do to everyone else?"

There's a brief pause.

"Did she answer the question?" somebody whispers.

"Was that it?"

"I don't think that was it," somebody whispers back.

"Oh my *goodness*," Ananya says, suddenly pushing her way to the front of the group with her hands. "Don't you guys know *anything*? That is Nicholas Kou Hidaka. Ret's long-term *boyfriend* and love of her *life*."

"*Yeah*," Liv echoes, shoving forward too, except a little less successfully. "You obviously don't know our Retty at *all*."

I stare at them both in astonishment.

OK: they have done some *serious* research. Nick managed to convince me that the middle K in his name stood for Koala for nearly six months, and Kookaburra for another two.

"How did you—"

"We can't *wait* to meet him," Liv breathes, gripping her hands together. "I ship you two so hard I can't even."

She *ships* us? Like, in a boat? Or a spaceship?

A spaceship sounds a lot more fun.

"Uh." I blink a few times. "I'm afraid we're not... I mean, Nick's not... I'm not..."

Apparently girls speak an average of 20,000 words every single day – I don't know where all mine have suddenly gone.

I just can't say it.

I can't say *Nick and I have broken up* out loud: it's lodged somewhere in the middle of my oesophagus.

"You are the *luckiest* girl in the entire universe, Harriet!" "Does he live in London?" "Does he ever pick you up from school?" "Does he have any *friends* you could introduce me to?"

"I…" I swallow painfully. "Nick's in Australia right now."

"On a shoot?" "I saw him on a bus a few weeks ago." "On a bus? Like, a passenger?" "Obviously not, idiot. As a poster. Boys like him don't take *buses.*"

"Uh." I swallow and try to find my voice again. Nick takes buses all the time. He's just a boy: not the Queen. "Actually, it's…" I swallow *again*. "I mean, there are times in our life when paths go in different directions and – uh. There's a fork in the road that…"

"Is she answering the question again?"

"I'm *so* confused."

There's a sharp voice at the back of the room.

"Right." A purple head appears from the crowd, and India walks forward, closes the magazine with a snap and hands it back to its owner with an icy expression. "This school dynamic is deeply disturbing and I think that's quite enough. Does nobody have any respect for privacy?"

Bizarrely, everyone immediately shuts up and I sigh with relief. I'm obviously not the only one who thinks

India might be royalty.

"*Yeah,*" Ananya sighs. "You guys are *vultures*. Ret comes to school to get *away* from all this stuff."

Liv folds her arms. "Such *hyenas*."

Actually vultures provide an invaluable service to the ecosystem by eating dead carcasses that are otherwise rendered inedible due to their bacterial content, whereas hyenas follow vulnerable animals and rip them apart while still alive.

It's really not fair to lump them together like that.

I'm just about to explain this in detail when the door swings open.

"Jasper!" Miss Hammond calls cheerfully from the front. I'm going to assume for the last ten minutes she's been gallantly taking the register and then answering it herself. "Better late than never! Join the crowd!"

He glances in surprise around the empty classroom, and then at the spot where every student is clustered in a mob around me.

My phone beeps and I pull it quickly out of my pocket.

Hannah darling! Kev THRILLED with Levaire shoot! Gucci director asked to see your book – call me!! Stephie xx

I'm too surprised at "Stephie" to hide my phone.

"No way!" somebody loudly squeaks over my shoulder. "*Gucci!* You're going to model for *Gucci!*" "Oh my God, that's amazing!" "Oh wow!" "Have you written a *book*, Harriet? What's it about?"

I flush in embarrassment, quickly shove my phone back into my satchel and look up again.

Jasper and I lock eyes for a few seconds and my stomach clenches slightly.

"You know what?" he says finally, still staring straight at me. "I think this particular crowd is quite big enough already, don't you?"

And he disappears again with a loud BANG.

"Jasper..." Miss Hammond says tiredly this time, scanning her register with a small sigh and then drawing a little tick. "Yes, Miss Hammond. Here, Miss Hammond. Have a lovely day, Miss Hammond."

The bell rings and everyone suddenly disperses to collect their bags, attention now focused on whatever their next class is going to be.

But I'm still staring at the door.

What is Jasper's problem? Why does he always have to be so horrible? I made him a dinosaur biscuit, didn't I? What more does he want from me?

More importantly, why do I even *care?*

61

The rest of the week can be summarised thus:

1. Under considerable duress, I surreptitiously teach a group of girls how to "catwalk" in double chemistry
2. Mr Harper tells me if I don't stop "stomping like an elephant" around the classroom he's going to give me a detention
3. I politely explain that I am, in fact, walking like a cat
4. Everyone laughs
5. I get a detention
6. Almost every girl in the year inexplicably wants to sit next to me for the next three lunchtimes.

Basically, I don't have a second to myself for the next five days.

In chemistry, I explain my "best beauty trick" to a big group of girls (toothpaste on my spots) and how to perfectly balance your dietary nutrition (chicken and

strawberry jam sandwiches). In maths we all have a long and apparently very interesting conversation about castings, and then everyone wants to see my 'book'.

So – flushed with pleasure – I get *Bleak House* out and show it to them all under the desk. For some reason they seem a bit bemused.

In physics, I start using Kirchhoff's Law to find the internal resistance of a cell. "Want to work this out together?" two of the new girls ask, pulling their graph paper over to mine. When I help them out, "You see?" one says triumphantly to the other measuring voltage, "Harriet knows everything!"

Eric wants to discuss Russians for a whole breaktime, Raya is adamant for three hours in double biology that Nick *must* have an identical twin brother and the sixth form netball captain thinks I'm *just the cutest* after I regale the team with a story about the world's most expensive coffee while waiting in line for the vending machine.

"But it's made from the droppings of an Asian palm civet," I clarify again, because I'm not entirely sure she's heard me. "That's poop. Basically mongoose poop."

"*Poop coffee!*" she exclaims, putting a delighted arm round me. "You are just so *adorable*."

On Tuesday I bring in all my extra Moroccan purchases and enthusiastically distribute them, and by Wednesday morning bright colours are scattered everywhere: silver earrings and bangles and scarves attached to people like bird feathers. Even the boys are participating: they're using spare bangles as tiny hoops to throw around cans and high-fiving me every time they succeed in their target.

Every morning and afternoon after school I meet the first years to hand over more of my books, like a private librarian service.

I have to explain – six times – to Stephanie that I can't take any more time off school to meet designers and she'll have to arrange interviews at weekends instead. Eventually she gets the idea and schedules something for the weekend after next.

By Friday, there are so many ticks on my Inner Star list it looks like one of the essays I used to write and then mark myself when I was seven. I have been confident, over and over and over again. I have been risky, repeatedly. I've been brave and limitless seven times, stylish three and inspirational at least twice.

And it has totally and utterly worked.

Whatever the opposite of lonely is, I've never been so *that* in my entire life.

I just haven't done any homework. At all.

No *wonder* I've got excellent grades for the last eleven years.

I had literally nothing else to do.

"Ret!" Ananya calls as I finally stagger out of the sixth form doors on Friday afternoon and blink sleepily in the sunshine. One of my pink scarves has been wound round her neck and a pair of my enormous silver earrings are glinting in her dark hair. "Retty! Where are you going?"

"We haven't seen you all *day*," Liv squeaks, wrapping her arms tightly round me. "Where *were* you? We *missed* you." I'm still finding her huge enthusiasm for me a little overwhelming, but it's nice that she's so affectionate.

"We're having a sleepover tonight at Indy's. It's going to be *ace*. You're coming, right?"

I freeze in surprise – have I just been voluntarily invited to my first ever non-Nat social outing? – then try to stifle a massive yawn.

Honestly, I had no idea trying so hard not to try hard could be so physically and mentally *exhausting*.

Fresh connections are made in the brain every time you form a new memory. Mine is now so stuffed full of new names and facts and conversations about body parts of celebrities I've never heard of before that I think I may have just run out of space.

"Of course I would *really* love to," I say politely, rubbing my eyes. "But do you mind if I come another time instead? I've got such a huge amount on this weekend."

Sleeping. Reading. Catching up on homework. Eating biscuits in my penguin pyjamas, hopefully with Nat, and watching documentaries about insects in case anything has changed in the last five days.

"See you on Monday?" I add with a little wave, and start wandering sleepily towards home.

Ananya's voice cuts through the air like a sword.

"Oh. Right. So it's like *that*, is it?"

I stop in confusion, and turn round slowly. "Huh?"

"We get it. It's *fine*, Harriet," she says with her arms crossed. "You've obviously got more *important* things to do than hang out with us now. We *totally* understand."

"*Yeah*," Liv agrees, folding hers too. "I mean, I thought we were a *gang*, but if you're too *busy*, Harriet, then just let us know. We wouldn't want to be *in the way*."

The words are nice, but something about the way they're saying them doesn't quite match. An unpleasant memory from last year is beginning to niggle at the back of my brain: one I killed and buried quite a long time ago.

At least, I thought I had.

"It's not that at all," I stammer, face starting to get hot. "I just haven't done any work this week and I'm really tired and there's a lot to—"

"No no," Ananya interrupts, holding up her hand.

"No need to explain, Harriet. You've got *so* much on, now you're a *celebrity*. I'm sure you have much *better* things to do than spend quality time with *us*."

And there it is.

With that word – *better* – the memory comes tumbling forward: out of my frontal lobes, through my hippocampus and straight into the middle of my forehead where it sits, flicking me hard with its fingers.

You really think you're better than everyone else, don't you? Who here hates Harriet Manners?

Put your hands up.

My entire body has suddenly gone cold, as if I've plunged myself headfirst into the freezer.

No.

No no *no*. Not again.

I can't do this again. Not again not again not again not again not again not again not again…

It suddenly feels like all my hard work over the last ten days is unravelling and I don't know why, or how to stop it. I must have deviated from the list, somehow. And now they seem to think I don't want to spend time with them…

And it's really *not* that.

I'm having *fun*. I'm just *tired*, that's all.

But as I stare at Ananya and Liv's tense faces, it suddenly

hits me that there is no time off from this plan. If I'm not extremely careful, the old Harriet Manners will return, and one by one all the hands that have come down are going to start going straight back up again.

Until finally I'm right back where I was last year, except worse.

Because this time it'll be all my fault.

And I'll know it.

"Umm…" I say, desperately trying to think. My brain is jittering around: picking up ideas and putting them down again. "Could we maybe do something awesome together next week? A… museum visit? An… art exhibition?" They're still staring at me. "A… little gathering or something?"

They glance at each other.

"OhmyGodohmyGodohmyGod," Liv squeaks, lobbing herself at me again. "*Really?* Doyoumeanitlcan'tbelieveit you'rethebestwillyoureallythrowusaparty?"

Huh? Where did a *party* come from? I meant tea and biscuits. Maybe a slice of chocolate cake.

"Well, I—"

"OhmyGodohmyGodHarriethowareyousoamazing howdoyou*live*tellmesolcanbreatheyourairandabsorb yourpowersandliveinyourmagickingdom*forever*."

"Wait," Liv blinks a few times. "Was that me?"

We all turn round simultaneously to see a pretty blonde girl, perched comfortably on a bollard behind us in silence. Like a hawk: the powerful kind with a pointy beak and muscular legs and a habit of tearing unsuspecting rabbits into pieces.

I haven't seen Alexa once all week. I'd almost forgotten she was in my year: that's how utterly invisible she's been.

She's not invisible any more.

And as she unsheathes her talons and looks at us steadily, I have a horrible feeling she's about to destroy everything.

62

In the 1970s, a man called Michael Lotito ate an entire aeroplane. Bit by bit, he chewed through every part of a Cessna 150: glass, metal, engine, leather and tyres. It took him two years but he finally swallowed all of it.

My hands are starting to sweat, but I'm somehow managing to keep my face composed.

After all, I've had more than eleven years of Alexa now. As Lotito proved, you can get through anything with enough practice and a decent set of teeth.

Be brave, Harriet.

"So," Alexa says smoothly, smiling as I push my shoulders back as far as I can get them and lift my chin, "how goes Project Reinvent Harriet Manners? Is she everything you hoped she'd be and more?"

Ananya and Liv take a step forward until they're standing on either side of me, like identical bookends. "Of course she is. We just totally *love* her."

"Harriet's the *best*."

"*Isn't* she just?" Alexa says, her cat-smile curving a little more. "Hasn't this last week been *so much fun*? I've *loved* watching Harriet transform into an icon right in front of my very eyes. It's like a Disney film or something."

My stomach suddenly feels like it's full of aeroplane too. What does *that* mean? Has Alexa been watching me the whole time?

Ugh. It feels a bit like pulling off a shoe and then discovering an enormous cockroach has been sitting inside it for the last six hours.

"Yeah, well, whatever," Liv says stiffly, putting her hands on her hips. "Harriet's having a *party*. A *big* party. An *amazing* party."

"Yup," Ananya says coolly, staring at her fingernails. "And guess what, Lexi? *You can't come.*"

OK: tea and biscuits is rapidly spiralling out of control.

"A big *party*?" Alexa says, hopping off the bollard. "Really? That sounds like such a *brilliant* idea. I bet you really blow everyone away. You've always had such an incredible imagination."

I stare at her in amazement.

I know it seems crazy, but it sounds like she really, genuinely means it. *Could* she mean it? Maybe an entire week of being ostracised has made Alexa realise how I've felt for the last six years. Maybe this is her way of making amends.

I'd have preferred a traditional apology – maybe a handwritten card with a dolphin on the front – but I'll take what I can get.

In a flush of hope, I step forward.

"Alexa. It's more of a… gathering, really. But if you want to come, then… you can. You're invited. I'd really like you there."

That last bit isn't true at all, but baby steps.

"Harriet," she says, breaking into a wide smile. "I would *love* to come. Thank you *so* much for inviting me. Let's try and put the past behind us, shall we? It's time we moved on, don't you think?"

Alexa kisses my stunned cheek.

"This is *so exciting*," she whispers into my ear. "I am *beside myself* with anticipation." Then she gives us all a little wave and saunters down the road, swinging her bag jauntily behind her.

I watch her walk away in bewilderment.

OK… Did my lifelong nemesis and arch-enemy just *kiss* me?

"Well," Ananya says grumpily when Alexa is finally out of earshot. "I don't see why you had to invite *her*. But I guess it's your party, so you can do what you want."

"Lexi won't come," Liv says confidently. "She always

says she will and then she never does."

An old, bright-purple car stops outside the school and India's head pokes out of the driver's seat. "Are you getting in or what, BANANA? I draw the line at being your private chauffeur service."

Wow. India must already be seventeen and she can drive: no *wonder* she has such an air of distinction and gravitas.

Also, she matched her car to her hair.

That is *so freaking cool.*

"Coming, Indy!" Ananya calls, waving. Then she turns to me. "This is *so* brilliant, Retty. You're too good to us, you know that?"

"Eeeeeep!" Liv squeaks, chewing on the end of her ponytail.

"Iwon'tbeabletosleepIcanalreadyfeelitohmygoshwhat amIgoingto—"

"*GET IN THE CAR, MUPPET!* Liv too if she wants," India shouts, slamming hard on the horn four times. "Are you coming as well, Harriet?"

I shake my head apologetically, and India nods and turns back to fiddle with the radio. Ananya and Liv give me a hug that threatens to permanently change the shape of my windpipe, then climb into the back of the car still chattering excitedly and drive away.

At which point the sixth form door opens and a familiar fluffy head appears, pauses for a few seconds and starts charging in the opposite direction.

So I take a deep breath, tug my satchel on to both my shoulders and begin racing after the only person in the year who *hasn't* spoken to me in the last five days.

Toby Pilgrim.

63

A mouse's tail is precisely as long as its body.

Toby is literally the only person I know who would find this fact interesting, and possibly try to hunt one down so he can measure it with a ruler.

Apart from me, obviously.

And – as I start shuffling after him in my little leather slippers – that's suddenly all I want to talk about. How every human has between two to four million sweat glands, and how on just one square centimetre of our skin live eight million microscopic animals.

All I want to do this weekend is play scrabble and debate in great detail which of the twelve Dr Whos is the best. Toby asked me to stay away from him until the end of this week, so I've obediently done exactly that. But his secret project should be finished now. It's time to spend some proper time together.

I had absolutely no idea how much I would miss him.

Unfortunately, I also hadn't realised how fast Toby was

capable of walking. By the time I've finally caught up with him, every one of my three million sweat glands has done its job and I'm covered in a fine film of water.

I suspect our PE class would be similarly surprised at his speed.

Had Tobes shown this kind of athletic capacity over the last five years, he could have spared himself a lot of wedgies.

"Toby?" I say for the fifteenth time. "Toby? Tobes? Toby Pilgrim?" He keeps walking, so I try to run in front of him. "Toby?"

Then I grab his arm. "Hello, *Toby*?"

"Oh, hello, Harriet," he says finally, taking enormous white headphones off and clipping them backwards round his neck so he looks a bit like a vicar. "I was busy listening to vocal and instrumental sounds combined in such a way as to produce beauty of form, harmony and expression of emotion."

I beam at him. Only Toby would say all that instead of *music*.

"How are you, Tobes? I haven't seen you at all this week. Did you finish your project? Did it go well? Because if you have, I was thinking maybe we could spend this evening—"

"I've got a new jacket, Harriet," he interrupts. "It's a

Secret Agent jacket, and it has thirty-five pockets. Here's one to warm my hands. One for a torch. One for ID. One for glasses. One for sunglasses. One for spare glasses…"

We may be here some time.

"Brilliant! Why don't you come to my house and have a cup of tea, and we can look at all of them together! We can find other things to put in them and…"

"Here's one for a laser."

"Yes…"

"And one for an iPod."

"OK."

"But I'm afraid I need no pocket in which to put the time I have for you right now, Harriet," Toby says, putting his headphones back on. "Because I sadly have none at all at this precise moment."

I stop walking and stare at his back blankly. "What?"

"I'm spending this evening with Jasper," he explains over his shoulder, while fiddling with his iPod. "We're going to fight."

For a few seconds, I'm not sure which of those two statements is more astonishing. "*Fight?* Jasper? You're going to fight *Jasper*?"

A wave of relief rushes through me.

I *knew* Toby would come to my aid eventually. I just

hadn't realised it would be with such uncharacteristic violence.

"Tobes," I say, running after him again. "That's so sweet of you, but just because Jasper and I don't get on it doesn't mean *you* have to dislike him too."

"I don't," he says in surprise, fiddling with his iPod again. "Why would I dislike him? He's a thoroughly nice chap with many interesting and valid points. We've become excellent friends."

I blink. "...Oh."

"Did you know that he's a purple belt in Jiu-Jitsu, Harriet? As I have just discovered Bartitsu, a classic gentleman's martial art from the 1800s, we're going to see which one we like best. It should be rather fun."

I blink again in response.

"Although," he adds slightly sadly, "my fighting involves umbrellas, snuffboxes and top hats and was used by Sherlock Holmes, so I will probably vanquish him effortlessly. Hopefully he won't hold it against me."

Then he clicks a button.

Giraffes have no vocal chords, and it seems neither do I right now. *Jasper?* Despite my noble statement thirty seconds ago, *obviously* I wanted Toby to dislike Jasper on my behalf. Of all the people he could have befriended, Toby's picked the one who hates my guts?

In a sudden rush of suspicion, I lean over and look at Toby's iPod. There's no light: just a dark battery picture, lodged in the middle of the screen.

Which means he could hear me.

Which means he carried on walking anyway; which means he was *ignoring* me.

I suddenly feel a bit dizzy. I'm now trying desperately to remember what was drawn on the paper he hid from me in the art room last week. All I actually *saw* was a rabbit and a badly executed outline of Darth Vader.

Oh my God. Is there even a science project?

Has there *ever* been one?

"What about tomorrow?" I blurt, racing after him again. I'm wrong: I have to be. This is *Toby*. "Saturday evening? Sunday?"

"I'll be very busy," he says, avoiding my eyes. "Super busy with many interesting and exciting things that don't involve you."

I stare at him for a few seconds, eyes beginning to prickle. "Toby, that's incredibly hurtful."

"Oh." He looks confused. "I'm so sorry, Harriet. I didn't mean it to be. What's a more sensitive way of saying I'm not allowed to spend time with you right now?"

Giraffes have nothing on me. An oyster is more capable of putting together a coherent sentence.

"Uh."

"Well, this has been a very interesting catch-up," Toby says finally as I stare at him in silence. "It was nice to see you, Harriet Manners. I hope you are enjoying all your brand-new friends."

Then, without another word, Toby makes an abrupt left and dives straight through a hole in a hedge.

And crawls out the other side, away from me.

64

I stand for a few minutes and watch Toby army-crawl across the grass as if I can't see him.

Enjoying all my brand-new friends?

Not *allowed* to spend time with me?

What the *sugar cookies* have Jasper and Toby been talking about for the last two weeks in the art room? How many *excellent and valid points* has Jasper made, exactly, and what about?

Or – more specifically – about *whom*?

I blink back the hurt as my ex-stalker attempts an enthusiastic somersault and disappears round a wall. He *asked* me to stay away last week, so I did. Why is he being so weird now? What have I done wrong? Is he angry with me for something?

Then I swallow and tighten my hands into little balls.

If Toby wants to take sides against me, *fine*.

He wasn't really part of my gang anyway: he was a late insertion, an involuntary addition who forced his

way in via totally socially unacceptable methods, such as stalking. If he's going to be like this, it can just return to normal again: Nat and I together, like fish and chips, or ketchup and mustard or banana and Marmite, which I quite like even though nobody else I know does.

Except…

I haven't really heard from my best friend all week either. We've exchanged a few messages – having a great time, super busy, etc. – but other than that she's been pretty quiet. I've been giving her some space to enjoy the first few heady days with her new boyfriend.

But I think I've finished doing that now.

So I get my phone out.

Hey – want to hang out this weekend? Hxxx

My phone beeps almost immediately.

You OK? ☺ N xxx

Brilliant! I just thought we could watch that model show you like. I think somebody gets punched this week. ☺ Hxx

Love to! But super busy again. ☹ Another time? ☹ Nx

Monday or Tuesday? Wednesday? H

Something in my throat is starting to hurt.

I may not understand relationships, but I understand punctuation.

This is rapidly growing tension composed entirely of kisses and passive aggressive emoticons. Three kisses to two to one to none: we're both getting irritated. Strategically placed smiley and sad faces: she's feeling guilty, I'm getting needy.

And there's really no way Nat's *that* sad.

She lives three minutes' walk away: not in the outer Hebrides.

I wait an inordinately long time – given that we are *in the middle of a conversation* – then my phone beeps.

Out every night this week too.☹ I'll ring soon?☹ Love you. Nat xxxx

I stick my tongue out at my phone – two sad faces and four kisses is really pushing it – then type:

No worries! Let me know when you're free! ☺ Hxx

Insincere winky face.

A part of me totally understands: of course it does.

I know exactly what happens when you meet someone you really, really like. I know how it feels as if the world is shutting down and opening up at the same time: as if it's somehow getting bigger, but only for the two of you. How every sentence of a book, every line of a song, every scene of a film, has a little fragment inside it just for you.

How anything that doesn't starts to melt away.

But no matter how much time I wanted to spend with Nick, I always tried to find a way to put Nat first. To include her. To make sure she didn't feel shut out. Always. Because falling in love doesn't have to mean dropping your best friend in the process.

Except – as I put my phone back in my pocket and start wandering slowly home again – I'm starting to realise I might be wrong.

Maybe sometimes it does.

65

Every hour in Britain we throw away enough rubbish to fill the Albert Hall. It looks like they've just found a new place to put it.

The house has exploded, yet again.

As I push the front door open slowly, I spot about eighteen different receptacles scattered at random all over every possible surface: cups, mugs, glasses, vases, the yellow bucket we normally keep in the garden. Tiny bits of debris are scattered all over the hallway, as if a particularly stupid Hansel and Gretel got lost somewhere near the entrance.

So far this week I've tidied the house every single night before Annabel got home.

And – frankly – I've had enough.

"*Dad*," I say, slamming my satchel on the floor. "Do you think we have *pixies* or something?"

"Don't be ridiculous." My father pokes his head round the corner of the living-room door. "I don't believe in

pixies, Harriet, or fairies either for that matter. I'm a fully grown man in his forties. Do I look like an idiot?"

I stare at him for a few seconds. I can't believe that appears to be a genuine question.

"You have a tea towel on your head."

"Yes, well." He sticks his nose in the air in a gesture I may have to stop doing sharpish. "Your sister and I have spent the day adventuring, and I was keen to give her as realistic an experience as possible."

"With a tea towel on your head?"

"I couldn't find my Indiana Jones hat, and Tabitha thought it was hilarious." He holds Tabby out from behind the doorframe. She has a tiny towel on her head and is grinning widely. "So, don't you want to know what we found?"

At any other time, I absolutely would: yes. I admit I'd be donning a tea towel and marching around the house with my compass.

But right now, I'm not really in the mood.

"No," I say a little too sharply, putting one foot on the stairs. "Feel free to discover-stroke-destroy the house without me, Father."

"First we found a half a hamster wheel in the shed, which is *very* mysterious given that this family has never had a hamster."

Another step and a sigh.

"We did, Dad. It ran away on day two."

"Ah. Smart little man. We *also* found a quarter of a person, which your sister thought was hysterical."

He pulls out the Hug Pillow Rin sent me from Japan a few weeks ago, straight after I got back from New York. It consists of half a torso, one arm and a pink T-shirt that says *I am made for the loving of us.*

"A gift from a friend," I say, taking another grumpy step. Then I turn back slightly. "Actually, give me that."

Dad throws it and I catch and hug it to my chest.

It might just be time to start using it.

"Don't you want to know what else we found, Harriet? They appear to be addressed to you."

"If they're flyers from the Chinese takeaway then it's because I told the man in the shop that fortune cookies were actually invented in San Francisco and…"

I stop.

Dad's grinning and wiggling his eyebrows.

With a sudden lurch, I glance back at all the glasses, mugs, vases and buckets. They're not randomly distributed at all: they've been placed carefully. And the debris looks like… petals and leaves.

Oh my God.

I *knew* it. I *knew* I'd hear from Nick again.

In a single day, one human heart produces enough energy to drive a truck twenty miles. As I leap back down the stairs and start following the trail, mine suddenly feels like it could propel me around the country.

The petals are scattered in the kitchen, out on to the back step and down the garden. I run after them, with Dad jogging carefully after me with Tabby in his arms.

Then I open the shed and my little sister gives a shout of happiness that's only very slightly louder than mine.

There are flowers everywhere.

Hundreds of yellow roses, pink alstromemeria, purple and white sweetpea, pink gypsophila, cream freesias and red carnations. They're arranged in bunches on every available surface: on top of the lawnmower, hanging off a large rusting fork and lined along the window ledge.

It smells like Granny Manners' house, except it doesn't come from a spray or a potpourri inside a particularly creepy teddy bear.

I open my mouth and shut it again.

"I spent all day arranging them for you," Dad grins from behind me. "They came with that."

He points at the old hamster ball, balanced haphazardly on a chair in the middle.

In it is a little yellow envelope that says:

HARRIET MANNERS

And my heart abruptly shoots like a truck to the moon.

66

I've never been sent flowers before.

Or I have – obviously – because I'm sixteen and what kind of self-respecting teenage girl has never received flowers?

I'm just not entirely sure they count if they're from your family, you're ten and you've just had your tonsils out. Gifts don't seem to mean quite as much if you have to chop a bit of your body off first to get them.

But as I run back into the house with my hug pillow over one shoulder, my arms full and my hand clenched tightly round the envelope, it hits me: these aren't just proper flowers, romantic flowers.

They're *fairytale* flowers.

The kind you send someone when they win an Oscar, or have their first opening night in a theatre, or break a world record.

Or if you love them unstoppably.

Hands shaking, I reach my bedroom, close the door

300

gently behind me and sit on the floor. I carefully place some cornflowers so I can stare at them, chest still zooming upwards.

Then I turn over the little yellow card.

With infinite slowness – the kind that really, really irritates Nat every Christmas – I peel it open. Carefully, delicately. As if I'm performing some kind of open-heart surgery.

Which, in a way, I kind of am.

Then I stare at the paper inside it.

My little Cinder-doll! I am sage and onioned with pride right now. Best hat I've ever found.
All my turtle dove.
Your F-G, Wilbur

And my nose abruptly starts to prickle.

Wilbur.

I feel like I'm splitting in half again: divided between being incredibly touched by this gesture, missing Wilbur so hard it hurts, and hating myself for…

For wishing it was from someone else.

No wonder I never get sent flowers. I'm a horrible, ungrateful hat and I deserve to have things cut out of my body without receiving any floral arrangements at all.

301

Blinking, I stare at the letter a little longer.

Then I give it a gentle hug, put it on the floor and fiddle with a blue cornflower petal while I wait for the annoying prickle in my nose to go away.

But it doesn't.

Slowly, it spreads across the bridge of my nose, along my cheeks, into my forehead and creeps between my eyebrows. Like ivy, it tendrils outwards: stinging and bristling and spiking all the way across my face until finally it wraps itself round my throat and crawls into my eyes.

I try to take a deep, calm breath: *It's OK, Harriet, it's OK, Harriet, it's OK it's OK it's OK it's OK…*

But it's no good.

The vines wrap tighter and tighter until I can feel the panic rising: my eyes wobbling, my chin crumpling.

I can't do this any more.

I need Nick here, right now. I need to put my head on his chest and have his feet on top of mine; I need the smile that goes all the way round; I need his calmness and his kindness. I need his fresh green smell, and the scar he got from a seagull, and the way he brings things down from high shelves in supermarkets for strangers without being asked to.

I need him to tell me things are going to be OK.

That he hasn't gone for good; that I can do this without

him. Because he's coming back.

But I just don't know if I believe any of it any more.

So I do the only thing I can to bring him closer. I sit up;
I wipe my face and grab a piece of paper and a pen.

And I start writing again.

Dear Nick,

I know we made this decision together.

I know we both thought it would be less painful
to break up before the distance did it for us. I really
believed it was the right thing to do: that it wouldn't
hurt as much this way. But I can't imagine anything could
be harder than this.

And I don't think I'm OK.

I came back from New York and I was so devastated
I shut myself away from my best friends, and now they've
shut themselves away from me too.

I've done everything I can to feel happy again. I've
been to Morocco and ridden on camels and danced in the
desert: I've chased my inner star. I've thrown myself
into modelling and done whatever it takes to make new
friends at school so I'm not alone, even though I don't
really understand them most of the time and I don't
think they understand me either. I'm trying <u>so</u> hard to

move on without you.

But I'm not, Nick. I'm not moving anywhere.

All the things I wrote in the last letter... they weren't true. Or they were, but it wasn't what I really meant. I was hiding behind facts and figures because I didn't know how to say this:

Every day you're changing, you're growing, you're living, you're out there being you, and the only thing staying the same is me.

I'm still here, holding on to you.

Stuck in the past. Trapped in it. Burying myself in it. Drowning in it. And I don't know what to do to make it better.

I miss you, Nick. I've missed you every day, every hour and every second since you've been gone.

And I miss the bit of me you took with you.

Harriet xxx

67

I have never run so fast in my entire life.

With my envelope in my hand, I fly down the stairs, out into the street and towards the postbox as if my feet are on fire.

As if there are tiny wings on my heels and six rocket engines on my back. As if I have a magical cape; as if I'm a paper aeroplane.

As if I'm a comet, or a falling star.

And as I run, I chase Nick.

Tokyo – June (4 months ago)

"3,358 seconds."

We passed through tiny side streets, past dark wooden houses with white fabric hanging from the doorways like half-open gifts, under little archways and curved roofs, popping out into bustling, noisy roads and then back into

the quietness again.

"3,247 seconds."

We raced past a little train station.

"2,320," I told him as we ran over a beautiful wooden bridge stretching across a canal, painted red and stuck with long, red flags. "Nick, where on earth are you taking me?"

He laughed and turned round.

"Harriet…"

As he turns, Nick's face flickers slightly: like a broken projection of an old movie scene. Then it melts, as if I'm passing through it like smoke.

Maybe I'm just not running quickly enough.

So I run faster.

I run until my thighs burn and my eyes blur and the world judders from side to side. Until my breath is coming in high-pitched squeaky noises and all I can hear is thumping under my feet.

Focus, Harriet.

"1,986 seconds." We jogged breathlessly through grey cement streets as skyscrapers started closing in around us.

"1,653."

Up some steep stairs. "1,454."

"Harriet…"

But Nick's starting to evaporate again.

Now I can't see the exact shape of his nose, or the precise shade of his eyes, or exactly the position of the mole on his cheek. I can't remember the angle his mouth turns down in just before he smiles, or the exact tone of his voice when he's tired.

So I frown and keep running.

Through the park with the roundabout where we spun in circles last summer.

Across the path where we kissed in the rain; down the road where my foot got wet and he gave me his sock.

Past the first postbox, where he posted my first ever letter.

"1,223 seconds," I said. "I don't understand where we're—"

"Harriet…"

Now his chin is gone, the shape of his ears, the colour of his back in the summer, the curl of his lips.

"Harriet."

I can't remember what his hand felt like.

"Harriet."

I can't remember the expression on his face.

"Harriet."

And I'm running as fast as I can: as if my legs are the wind-up handle on the old movie projector, and maybe all I have to do is get them moving quickly enough for long enough, and – with a little click – I'll be able to see him again.

Smiling and waiting for me to catch up.

But it doesn't work.

Every time Nick turns round, his face flickers and fades a little more.

And as I come to a juddering stop by the second postbox, it finally hits me just how pointless this is. My letters aren't being read. They're not being answered. What's left of Nick is all in my head, and when that goes dark, so will he.

Whether I'm ready or not.

Over the past year, Nick has disappeared so many times.

But this is the first time he's actually gone.

68

I post the letter anyway.

I've run so far and so hard it seems silly not to.

Then I slide breathlessly down the postbox until I'm sitting on the floor with my head in my hands. Nat and Toby don't want to see me. Rin, Bunty and Wilbur are thousands of miles away.

Nick isn't here.

And now I have two whole days stretching ahead of me that seem impossibly empty.

Forty-eight hours of homework and documentaries and hiding in stories that aren't mine again. Two days of rearranging the cans in the kitchen into reverse alphabetical order and trying to wiggle my earlobes when I'm pretty sure I don't have the necessary muscles.

A full weekend of being the old Harriet Manners.

And something inside me snaps.

I wait until I've got my breath back, which – I'll be honest – takes longer than the NHS says it probably

309

should for a girl of my age and size.

Then I grab my phone out of my pocket.

As fast as I can, I click on every number I've carefully collected over the last week at school: Ananya, India, Liv, Chloe, Mia, Raya, Eric, Robert and a plethora of other people whose names I couldn't quite remember. (They're A, B, C, D etc. in my phonebook, because it seemed rude to tell them that.)

I grit my teeth together.

Then I write the following text message:

I'm having a big party next Friday and would love you to come! Details on their way.☺ Harriet Manners xx

There are 250 different types of bees in the UK. Over the following two minutes it sounds like they're all trapped inside my phone.

Buzz.

Yes! I'm in! You're THE BEST! X

Buzz, buzz, buzz.

No way! You rock! Xx

You legend! Bringing the whole footie team!

Epic! Can I invite the boys' school? x

Buzz buzz buzz buzz buzz buzz buzz.

And as replies start rolling in by their dozens – even from people I haven't sent the message to – I put my still vibrating phone back in my pocket and stand up.

I know what it is I have to do.

I'm going to throw the partiest party the world has ever seen. It'll be huge. Enormous. Prodigious, humongous, jumbo, bumper, almighty. A monstrous, princely, towering and stupendous party to end all parties.

And when it's over, the old Harriet Manners will be gone forever and she won't be coming back.

Because this isn't a game any more or a fun chance to tick things off a list. It isn't a way to distract me, or keep me busy, or help me forget the people I miss.

The glittering version isn't just the life I've chosen any more.

It's the only one I have left.

69

I spend the rest of the weekend planning.

With Tabby perched on my lap, I spend three hours in Dad's home-office: typing, formatting and printing out two hundred individual invitations on different-coloured paper.

Then I hand my sister back for health and safety reasons and spend another four hours carefully cutting all my invitations into cool shapes and drawing really relevant images all over them.

I make a dozen phone calls, compile six different planning lists and do a little shopping.

I even borrow some of the money I made on my Moroccan job from Annabel, on the strict understanding that I pay it all back just as soon as it comes through.

My stepmother is surprisingly on board, actually.

"A *party*?" she says, lurking in the door of the office as I start enthusiastically laminating all my various bits of paper. Everybody knows that a party isn't official until all

the invites are rendered completely waterproof. You just never know what's going to get spilt on them, further down the line.

"Yes," I say firmly, taking a warm piece of plastic out of the machine. "I need one, Annabel."

Then I add one of the little gold stickers I normally save for myself when I get an A+ on an essay.

There's a short silence.

"Would you like some help?"

I glance up at Annabel in surprise, and then at the bullet-pointed argument I carefully prepared for the moment I had to fight her on it. I'm starting to wonder if having a baby has relaxed my stepmother a little too much: she seems to have become alarmingly easy-going.

The moment she starts doing yoga, I'm calling the authorities and asking for some kind of brain scan.

"I think I need to do this on my own," I say gratefully. "But thank you."

Plus there's always a risk she'll make everyone sign some kind of legally binding contract before they get through the door, and that's just not the look I'm going for.

In the meantime, Dad is bouncing around the house as if all two floors have become a trampoline overnight.

"I *love* parties. What's the theme? Can we make it

food-related so I can dress as an Italian chef and turn Tabby into a lobster and carry her around in a really big pot?"

I look at Annabel in alarm.

If my father so much as shows his face, my hard-earned new image is going to go up in flames. Especially if he's wearing a fake moustache and pretending to boil my sister.

"No, Richard," Annabel says firmly. "If Harriet needs us we'll be on hand, but otherwise we're staying very much out of it."

Seriously: any minute now she's going to tell me quinoa is pronounced *keen-wa* and start extolling the virtues of meditation.

"*So unfair*," Dad says for the six billionth time. "Well if you change your mind, I've got the costume anyway. Harriet wore it fifteen years ago and made a very charming crustacean. She used to cry when we made her take it off."

Which – now I'm thinking about it – explains more about my life than I'd like it to.

By the time I get to school on Monday morning, I'm pretty much ready. I don't want to sound smug, but this is going to be the most awesome party anybody has ever seen in the history of social gatherings.

I'm even getting pretty excited about it myself.

And I'm not the only one.

"No *waaaay*," Lydia and her little friends squeak as I hand them invitations, tucked into my latest *Giant Bathroom Reader*. "For *us*? We can come? *Really*? You're the *best*, Harriet Manners!"

"*Amazing*!" Chloe beams at me, studying it carefully. "You're so *adorable*!"

"*Ace*," Eric and co grin as I hand them all shiny slips of plastic. "This is *so cool* of you, Retzer."

(That's my name now, by the way. Retzer. I sound like something you take when you've got a funny tummy.)

Liv takes one look at the invitation and immediately starts hyperventilating.

"Look! LooklooklookIcan'tbelieveitwhatamIgoingto wearthisisamazingI'mjusttotallygoingto—"

"*Olivia*," India snaps, rolling her eyes. "Calm *down* or you're going to pop something."

"It's just the best idea *ever*, Ret," Ananya says, giving me a huge hug. "Is *everyone* coming? Will I know them all?"

I beam at her. "Hopefully! They all texted back straight away so it looks like it!"

Ananya and Liv both squeak.

"I'm going to take *loads* of photos," Liv says, kissing my invite. "This is *so exciting!*"

Six hours of burning my fingertips on melting plastic were *totally* worth it.

Everyone loves them. So much so, even I am a little surprised. The last time I saw my peers this excited about anything, we were six and Father Christmas took an impromptu assembly with three real-life reindeer.

I'm handing out invitations in form time and biology, maths and physics and chemistry. I stand outside French and English and history, even though I don't take those classes. I do the rounds in the dining room at lunch, and construct a little booth in the common room at breaktimes.

The most important thing is I don't leave anybody out.

Even if that means giving one to Alexa.

Then – slightly less courageously, because she's still staring at me in silence – running away again.

Finally, when almost all my bits of laminated plastic are gone, I head to Toby's form room. Despite still being cross with him, I'm kind of hoping he'll get over it eventually. Hopefully by Friday evening: I spent extra time drawing on his invitation, and used all of my very best stickers.

"Thank you for this, Harriet Manners," Toby says rigidly as I jump out from behind the door and thrust it in his face before he can spot me and run away again. Except he's still not meeting my eyes and it's impossible not to notice. "I'll need to check first. I'm afraid I don't think I'll be allowed."

I nod sadly.

Then I glare daggers at Jasper from across the hallway until he blinks and looks away again.

By Wednesday morning, I can't move a single step down a school corridor without being high-fived, hugged, kissed and affectionately pretend-punched on the top of my arms.

"Hey, Ret!" "Yo, Retty!" "Retzer! How's it going?" "Looking *cooooool* today, Retty-girl!"

And as the lower school starts to slowly fill up with sequins and bright scarves and red leather satchels, I realise in bewilderment that maybe I was right.

Maybe it really is this easy.

Because as I smile confidently and wave bravely – as I laugh riskily and high-five people carelessly back – it occurs to me that maybe I've finally found my Inner Star.

And it wasn't as far away as I thought.

<u>70</u>

By Thursday afternoon, *Harriet's party* is the only thing anyone can talk about.

My entire biology class has been moved outside to the netball courts while we wait for the two other classes to join us, and it's raining hard. We're all standing in the cold: huddled and shivering under little umbrellas.

But nobody seems to have even noticed.

Everyone is using the extra time to animatedly discuss their favourite parties over the years. Apparently there have been a plethora of imaginative themes, ranging from 80s Lycra to toga to Halloween, and they've all had varying degrees of success.

Which I wouldn't know, obviously, because I wasn't invited to any of them. I'm getting as involved as I can, but apparently Tudor regalia isn't as cool as I thought it was, and neither is 'Victorian Orphan'. 'General home appliances' isn't cutting it either.

"But honestly, Ret," Chloe says as we stand in a little

group of girls. "I think your one on Friday is going to be better than *all* of them."

"It's *such* a cool idea. What made you think of it?"

I consider this carefully. "It's just nice to share the things you love with other people, you know?"

"*Totally.* Oh my God, that is *so true.*"

"It's *so* kind of you to share them with us."

"*Girls*," Mr Collins says as the second sixth form biology class walks out of the building to join us in the rain, "I've asked you to stand in silence, please."

"So what should we wear? Something shiny, right?"

"The last party I went to I had this awesome bee costume with adorable antennas that wobbled when I danced."

Huh. I didn't know Attractive Animals was a socially acceptable dress theme.

In fact, I thought it was kind of illegal.

"Oooh," I interject excitedly. "Research shows that bees use their right antenna to determine whether another bee is friend or foe. Did you use that to flirt with boys?"

They all stare at me for a few seconds, and then burst into loud laughter.

I wasn't joking at all – I thought it would make an excellent icebreaker – but I can now feel myself puffing up so hard I may need to hold on to the school fence to stop me floating away.

I *love* being so unexpectedly funny.

"*Girls*," Mr Collins says again, frowning, "what did I just say? Am I talking to myself? Can anyone actually hear me?"

"*Or*," I continue, thinking hard, "a honey bee uses its dance to communicate information about the location of food. You could have choreographed one around the snack table!"

They laugh even harder. "Hilarious!"

"Or you could have worn a tiara and acted like a Queen Bee and—"

"Girls," Mr Collins sighs, trundling over to us. He has a large, round chest, a rolling gait and has always reminded me slightly of a disconcerted badger. "*What* is this commotion?"

I look at the sniggering group and suddenly feel slightly light-headed. "Sorry, sir," I say, winking at them, "we didn't see you *bee*-hind us."

They giggle harder and I beam.

"Did you not?" Mr Collins frowns. "I'm sure you were facing this way."

"*Bee* serious, sir," I say, wiggling my eyebrows. "That's just un-*bee*-lievable."

The girls are now howling in hysterics.

Mr Collins is starting to look annoyed, but I'm far too giddy to stop now. I want *more. More* laughter. *More* approval. I *knew* my fondness for clever puns would come in handy one day.

"In fact, have you heard the Beatles song, *Let It Bee*, sir? It's really *bee*-eautiful. It really helps us *bee*-have."

Something in Mr Collins' face suddenly twitches.

"*Right*," he snaps, pointing to the middle of the playground. "I've had enough. Get over there, Harriet. *Now*."

I blink. "But—"

"This is because I have honey sandwiches every day, isn't it? They're simple to make and easy to pack and I will *not* be mocked for my eating habits by a sixteen-year-old. Frankly, I don't know what's come over you this year, young lady. Mr Harper and Miss Lloyd say you've been causing trouble in their classes too."

And – just like that – geeky Harriet Manners reappears again with a *pop*.

I feel a bit sick.

Now the *teachers* don't like me? Why is it so impossible to keep everybody happy?

"Oh no, sir," I say desperately, cheeks flushing, "we weren't laughing at you. We were just talking about this

321

party I'm going to be—"

That does it.

"I SAID GET IN THE MIDDLE, HARRIET," he yells flatly. "RIGHT THIS SECOND."

I glance to the side, but the girls now have totally straight faces: my hilariousness has evaporated.

Swallowing, I put my head down.

Then I start shuffling awkwardly through the rain towards the yellow circle drawn in the middle of the netball court. Somewhat ironically, centre is a position nobody would ever give me voluntarily in a million years.

Then I stand in silence and wait.

It's really pouring now, and I'm getting soggier by the second. Within a minute, my hair's plastered to my head, water is running down my cheeks and dripping off the end of my nose, and my leather pumps are making little squelchy sounds every time I move.

Of all the days I picked to be accidentally naughty, I could have at least chosen one with slightly better weather.

Slowly, Mrs Harris and the final biology class join the crowd at the edge of the court: a total of thirty-three freezing students.

Every single one of whom is staring directly at me.

In tropical and subtropical oceans all over the world,

you can find a frogfish of the family *Antennariidae*. It is bright red and silent, and notable because of its penchant for creeping slowly along the sea floor on its pectoral fins.

We're now basically indistinguishable.

I'm so embarrassed, I am literally centimetres away from dropping to the floor and shuffling off on my belly too.

India's standing under a bright yellow umbrella, and she gives me a little *What's going on?* frown.

I respond with an *I did a bad thing* wince back and shrink a little smaller.

"Right," Mr Collins says angrily, blowing a whistle. "We are all grouped here together today to practise sampling and classification for your Biology AS-level coursework."

"Yes, sir," everyone says, still staring at me.

"But *some* people seem to think they have more important, exciting things to talk about right now. Apparently this is an inconvenient distraction from their social calendar."

My biology teacher points at me unnecessarily: the entire department is already focused on the middle of my forehead.

I stare at the floor, suddenly grateful it's raining.

I'm so humiliated, it's the only thing that's going to stop me bursting into spontaneous flames.

"If you can't show this class and your teachers the respect and focus they deserve," Mr Collins continues clearly, "then you can stand in the rain with Harriet Manners. Am I crystal?"

"Yes, sir," say thirty-three students.

Water drips off the end of my nose and my cheeks feel like they're on fire.

I'm just trying to work out if there's a way of harnessing the rain and dissolving completely like the Wicked Witch of the West when a throat clears.

And a hand goes up.

71

"I just have a quick question, sir."

There's a short pause as Mr Collins frowns and peers at the speaker through his glasses. "Yes, Miss... Sorry, I don't know your name."

"India," she says smoothly. "India Perez. I moved here from Leeds at the start of term."

"Ah." Mr Collins nods. "Yes. I've heard your name in the staffroom. What would you like to know?"

"Sir, are your atoms, molecules or ions arranged in a highly ordered, microscopic structure?"

He blinks. "Excuse me?"

"Have you ever known yourself to form a lattice shape, and under a microscope are you largely geometrical?"

"Sorry?"

"Are any members of your family a) a snowflake –" India's now ticking off on her fingers – "b) a diamond or c) table salt?"

"*India*," Mrs Harris whispers nervously.

325

"I'm sorry, but this *teacher* wanted to know if he was crystal. I'm simply trying to find out by means of classification. We *are* in a biology class, aren't we?"

All three classes have started sniggering, and Mr Collins is slowly turning the same colour as India's hair.

"Oh, *another* funny one," he snaps. "We're a veritable stand-up comedy show round here, aren't we. Get in the middle too, Miss Perez. Go on. In."

India slowly closes her umbrella and walks towards me through the rain.

I watch her approach in bewilderment.

Honestly, I kind of thought India didn't like me very much. I've caught her looking at me with disdain *way* too many times for it to be a coincidence.

"I don't think he's crystal at all," she says as she stands next to me. "It's extremely disappointing."

I smile soggily at her. "You didn't have to do that."

Her hair is getting steadily darker and a raindrop is collecting on her nose ring.

"Yeah," she says flatly. "I kind of did. He shouldn't have picked on you like that."

In the meantime, Mr Collins' temper seems to be slowly winding down again. "Right," he says sharply, picking up his clipboard once more. "Anybody else fancy getting wet today? Or can I get on with my class now?"

There's a moment of silence.

The kind of silence you could slide down, should you be interested in sliding down silences.

Then two of the boys put their umbrellas down. "Yeah, go on then. It's getting a bit dry here anyway."

"Yup." Another umbrella disappears. "I fancy a bit of rain action."

"Me too. Mutiny!"

"Well, if everyone else is then…"

One by one – slowly at first, and then with increasing speed – all three classes close their umbrellas and start walking towards me through the rain. My heart is now expanding so quickly it feels like it's going to squeeze out between my ribs in ribbons, like the red plasticine in a Mr Potato Head.

Because it doesn't seem possible. It *can't* be possible.

But it is.

Slowly but surely, the entire playground moves from one side to the other until every biology student in the year is in the middle of the playground, soaking wet.

Standing behind… me.

72

All but one.

I didn't even know Jasper *did* biology until this moment. That's how quiet he is, and how far at the back he's been standing.

"Oh for the love of…" he sighs from his solo position by the fence. "Seriously, what is it with this girl? Is she made of chocolate or something?"

And without warning, a hot, red firework of anger starts fizzing inside me like a spinning Catherine wheel.

I *hate* this boy.

This is one of the most triumphant, glorious moments of my entire life and Jasper's *ruining* it. *Again.* He's already taken Toby away from me. Why does he have to try and take the rest of the year too?

Why can't he just leave me *alone*?

"*Actually*," I snap, folding my arms furiously. "There is a *direct* correlation between the amount of chocolate a country consumes and the number of Nobel laureates

328

they produce. So *there*."

Yeah, I know.

Everyone is looking at me: I panicked.

"That doesn't even make *sense*," Jasper exhales. "You literally just took one word out of what I said and attached an unrelated fact to it."

Sugar cookies. That's exactly what I did.

"So?" I manage, the firework fizzing again. "What do *you* know about chocolate?"

"An average of eight insect parts are found in each bar," he says flatly. "Which makes it a lot less nice than everyone thinks it is. Hey – maybe you're made out of chocolate after all."

My cheeks flame. That is *very* hurtful.

And scientifically accurate, which makes it even worse.

"Well the compound *theobromine* is found in chocolate and it can be lethal in large quantities. So maybe you have something in common with it too."

Yup: I panicked again.

"I am so confused right now," somebody whispers. "What are they talking about?"

"Now…" Mrs Harris says, stepping forward and gripping her hands together anxiously. "Let's be nice, you two. We're here to… to… study ecological diversity, so why don't we all grab a clipboard, a white tub and a bit of rope and…"

There's a cough.

"Just hang on a second," Mr Collins says, stepping between us and rubbing his chin with his hand. "Am I right in thinking that you, Jasper King, do not like Harriet Manners?"

"No," he agrees, glowering until something inside me does an angry little flip backwards. "I think it's fair to say I do not."

"And would I be correct in assuming that you, Harriet Manners, are not terribly fond of Jasper King?"

"Correct," I say, narrowing my eyes at him until my eyebrows hurt.

Mr Collins breaks into an enormous grin: as if all his Christmases have come at once, along with half his birthdays and a couple of Hanukkahs too.

"Excellent," he says, zipping up his jacket triumphantly. "That saves me giving the entire class a detention. Harriet Manners, maybe you need to spend a little time with somebody who understands what kind of behaviour this sixth form expects from its students."

Jasper and I glance at each other in confusion, and then my stomach goes rigid.

No. No no no. *No no no no NO.*

"Harriet and Jasper will be working together for the rest of the day," Mr Collins confirms cheerfully. "Have fun. Class dismissed."

73

Here are some classic enemies in popular culture:

1. Captain Hook and Peter Pan

2. Shere Khan and Mowgli

3. Maleficent and Aurora

4. Ursula and Ariel

5. Scar and Mufasa

And yes, they're also all Disney characters but I still think cartoons perfectly reflect the modern world and all its conundrums and aren't just intended for young children at all.

Whatever Nat might say.

Or the British Board of Film Classification.

332

But as Jasper and I silently grab our roll of string and clipboards and start heading into the long, wet grass at the bottom of the field, I can't stop wondering which one I am: the villain or the hero.

After all, *I'm* the one in trouble and *he's* the one I'm supposed to be trying to emulate.

But I'd *know* if I was the bad guy, wouldn't I?

"Would Your Highness like me to take my coat off and throw it across a puddle for you to tread on?" Jasper growls as I pick my way precariously through the muddy grass. "Or should I carry you on my shoulders while playing some kind of celebratory trumpet?"

This is so typical.

I've spent the majority of my life stomping across mud in supermarket trainers, looking for flowers to press/dandelions to wish on, and now I actually have to do it for grades: *now* is when I'm wearing soggy cotton and little leather slippers with no grip at all.

By comparison, Jasper is dry, warm and comfortable in waterproof boots, jeans and a light blue anorak.

I really, really despise this boy.

We reach a particularly thick section of grass next to a big oak tree and stop. The rain has finally slowed down, and everything is starting to sparkle slightly.

"First of all," I snap, unrolling a piece of blue string

and pinning it to the floor with a metal spike. "I am not Queen Elizabeth the First, despite similar colouring. Second of all, you *wish* you were the famous explorer Sir Walter Raleigh. And third of all, the cloak across the puddle story is fiction made up by clergyman Thomas Fuller so…"

So what?

"Stick that in your face and stuff it," I finish lamely.

"That's the worst comeback I've ever heard. And why would I want to be Raleigh, anyway? He had his head embalmed and given away in a bag."

"Well, I don't know about everyone else," I retort, forcing another stake in the ground, "but my fingers are firmly crossed for a repeat performance."

"Ouch. Historical burn." Jasper glares at me as I start stalking off with the roll of string. "Where are you going, princess? That's not a right angle. You know we need to section off a perfect square to get an accurate area."

"This *is* a right angle."

"It's seventy five degrees, at best," he says, taking the string off me. "Do you even understand what a right angle is?"

Oooooh.

"How *dare* you," I snap, taking the string back off him. "I knew what a right angle was before you were *born*."

"When were you born?"

"…August."

"Right. So you must have been one of those genius unfertilised eggs everyone talks about." Jasper pulls the string into the final fourth side of the square. "Why don't you just sit on a log and contemplate how amazing you are while I start measuring the diversity of species in our area?"

Another little flash of fury pulses through me.

Made significantly worse by the fact that my feet are now so cold and wet that sitting down for a bit actually sounds quite appealing.

"I've found an insect," Jasper adds sharply, crouching on the floor. "Wings."

I look at the key we've been given. "One pair or two?"

"Two."

"Membranous or hard and leathery?"

"Membranous."

"Covered in a kind of white powder?"

"Think so. The wings are held over the body, not lying flat to the sides."

"Then it's a lacewing. A *Neuroptera*, actually." Then – before I can stop myself – I blurt: "Did you know that lacewings can detect bats using hearing apparatus in their wings?"

"I did, yes," Jasper says, unrolling the string to its final corner. "Because I, too, am a sixth form biology student. But thanks for the patronising information."

Another little dagger of anger flashes through me.

"Why are you even *doing* biology?" I bend down and peer into the grass. "I thought you were an *art* student. Write down frog."

"What kind of frog?"

"Smooth moist skin, green, stripes on back legs, hops. *Frog*."

"Are you sure?"

"It's a *Rana temporaria*," I snap. "I know a common frog when I see one."

"Maybe you should try kissing it then, Your Highness. See if another prince pops up."

My cheeks go bright red. I have no intention of kissing anything, frog or otherwise.

But I resent the implication that I might.

"And I like biology," Jasper adds, kneeling into the grass. "Write down earthworm."

"Maybe you should kiss *that*," I say fiercely, scribbling it on my clipboard. "See if yet another slimy creature without a proper functioning heart pops up."

Jasper makes a weird snorting sound, and I glance up. It sounded like a laugh, but his face is completely composed again.

"Work on that one," he says sharply, standing up. "One day it could develop into an actual joke."

Oooh.

We're only a metre away from each other now, and I'm so angry I'm trembling slightly. For the first time, I'm close enough to see that there are six freckles scattered across the bridge of his nose and his eyes aren't two different colours at all. They're both bright blue, but one has a large splodge of brown in it. As if somebody dropped a little splash of the wrong paint on wet paper.

It's really pretty, actually, which makes me even angrier. Jasper doesn't *deserve* interesting, genetically rare eyes. This horrible boy should have boring matching ones, just like everybody else.

We stare at each other for a few seconds.

A line of blue string is running round us in a perfect square, and we're in the middle: tense and pulsing with anger.

Exactly like a boxing ring.

Any minute now a man in a tuxedo with a microphone is going to jump out from behind a tree.

3. 2. 1. FIGHT!

At that precise moment the whistle blows – calling us back for our first round of results – and Jasper turns abruptly, rolls the string back up and hands it to me.

"Torture's over," he says sharply, before pounding across the grass towards school. "I hope that lesson was as illuminating for you as it was for me."

And I've had just about enough.

"Why do you hate me so much?" I say angrily, running after him. "Is there a particular reason, or is being nasty just a fun extracurricular hobby?"

Jasper keeps walking.

"I don't hate you, Harriet. I just don't like you very much."

I know that should be a relief, but for some reason I don't quite understand, it feels kind of worse.

"But *why*?" I say breathlessly, still running to catch up. "I know we didn't get off to the best start but—"

"Everyone in the entire world doesn't have to worship you, Harriet," he sighs. "Gliding through life surrounded by fans, with your *I'm-so-cute-and-quirky* dinosaur biscuits and random facts. I just find you a bit full of it, that's all. I'm only one person and very much in the minority. Why does it matter?"

I stop running and flap my mouth a few times.

Full of *what*, exactly?

And I can't believe I've spent my entire life being ostracised and now I finally have lots of friends it's being used against me. Plus – I'm not trying to be cute. I just really, really like dinosaurs.

This is *so unfair.*

"Well I may not be *your* cup of tea," I say, trying to run past him, "but I've *always* been Toby's. So why have you told one of my best friends not to play with me any more?"

Then I flush.

Great: I just made myself sound about six years old. As if somebody took my favourite teddy bear off me and I'm getting a bit hysterical about it.

Probably because that's exactly how it feels.

"If somebody doesn't want to be part of your fan club," Jasper says tiredly, "it has absolutely nothing to do with *me*."

He pointedly lifts an eyebrow.

And that does it.

The little angry firework stops twisting in my stomach, and – with an abrupt *whoosh* – bursts up through my chest, into my head and out of my ears in a shower of sparks.

"I *hate* you," I hiss, spinning round and whipping the blue string through the air at him. "You mean, horrible, unkind—"

But I don't get a chance to find the right noun.

Jupiter has the fastest spinning rate of any planet in

our solar system at 28,273 miles an hour. Not for the first time this term, I may have ended up there.

Because as I watch the string sail through the air – two metres to Jasper's left – I just keep right on rotating.

Round and round and round.

And as my hand clutches at nothing and my silly slippers try to find some traction, I give a little squeak and slip forward, still spinning slightly.

Straight into the mud.

74

There have been a lot of embarrassing moments in my life.

The time I walked around the supermarket with my skirt tucked into my knickers until a sales assistant had to point it out to me. The time I had cinnamon powder on my top lip and everyone thought I'd grown a "little ginger moustache".

Peeing myself during storytime when I was five because I got too excited about *The Faraway Tree*.

(I lied: it wasn't milk.)

Lying flat on my face in mud in front of a field full of thirty students, my new nemesis and three teachers is an event now very much on that list.

"Crap, are you OK?" Jasper jumps forward. "You're not hurt, are you? Nothing's broken, is it?"

I stare coldly at the hand he's holding out.

My palms are stinging, my knees are stinging, my eyes are stinging and my cheeks are stinging: all the familiar symptoms of humiliation and falling over.

341

In my peripheral vision, I can see groups around the field, starting to head in this direction.

Am I hurt? No. Am I angrier than I have literally ever been in my entire existence?

Absolutely.

"Oh you know me," I snap, shakily trying to get to my feet. "I'm so *full of it* I can't even stay upright. *Don't* touch me."

Jasper grabs my arm anyway. "At least let me help you up, Harriet. We don't have to be friends, but I'm not a monster. Let me get you off the floor."

"I said *do not touch me.*" I shake him off furiously. "*Ever.* The next thing you hold out gets bitten off."

He laughs, and it takes everything in my willpower not to lean forward and scrabble at his face with my little dinosaur claws.

"Fair enough," he says, shrugging. "Sorry. Maybe I should have put down that cloak after all. Could have provided a bit of padding."

"*Ooh,*" I say, getting on to my knee. "I'll get a bit of padding and stuff it right in your—"

But I don't get any further.

My foot hits another slippery spot, and this time I slide backwards.

Into the mud again.

75

You know what? I think I'm just going to stay here.

The universe seems to be strongly suggesting that lying on the floor, covered in 360 degrees of wet dirt, is exactly where I'm supposed to be.

The bell for breaktime rings.

With a clatter, people burst out of the sixth form doors, pause and then a large number start running towards me.

I automatically close my eyes and wait for the inevitable laughter. *Geek. Loser. Idiot. Why do you always make a mess of everything, Harriet?*

"Oh my God, are you all right, Ret? What happened?"

"You poor thing, you're totally *dripping*."

"The biology department should be ashamed of themselves, sending us out in this weather. My parents are going to write in and complain."

Cautiously, I open one eye.

Dozens of faces are now hovering over me, creased with concern. There isn't a glimmer of laughter: not a

single sign of a snort, an eye roll or a chuckle. Nobody's whispering or taking photos and videos and then uploading them straight on to the internet.

Seriously?

I slipped over into wet mud *twice.* I'm one banana skin away from being a Charlie Chaplin film.

India silently helps me up.

"I... umm." I wipe a strand of hair out of my eye, almost definitely making the mess worse. "I thought it was important to get a close-up view of our biology project. From... you know. Ground level."

Everybody laughs.

A clomp of wet mud and grass falls off my knee with a *plop* on to the floor and there's a sympathetic *awwwww.* Somebody hands me a useless but well-intentioned tissue.

"In fact," I say, my cheeks gradually starting to return to their normal colour, "baby elephants have been known to throw themselves into mud on purpose when they're having a temper tantrum. That's pretty much what I was doing too."

It's not that far from the truth, in fairness.

There's another laugh. I head towards the sixth form block to try and dry off, and the crowd begins to disperse. But just as I'm walking off, Liv arrives.

"What *happened*, Retty?" she says breathlessly, running to my side.

"She got pushed," Ananya says, barging through. "I *saw* it. That *freak of nature* lost his temper and shoved her over, then he *laughed*."

She points at Jasper, and some of the remaining students abruptly turn back towards him.

"Oh my God, what a *weirdo*." "What is *wrong* with you?" "Douchebag!"

"Such a *mutant*," Ananya says fiercely, crossing her arms. "Where did you come from, anyway? Is one of your eyes made out of glass or something?"

"*Yeah*," Liv hisses. "Freakazoid. No wonder you hide in the art room on your own like a total loser."

The sudden vitriol is so thick, so intense, it feels like you could open your mouth, take a chunk out of the air and swallow it.

African wild dogs are one of the most efficient pack hunters in the world. When working together, they have a successful kill rate of eighty per cent.

Some of my classmates' ratio may be even higher.

I look in surprise at Jasper.

Is this what they're always like to him? Is this why he's in the art room all the time? Is this why he's so angry and hostile constantly? How hadn't I noticed?

Jasper lifts his chin, clenches his jaw and glares at me defiantly. *Go on then*, he seems to be silently saying.

Do it.

This is my chance, and we both know it.

All I have to do is say four little words – yes, he pushed me – and I'll have the ultimate revenge. This horrible boy has insulted me, called me names, judged me and twisted my friend against me. Now it's my turn.

After all, he *started* this, didn't he?

Except…

Except as I stare silently at Jasper's round face, with a lurch I suddenly recognise it all. The tenseness of his jaw. The too-brightness of his eyes. The twitch in the muscle next to his mouth. A group of people facing one way, and only one facing the other.

He's pretending he doesn't care, but he does.

I know, because eight days ago – and for eleven years before that – it was me.

"Jasper didn't push me," I say quietly, still looking at him. "I slipped twice because I'm an idiot, and he was just trying to help me. And he's not a freakazoid, so please don't call him that. The chances of having *heterochromia iridium* are six in a thousand, so – to quote Professor Xavier – it's actually a very groovy mutation."

Jasper blinks.

"Also," I say, reaching firmly into my trouser pocket, "here's your invitation to my party, Jasper. I'm sorry I didn't give it to you earlier."

I pull out a piece of muddy plastic and wipe it clean on my scarf. *Ha. Told* you laminating everything was a good idea. When you fall over as much as I do, you learn to take precautions.

Still dripping, I hold the invitation out and Jasper takes it in silence. His face is slowly turning from pale to a strange, mottled pink.

"*Well*," Ananya says, uncrossing her arms. "We were only *defending* you, Retty. As long as you're OK, that's all that matters."

"Definitely." "We didn't *mean* it. We were only *teasing*." "He should *totally* come to the party."

Jasper's face still hasn't moved.

We look at each other for a few seconds.

Then I resume limping soggily back to school.

The last thing on my list is *believe in yourself,* and this is exactly what it means, isn't it?

It means knowing who you are, even when it's incredibly tempting to be someone else instead.

I'm not Hook, or Khan, or Ursula, or Scar.

Maybe in another life, I might have been.

In an alternative universe – one where everybody

always laughed at my jokes and invited me to parties and never hid my pencil case at the back of a toilet cistern – maybe it would have been harder not to hurt somebody who's hurt me.

But for the first time in eleven years, I'm glad I've spent a lifetime with *GEEK* written all over my satchel. I'm glad I know exactly how it feels to always be on the outside, looking in.

I might finally be on the inside now.

But I am not – and never will be – the villain.

76

Which means there's one more thing I have to do.

"Harriet!" A blue front door swings open and a face coated in thick brown gunk pokes out. "Darling! Just look at the two of us! Snap!"

Nat's mum holds her hand in the air, so I high-five it.

It seems churlish to point out that only one of us is covered in mud intentionally.

"Hello, Miss Grey," I smile, picking a bit of wet grass from my hair and flicking it into a bush. "How are you?"

"I'm just *dandy*, sweetheart. No botox in six months and I've got so many expressions I'm terrifying the postman." She wiggles her face and grins. "I don't think I've seen you since you got back from Nooo Yowwwk, darling. Are you *terribly* glamorous and sophisticated now?"

I look down.

Nearly a year ago, Toby vomited on me and I was

forced to walk around Birmingham wearing little blue nylon shorts, a yellow T-shirt with the number 9 on the back and knee-high green socks.

I am now in a boy's football kit again, complete with little studded boots. You can say what you like about the universe, but it obviously has a very symmetrical and ironic sense of humour.

I just wish it wasn't always aimed at me, that's all.

"Absolutely," I grin. "Or as good as I'm ever going to get, anyway."

Then I clear my throat.

After I'd raided the PE lost property box, I took a deep breath and raced to Nat's house as fast as I could. I still haven't given her an invitation to my party, and it doesn't matter how hurt I am by her, she's my best friend, I love her, and I need to make sure she has one.

Two, actually: one for Theo as well.

He'd seriously better be worth all this trouble. I'm going to be very annoyed if he's as drippy as François.

"Umm." I step into the hallway and hand Nat's mum two pieces of laminated plastic. "I just brought these round for Nat. Can you give them to her? Also, is it OK if I run upstairs and get something from her cupboard?"

Every fun thing I own in the world is currently in a cardboard box that has NAT AND HARRIET'S WORLD OF

FUN written on the side in purple Sharpie.

My party doesn't need it – obviously – but it's always nice to have a fall-back plan.

"Of course, darling," Nat's mum says as I tug off a football boot. I might look into getting some for myself: they're remarkably grippy. "But why don't you just give them to her yourself? She's in her bedroom, watching a film."

I pause, still holding on to a red lace. "What?"

"*Roman Holiday*, I think. She said it's for her course but I'm not entirely convinced it isn't just an excuse to watch Gregory Peck drive a scooter."

"But…" I blink a few times. "Nat said she was out every night this week."

Nat's mum laughs. "In that case, she's been climbing up the chimney like Santa Claus. To the best of my knowledge, Natalie has barely left the house for anything but college in a fortnight."

My stomach flip-flops.

"Then I must have misunderstood," I say slowly as I take the other shoe off and start climbing the stairs.

"You definitely have some kind of wires crossed," Nat's mum says brightly.

"Huh," I say, frowning. "Weird."

But as I climb the stairs, I check my phone again: just to make sure.

I'm out every night this week.☺ I'll ring soon.☺ Love you. Nat xxxx

Two sad faces, four kisses.

And she never rang me.

So you can analyse and pull it apart as much as you like, but there isn't a lot of ambiguity in that sentence.

I don't think I've misunderstood at all.

77

The Birch and Swinnerton-Dyer conjecture is one of six unsolved Millennium Prize Problems. It's regarded as one of the most challenging mathematical problems in the world, and it's so hard there's a $1,000,000 prize for the first one to solve it.

By the time I reach my best friend's room, three floors up, I've decided I'd rather be giving that a shot right now than trying to work out what's going on here.

None of this makes any sense.

Nat has repeatedly told me she hasn't got any time to see me, but she's been in *every night*? What the *sugar cookies* is going on?

Has Jasper got to her now too?

Maybe he's written a list of my failures as a human being in the sky with plane smoke and trailed it all over Hertfordshire.

Frowning, I lurk anxiously outside Nat's bedroom for a few seconds.

353

Then I knock politely on the door. We normally have a strict no-knocking policy, but I no longer feel totally comfortable just walking straight in.

"I said *in a minute*!" Nat yells through the wood. "I'm still drying, Mum! You know I can't eat pizza with wet nails! Enamel is not a topping!"

"It's not Mum," I say in a slightly bewildered voice. "It's Harriet."

There's a short silence and a little clatter.

Then the door swings slowly open.

Nat's wearing a bright green dressing gown with cotton wool balls stuck between each of her toes, fingers spread wide in the air in a large Y shape and a white blackhead strip plastered across her nose.

"Harriet! What are you doing here?"

"I could ask the same of you," I say, folding my arms tightly. My throat is starting to hurt again. "You said you were out all week, and yet... *here you are.*"

A familiar, guilty red pattern has started making its way across Nat's collarbone and I watch it travel suspiciously up her neck and on to her jawline.

"I'm just... getting ready to go out again."

I fold my arms a bit tighter. "Funny, because your mum just told me you haven't left the house much in weeks."

"Right." The pink rash climbs a little higher on to her

cheeks. "Well, I've been sneaking Theo in. You know…
without Mum knowing."

My shoulders relax a little bit, but not entirely.

That might be true, but Theo's certainly not here
right now: I've known my best friend skip a maths exam
because she had an unsightly blocked pore. She's not
going to be sneaking in a boy while dressed like Kermit.

"OK," I say slightly stiffly. "Well…" There's an
uncomfortable pause. "If he's not here now can I come
in, then?"

"Oh." Nat nods and opens the door properly. "Yes,
please do come in."

"I will," I say awkwardly, walking forward and taking
an uncomfortable seat on the edge of her bed like an old
matron aunt. "I'll come in. Thank you very much."

Then I twiddle my thumbs.

"Nice weather we're having," I say experimentally,
even though it's been raining all day. "Unseasonally
warm."

"It… umm. Is," she says. "They say there's a storm
coming."

I've never, ever felt like this around Nat before.

Together, we've made it through eleven years, three
countries, three break-ups, six million fights and three
hundred chicken and jam sandwiches, but there's never

been this kind of distance between us before.

I just don't understand where it's come from.

"Well." I stand up and clear my throat. "I thought you should know that I'm having a party tomorrow, Natalie. You are most welcome to come."

Natalie. I just called my best friend *Natalie.*

"A *party*?" Nat stares at me for a few seconds. "You're having a *party*?"

"Yes."

"Like, a proper party? With proper people? *Real* people?"

"Yes." I'd be offended if ninety-five per cent of our guests in the past hadn't consisted entirely of teddy bears, Mickey Mouse and a shaved-headed Barbie doll. "Real people."

Nat's eyes are so round she looks like an ocelot. "A physical, real-life party, with people and music and food and lights and—"

"I understand the basic concept of a party, Nat." I'm getting a bit irritated now. "Yes, a *party*."

She frowns and stares into space.

My stomach suddenly flips, and every single bit of stiffness abruptly melts away in a wave of guilt.

"Oh please don't be angry with me, Nat," I say, jumping off the bed and grabbing her hands. "I know I didn't tell you, and I know it's normally just us, and I know we normally arrange it all together and it's a tradition, but you weren't around and I didn't know what else to do and... *Please* don't hate me, Nat."

Nat blinks a few more times. Then her face clears.

"What on *earth* are you talking about? I couldn't be more delighted. A *party*. Harriet Manners is throwing a *party*!"

Like a soldier she drops to the floor and starts rummaging under her bed until she's dragged out a huge, familiar cardboard box.

Then she hops up and claps her hands.

"So," she says brightly, rushing across the room and flinging open her cupboard with a flourish, "we'll need to sort you something to wear, obviously. It's important to get it *exactly right,* because otherwise... tragedy. Chaos. And we can't have that."

She pulls out a yellow dress, holds it up critically, then shakes her head and lobs it on the floor.

I can feel every single cell in my body starting to uncurl. It's all going to be OK again. The Super Team are back.

"You really don't mind? Really?"

"Of *course* I don't mind, you silly billy. A *party*." She laughs. "An actual *party*. Who'd have thought it?!"

"Not me," I say fervently, starting to laugh too. "I'm

throwing a party. *Me*. Can you believe it!"

We're both snorting with laughter now.

"Hey, what's that big party you've heard of?" Nat chuckles. "Oh it's *only* Harriet Manners'! Biggest party of the year, dontcha know."

"What's that?" I giggle, holding my hand up to my ear. "Want a ticket to the bestest party of the year? Well, you only need to speak to *Harriet Manners*."

"Hahahahahaha!" Nat shakes her head as she drags an orange dress out of her wardrobe and then lobs it on the floor too. "Unbelievable! So who's coming? How big is it? What's the plan? How did this come about? I need to know *everything*."

"*Well*," I say excitedly as Nat pulls a green dress out and holds it against me with narrowed eyes, "it's going to be pretty amazing, Nat. I've thought of *everything*, and almost everyone in my form has RSVPd, I think. Quite a lot of the boys' football team, the girls' netball team…"

"Maybe with blue shoes," Nat murmurs, now lost on Planet Fashion. "Silver? Black?"

"Most of my biology class," I continue happily, ticking them off on my fingers. "Physics and maths. Lydia and her friends."

"*Gold*," Nat says triumphantly. "Gold shoes, green dress, earrings in… silver?"

"And then my new gang, obviously." I hold my hands up thoughtfully. "So that's India – she's new and she's got this really cool bright-purple hair I think you'd love – Liv and Anan—"

Both Nat and the green dress suddenly go very still.

Oh my God.

What is *wrong* with me? Why isn't there a draft box in my head to save statements like that before I say them? We were doing *so well.*

"What?" Nat says sharply, all signs of giggling now gone. "What did you just say?"

"Uh." I stare past my best friend's left ear for a few seconds, brain now scrabbling desperately. "Liver and onion, that's what India and I call ourselves. We're all like, *Hey, Liver and Onion! How you doing, Liver and Onion?"* I cough. "It's an… umm… Leeds thing."

Sorry, Leeds.

In April 2005, a pond in Hamburg made international news when toads started exploding for no apparent reason. Judging by the colour my best friend's face is now turning, exactly the same thing is about to start happening here.

I bend down quickly and pick up the cardboard box of fun.

"Liv and Ananya? Did you just say your new *gang* is

Olivia and Ananya?"

"Well…" I'm sidestepping out of the room now like a nervous morris dancer. "It's not a *gang* exactly, Nat. That was a bit of an overstatement. It's more like an… informal group. A good thesaurus might say it was a squad, or a troop or even a—"

And Nat promptly goes BANG.

78

Fact: the toads didn't explode for no reason at all.

Everyone just *thought* they did.

Eventually a top amphibian expert, Franz Mutschmann, realised crows had pecked out and eaten their livers, leaving the toads to explode from their own protective swelling.

Which is a bit disgusting, so I'm sorry about that.

Although it's worth noting that maybe the collective noun is a *murder of crows* for a reason.

What I'm trying to say is: Nat's not exploding inexplicably. It might look to the untrained eye like she is, but I am an expert on Natalie Grey and I understand it perfectly.

It's only ten steps to the bedroom door.

If I can use this cardboard box as a protective shield there's a remote chance of getting out of here without being blown to shreds first.

"ANANYA AND LIV?" Nat yells as I quickly trundle

361

towards the exit. "YOUR NEW BEST FRIENDS ARE ANANYA PEREZ AND OLIVIA WEBB?"

"Girls?" her mum calls up the stairs. "Keep it down or take it into the attic."

"Alexa's *henchmen*?" Nat hisses in a lower voice.

"They're not her henchmen any more," I try to explain, shuffling another step. "Actually, they're on my side now."

"Why would you *want* them on your side? They're *horrible*. And I don't know who this 'India' girl is, but if she's hanging about with them I guarantee she's just as bad, if not worse. She probably *wants* something from you. Are you doing her homework for her, or something?"

My cheeks are getting hot and my stomach feels like I've been eating aeroplane again. "That's a terrible thing to say, Nat. You don't know them."

"I totally *do*, Harriet. They've been cheerleading behind Alexa for the last eleven years. Sneaking around, yes sir, no sir, three muppets full, sir. Next you'll be telling me *she's* coming to your party too."

There's a short silence.

"Alexa really wanted to come," I say defensively, taking another step towards the door. "She told me she did, she said we could have a clean start and—"

"*No*," Nat says, eyes widening. "Oh my God, you have

got to be kidding me. This isn't what I... It wasn't in the... Have you forgotten *everything they did*?"

"Of course not." My cheeks are getting hotter and hotter. "But they're all sorry, Nat. I'm sure they are. We were only children – everyone should get a second chance and people *change*, don't they? I mean, *I* have so—"

"No, they *don't*." Nat grabs the edge of the cardboard box closest to her and tugs it, hard. "When are you going to learn this lesson, Harriet? *People don't change.* You're not having a party with them. No. Nu-uh. I *forbid* it."

I try not to think about Ananya turning on Jasper earlier – she was just worried about me, she didn't mean it – as something in my chest starts to burn.

I can hear Alexa's voice again: *You think things are going to change? You think things are going to be different now?*

Has everything I've done been for *nothing*?

"You *forbid* it?" I tug the box back. "I'm sorry, are you the entirety of the British legal system?"

"Don't be so incredibly naive, Harriet." Nat tugs on the box again. "They're *using* you. A total *idiot* could see that."

My chest burns a little bit more.

"Using me for *what*? And I'm naive for thinking people might actually just *like* me? I'm an idiot for believing I'm worth spending time with?"

"That is not what I…"

"So you're allowed new friends and a new boyfriend and a new life, and I just have to sit on my own for the next two years, is that it?"

"Why are you being like this?" Nat frowns. "Is this really about Nick? Because if it is…"

And – with an enormous eruption – the burn in my chest comes roaring out of me like a volcano.

"*This is not about Nick!*" I yell at the top of my voice. "Everything in the world is not about Nick! HE IS GONE AND HE IS NOT COMING BACK. This is about *me*, Nat. *Me!* My story is not over just because *he's not here*."

Nat blinks, but it's all still bursting out like lava in one steady, bubbling stream. "And I'm trying as hard as I possibly can to move forward, and now you're taking it all away from me! You're *ruining* it!"

"Harriet! How can you even *think* I…"

But I've been holding on to this for too long now and there's nowhere left inside me to keep it all.

"You *left*, Nat." My chin is starting to wobble and I tug on the box more sharply. "Don't you understand that? You *left me on my own*. You chose college, then you chose Theo, and now you're always busy and you're never around and *what was I supposed to do*?"

I tug the box again.

"But Harriet I only said I was busy because—"

"And you know what?" The flames are rising up: into my cheeks and flicking between my eyebrows. "Maybe I'm *glad* you're gone. Maybe I'm *glad* you're not around. Maybe this is what we both needed, because maybe *you're* the one who's been holding me back in the first place."

Nat goes very still. "*What?*"

I want to stop. I need to stop.

But the lava is hurtling down the mountain. It's burning everything and everyone who gets in its way, and there isn't a single thing inside me that can halt it.

"My life is better without you in it, Nat. I'm more confident. I have friends. People *like* me. I've moved on. Maybe this is what's supposed to happen. I mean, it's not as if we have anything in common any more anyway."

The colour suddenly drains from Nat's face, as if somebody's pulled some kind of plug inside her. She stares at me in silence for a few seconds, then her eyes get very bright and very hard.

"Right," she hisses, tugging hard at the box. "I've heard enough. This isn't yours – let go."

"No." I tug back. "It's not yours either. *You* let go."

"Let GO."

"*You* let go."

"YOU."

"*You.*"

"HARRIET. LET. GO. OF. THE. BLOODY. BOX."

And – with one almighty rip – we both tug on NAT AND HARRIET'S WORLD OF FUN at exactly the same time and it splits right down the middle.

Exploding on to the floor between us.

79

We stare at the mess for a few seconds in silence.

Scrabble tiles and Monopoly hotels have gone everywhere. Face paints have smashed into pieces. Deflated balloons with little eyes and mouths have rolled under the bed and a tail from an old donkey is lying on top of my foot.

Organs have been spilt: there's a kidney and pancreas from an old game of Operation still rocking back and forward slightly on the floorboards.

Old blue glitter is spread across the rug.

Then – with astonishing speed – Nat bends down and sweeps it all up into her arms. The Maglev train in Shanghai is the fastest train in the world, but at this moment I feel like Nat could probably beat it.

She runs towards the door.

"Don't!" I shout after her, because I know exactly what she's going to do and if she does I don't know how we're going to fix it. "DO. NOT. DO. THIS!"

But Nat does it anyway.

Without a word, she runs to the bathroom and lobs every house, every chess piece, every card, every paint, straight into the toilet.

Then she pulls the chain.

Slowly at first, and then with increasing speed, eleven years start to disappear in front of us.

Every late-night giggle. Every shared nose snort.

Hours and hours of *Cinderella* and *Shrek*. Hundreds of soda floats and pizzas and muffins.

Years and years of hiding under a duvet together, with a torch, so we could stay up a little later. Doing whatever we could to make the night last longer. To spend a bit more time together: just the two of us.

All spinning and turning until they've totally vanished. Gone.

"There," Nat snaps, facing me coldly. "*Now* we don't have anything in common any more."

We stare at each other, shoulders heaving up and down.

"Maybe you shouldn't come to my party after all," I say finally. "I think maybe we need some space."

"I agree," Nat hisses, face completely white. "After all, I wouldn't want to *hold you back* any more than I have already."

And with a firm kick of the radiator Nat storms out of the bathroom, slamming the door behind her.

Now, I know a lot about space.

I know it's big, and dark, and lonely, and we don't really understand it. I know that all stars are moving away from each other, and that the galaxies at the outer reaches of the universe are racing away from us at ninety per cent of the speed of light.

But as I let myself out of the bathroom and start charging angrily home, I can't help wondering if maybe that's what is happening to Nat and me too.

Because it feels like my universe and everything in it is slowly pulling apart.

And there's nothing I can do to stop it.

80

There's an altitude point that occurs between 18,900 to 19,350 metres above sea level, called Armstrong's Line. It's the exact level where atmospheric pressure becomes so low that water boils at 37°C.

In other words: precisely the temperature of the human body.

My blood is now bubbling so fast I suspect I may have crossed it.

In a fury, I rip home and charge straight up the stairs.

I fling open my cupboard and get my Arts and Crafts kit out. I pull out my baking kit and my notepad. And I start party-preparing like I have never prepared for anything before in my life.

And as I prepare, I chatter angrily.

"Oh I'm *sooooo* fashionable and cool," I snap as I start blowing up balloons and squeakily drawing on them with pens. "Oh I know *sooooo* much about eyeshadow," I mutter as I cut little shapes out of shiny paper. "Oh I

am just *sooooo* pretty with my swishy black hair and my glowing brown skin and I never ever get zits because I eat *allll* my vegetables and drink two whole litres of water a day."

Then I realise I'm essentially just being really nice about Nat under my breath, which isn't making me feel any better at all.

So I focus my anger and give it another shot.

"Fickle and disloyal," I hiss as I mix flour in with eggs. "Volatile," I complain as I shape ham and cheese sandwiches. "Nowhere *near* as good at Jenga as she thinks she is."

That's more like it.

In an angry whirlwind – not unlike the Tasmanian devil, the world's largest carnivorous marsupial and generally deemed to have one of the worst tempers on the planet – I whizz round the house: cutting and sticking, baking and mixing. I paint and blow up, pop accidentally and blow up again. I attach strings and ribbons and twinkle and put things in cardboard boxes.

But it's still not enough.

By the end of Thursday night, I'm nowhere near ready, and I'm definitely not calm. In fact, I'm more charged up than ever. Instead of defusing, the anger is just hardening and stiffening like cement between each of my cells until I lie awake all night, staring at the ceiling because I'm now too rigid to roll over.

This isn't just a party any more. It's a *battle*.

A battle made of streamers and balloons and music and carefully arranged snacks, and I have to win.

I'm going to show Nat.

She's going to *rue the day* she ever doubted me. I'll throw such a successful party, such an *amazing* party, that she will be forever known as The Girl Who Had Nothing To Do With It, Actually. For the rest of time, Natalie Grey will be asked where *she* was the night Harriet Manners triumphed socially, like the first time humans walked on the moon.

And any ideas I had for Friday night – which were quite a few anyway – are now accelerated, heightened, turbo-charged.

There is *nothing* I will not do to make my party victorious.

With a bolt of defiant adrenaline, I bounce out of bed on Friday morning and carefully pack everything away neatly in the car so that Dad and Tabby can help me drive it to The Venue.

I remind my father, for the billionth time, that he's not invited.

I listen to *It's so unfair* another 1,298 times.

Then I use every breaktime, lunchtime and all of my free periods at school to run out and start setting things up. I specifically hired a venue as close to school as possible so it would be convenient for everyone to get there.

Not least me.

"Can't we *help*?" Ananya says as I trot out of the front gates for the third time, holding a pair of scissors (upside down, obviously – I don't have a death wish). "Are you sure there isn't anything we can do? Can't we at least be at the gates to greet people?"

"We *so* want to be involved," Liv explains, chewing on a nail. "It's the best theme *ever, I can'twaittoseewho comesandwhatthey'rewearingand—*"

"*Olivia*," India sighs, putting a hand over her eyes. "Stop. Only killer whales can hear you now, and as far as I know, none of us are members of the orca family."

"Sorry, Indy. ButI'mgoingtofangirlsohardandohmyGod I'mbringingmyphoneandcameraand…"

India slowly lifts her bag and puts it in front of Olivia's face until she stops talking.

"That's so nice of you all," I say, shaking my head. "But I really want this to be a big surprise for everyone, so I'd like to do it myself, if that's OK?"

"Absolutely," Ananya says, nodding sweetly. "Just

know we're here if you need us. For *anything.* Anything *at all."*

By my fourth visit, I can feel the cement running through me starting to soften again.

The Venue has finally started taking shape.

As each table goes up, as food gets carefully laid out in strategically planned and organised patterns, as decorations get pinned to the walls and the ceiling, lights are unplugged and re-plugged, and a corner is set aside for a dance floor, I start to fill with a warm, confident glow of satisfaction.

And by the time I've quickly run home, jumped into the shower and tugged on my brand-new outfit, there's no question in my mind that I've done the absolute best I can possibly do.

Now there's nothing left to do but wait.

81

You already know what the theme is, by the way.

Of course you do.

If you've been paying attention, and if your mind works like mine does – in a logical, strategic, slightly obsessive-compulsive kind of way – there was really only one possible choice: one area I knew I could shine in.

But – just in case you've missed it – here's the invitation:

Night of Stars
8pm 'til late
132 Earl Street
Dress code: All That Glitters

Let's be honest: it was the only option that wasn't dinosaurs or group-solved crossword puzzles.

And yes, I know the Shakespeare quote is from *The*

Merchant of Venice and is technically "all that *glisters*" but glisters sounds a bit too much like *blisters* and I don't want people at my party getting accidentally confused and coming as one of those instead.

At 7:59pm exactly, I count down the last ten seconds of the hour as calmly as I can.

Ten, nine, eight, seven, six, five, four, three, two –

Then I fling the doors open wide.

I'm wearing a gold T-shirt customised all over with black star stickers, black leggings individualised carefully with tiny gold stars and a black headband with a large cardboard gold star stuck to the front. And I've used every single make-up trick I learnt in Morocco to help make me look suitably celestial.

Gold eyeshadow and eyeliner, highlighter, a bit of twinkle spray that's supposed to be used on trees at Christmas.

Behind me are reams and reams of hand-dyed black sheets, hanging from ceiling beams, with white fairy lights also borrowed from our family Christmas box wound carefully round them. The floor is covered in little hole-punched silver circles, and precisely three hundred and fifty hand-cut gold and silver paper stars are stuck to the ceiling in accurate constellations: *Chamaeleon, Octans, Reticulum, Indus, Pavo, Norma, Carina, Volans.*

Balloons are bunched in the corners with stars drawn on the front in Sharpie, and from the rafters hang two round red rubber balloons, two yellow, two blue, a teeny tiny brown one and a green-and-blue-mottled one I coloured in myself.

On the tables – on top of black sheets covered in little dobs of white Tipp-Ex – is an array of appropriately themed foods: sandwiches cut into stars, jellies shaped into stars, cupcakes with icing stars stuck on top, pizzas cut into stars, biscuits cut into stars, melon pieces cut into…

Well. You get the drift.

Let's just say I really made the most of my new star-shaped cookie cutters.

Bowls of Mars bars and Milky Ways have been distributed at random for the peckish and non-diabetic, the lights have been turned down low and in the corner is Tabitha's little fluffy turtle night-light, borrowed for a few hours: shining bright white and moving stars on all the walls.

(I obviously have a glow-in-the-dark constellation in my bedroom too, but the stars are stuck on the ceiling with superglue and Annabel wouldn't let me "dismantle the house" despite my desperate pleading.)

And – in the middle, at the back – is my *pièce de*

résistance. The main meal: the showpiece, the highlight, the pinnacle of all my achievements.

My own, personal DJ.

Hovering over a table with huge earphones on, looking as cool as can be and ready to hit the music just as soon as the first people arrive. Because that's the great thing about having so many friends: you can call in little favours.

Believe it or not, I haven't had to pay for a single thing: it's all been offered for free, out of the kindness of people's hearts.

Which includes the perfect venue.

Precisely seven years, three hundred and three visits, seven orienteering holidays and a camping trip where I was chased by a very large cow across a field have finally come to full fruition. One quick phone call and the head of the Girl Guides Association was more than happy to lend me their local wooden hut for the evening.

"Harriet," she said when I asked how much it would cost, "according to my memory, you got a hundred and two badges as a Brownie and Guide, not including whatever you achieved as a Rainbow."

"Seven," I said immediately. "I got my I've Had An Adventure Badge, my I've Been On A Sleepover Badge, my Aim High Badge, my Happiness Badge, my Loyalty

Badge and—"

"Stop stop stop," she laughed. "The hut is on us. I think you've earned it."

And as the first sounds of footsteps and giggles can be heard in the dark outside, I turn round quickly and stick my thumbs nervously in the air.

"All set?" my DJ calls from the back of the room, finger poised over the GO button, or – you know. Whatever the trendy disc jockey equivalent of that is.

Timing is paramount, so I wait a few seconds until the voices are so close I can hear them whispering *"You* go first," "No you," "No *you"*.

Then I take my deepest breath and nod. "*Go!*"

With a flourish, Steve the caretaker hits a button.

As the air fills with the buoyant, triumphant perfection that is *The Planets* by Gustav Holst, I can feel my smile getting broader and broader until my whole face feels like it's glowing from the inside out.

As if it has its very own source of solar energy.

And as the music swells and I swell with it, it's all I can do not to lift into the air too.

That's how brightly I'm burning.

"Hello," I say at the first small and polite knock on the door, "and welcome to the stars."

82

The first head round the door is Lydia's.

"Oh *wow*," she squeaks, jumping out with her bright orange hair flying and running into the middle of the room. "This is what I think *heaven* should look like. Because a) it's awesome, b) there are stars everywhere and c) cake!" She spins round a few times and runs over to the table. "AND *MARS BARS!*" she shouts. "THERE ARE MINI MARS BARS!"

Then she opens two and crams them both into her mouth simultaneously.

Yup. She's my spirit animal.

"*Lydia*," Fee hisses, poking her blonde head round too. "You're *so* embarrassing. *Try* and remember we left primary school four whole *months* ago."

Two more familiar little heads appear. "We're *so* sorry, Harriet Manners. Please don't send us home again, Harriet Manners."

I smile affectionately and beckon them in. They shuffle

forward shyly, self-consciously tidying up little spangly skirts and straightening their T-shirts with sequins that say LOVE, PARIS and MEOW.

Lydia's wearing a jumper with a sun on it and is now rocketing round the room with a mouth full of chocolate, prodding things at random.

"Oh, look! Balloons painted to look like planets! That's so clever!" She spins the little brown one round. "Except planets aren't stars, are they, Harriet? I thought they were celestial bodies in orbit? Did you cheat on the theme?"

I think I've just found the missing link between me and Tabitha. I may have to ask my parents if they've misplaced a child at any stage in the last decade.

"Planets are in between us and the stars," I explain, resisting an urge to high-five her. "So they represent the journey we take to them."

And also because let's be honest: there aren't that many snacks called *Fomalhaut* or *Kornephoros*. Mars Bars were much easier to source.

"*Ooooooooohhh*," all four say, clasping their hands together and gazing at the ceiling with round eyes. "*Cooooliooko.*"

Then they start skipping around the room, examining every detail – the tiny star candles, the big star cake, Tabby's fluffy night-light – and waving at the DJ booth.

"Hey, Mr Barker," they say cheerfully, stuffing sandwiches in their mouths. "You look *so* cool out of your overalls."

"Darn right I do!" Steve grins, taking his orange trilby hat off and doing a little bow. "Now let's party, shall we?" And he starts smashing his head to a particularly rambunctious cello solo.

In the meantime, I'm lurking anxiously by the entrance, staring at my watch.

The invitation said 8pm, and it is now 8:03pm.

Where *is* everyone?

Maybe they're not coming. Maybe this was a huge mistake. Maybe this is going to be like when I had a big order of books delivered and they said they would be there on Saturday afternoon and I waited all day on the sofa and they didn't show up at all.

Except, you know: a billion times worse.

Because that wasn't utterly humiliating or emotionally devastating or a waste of cupcakes and it's not like I was actually intending to leave the house all day anyway.

I check my watch again as the first years start dragging Twister from the Games Corner and laying it out on the floor, then again as they begin giggling and shouting colours and directions at random.

Then again.

And again.

Brain-imaging studies have shown that our perception of time stretches backwards when our eyes shift from one point to the other, meaning that the second hand on a clock feels like it's taking longer than a second to tick if we stare directly at it.

My second hand doesn't seem to be moving at all.

Like: at all.

It's apparently been 8:05pm for the last three hundred years.

Cheeks starting to flush, I sit on a little chair by the entrance and try to breathe as calmly as I can. The stomach of a hippopotamus is three metres long, and mine is now dropping so fast it feels like it may have stretched to similar proportions.

Then I hear it.

Another wave of noise outside the door: faint at first – a few giggles, a few faraway shouts – and then louder. Louder and louder and louder until the gravel in front of the Guide Hut starts crunching noisily.

I look up.

"Is that *them*?" the first years whisper with round eyes, frozen in terror with their feet and hands in the air. "Is that *the sixth formers*?"

Eyes widening too, I nod.

There are three tables in this room right now and for a brief second it takes all my willpower not to crawl under one of them.

Instead, I straighten my shoulders.

Be confident, Harriet. Be brave.

Harness your Inner Star.

And with a loud burst, my entire year comes pouring in.

83

Within moments, my classmates have flooded the room and settled all over everything, like one of the plagues of Biblical Egypt.

Except instead of locusts or frogs or lice or flies, it's sixteen-year-olds.

And instead of boils they've erupted into sequins.

Seriously, there is sparkle *everywhere*.

Never mind embracing the theme: this lot have wrestled it to the floor and got it in an aggressive headlock.

Almost all of the girls are wearing dresses, and some of them are in full evening gowns, covered in beads and twinkle and glitz. There are a few big net skirts, a number of tiaras and huge earrings and quite a few wobbling knees thanks to enormous heels: the entire female population has grown five inches in the last four hours.

Most of the boys are in shirts and black trousers; a few are in ties, and a couple have donned black tuxedoes with little sequin bow ties like magicians.

Lips are red, enormous eyelashes are stuck on, hair is carefully curled or straightened, messed up or cleanly shaven. (Apart from two little cautious moustaches: Robert and Adam.)

My gang have really gone for it: India's in a knee-length purple dress – like a very beautiful Barney the dinosaur – and Ananya and Liv are resplendent in floor-length satin red and pink gowns.

Honestly, I've never seen them all look so lovely.

So glamorous. So *glitzy*. It's like they've come to a prom, or a ball, or maybe the party Cinderella threw after she became a princess.

And they've made all this effort for *me*.

I mean, it's a little more glam than I was expecting for the Guide Hut, but the support is seriously appreciated.

I can feel a lump starting in my throat as the year spreads through the now relatively tiny room as if by osmosis, staring at the decorations in astonishment. They've gone very, very quiet. They must be *so* impressed.

I have obviously blown their minds.

"This is…" "Wow." "…Unexpected." "*Retro.*"

"Crikey." Raya picks up a little cup of jelly and blinks at it. "Is this *jelly*? Like actual jelly? With *glitter*?"

"Yes, but don't worry," I say quickly as her eyes widen. "It's totally safe to eat. I checked."

"Cu-ute," she says slowly, putting it down again.

"So where are the drinks?" Chloe asks, rubbing her hands together. "We're *parched.*"

"Over there." I beam and wave my hands with a flourish at the table on the left. "We have everything you could possibly want. Lemonade, cola floats, ginger beer, fizzy orange and my very own personal invention, Milkywayshake."

Then I snigger slightly.

"See?" I explain as she continues staring at me. "It's a space-themed play on words. Milkshake? Milkywayshake?"

"Oh," she says, not taking any of them. "Yeah."

The rest of the group is still staring in silence around the room, amazed at how creative I've been. The music is getting louder, and a few people are cocking their heads to the side curiously.

"What *is* this? Is it some kind of hymn?"

I turn to Steve and quickly make the international *next track* circle-finger gesture. The entire crowd follows my eyes.

"Is that your *dad*?" "Your *dad* is the DJ?"

"Don't be ridiculous," I laugh, shaking my head. "Please! As if I'd invite my *dad* to my own party! That's Steve."

"Steve… Steve the school *caretaker*?"

"All right there, spring-chickens!" he yells, bopping up and down to what is now *Waiting For a Star to Fall.* "DJ Earthling rocking the microphone for the free-range stylers!"

There are a few giggles.

Steve's *spinning* skills may be top-notch but I might quietly ask him to hold back on the comedy.

"Isn't it *brilliant*?" Lydia says, picking up the night-light and holding it in the air. "Isn't this just the best party *ever*? When I'm in sixth form I'm going to have one *exactly* like it except with even *more* chocolate and also *Galaxy* bars because Harriet forgot about them."

There's a short silence while everyone in the room stares at her. "Hang on – is she…" "Are they *first* years?" "Are there *eleven*-year-olds at this party?"

"She's twelve, actually," Fee says, pointing at Keira, the quietest of the four. "She was twelve last week."

"*Lydia?*" Chloe says in alarm, stepping out of the crowd in a glitzy blue strapless number. "What the hell are *you* doing here?"

Lydia folds her arms. "Mum said I could come as long as she could collect me at half nine and you're not allowed to say *hell*, Clobo, so *there.*"

"*Mum's* turning up at half nine?" Chloe's cheeks are going purple and she turns round to a now-giggling-again group in a fury. "*Shut* it. I'd like to see *your* kid sisters turning up to ruin everything."

I can feel my stomach starting to get tense and cement-y again. It hadn't occurred to me that my peers might not actually want the first years here. Isn't the expression *the more the merrier*? I mean, we were all first years once, weren't we? Exactly how much can change in five years, anyway?

Quite a lot, judging by my classmates' expressions.

"I invited them," I start protectively as the four begin to look in a panic at the exit. "It's my fault, they're here because I asked them, and they're actually really sweet and—"

"And they're welcome." India walks firmly to my side. "This is a great party, it was kind of you to invite everyone and we're all really happy to be here, *aren't we*."

This isn't a question, by the way. She's telling everyone they're happy to be here.

It seems to work. Some of the netball team start to mill by the drinks table, Robert picks up a sandwich.

"But of *course* we are," someone says. "We didn't mean it like *that*, Retzer! Don't be silly!" "We were just surprised, that's all." "It's a really *nice* gesture, Retty." "This is the *sweetest* party ever!"

"It's so *awesome*," Ananya says loudly, pushing

through to my other side and linking arms with me. "We're *so* impressed, Ret. With your… er… outfit too. And I love what you've done with the theme! Such a clever pun!"

"*Hilarious!*" Liv agrees, standing slightly behind me. "You're *so* smart, Retty. And *so* generous."

A flush of intense gratitude rushes through me.

Nat was wrong. I'm not sure what she thought these girls were using me for, exactly, but these are my comrades. My posse. My gang.

My *friends*.

Although – I have to be honest – not for the first time I'm not entirely sure what Ananya's talking about. *What* clever pun?

This party is the most literal thing I've ever done.

"Ah *shoot*," Steve says, looking around him in confusion. "I've left my box of CDs at home. Back in twenty mins, party people. I've put Now Eighteen on to keep you all going in the meantime."

There are a few more little sniggers as he tries to high-five three or four students on the way out.

"*So*," Ananya says as Steve disappears out of the wooden door. "*Tell* us all about the stars, Retty. Everyone is just *dying* to know."

Really?

I beam at the now silent, awestruck crowd in front of me. I've been preparing for this question for ages.

All my life, some might say.

"OK," I say happily, taking a deep breath. "The closest star to earth is obviously the sun, which is four point six billion years old and a yellow dwarf measuring one million, three hundred and ninety-two—"

"You're so *hysterical*, but I mean the *other* ones."

I stare at Ananya. "What other ones?"

"The *other* stars."

"Umm." She's very impatient: I was just getting round to them. "Uh, OK. There's Alpha Centauri, which is the second closest star… to earth but… actually consists of three…"

I gradually slow to a halt.

Everybody's looking really confused now. What on *earth* is going on?

Why does everyone keep glancing at the door?

"*Harriet*," Ananya says finally, putting a hand on my shoulder. "Just tell us when all the celebrities are getting here."

84

In 1961, the Museum of Modern Art in New York hung Matisse's painting *Le Bateau* upside down for forty-seven days before a stockbroker finally noticed.

That's exactly how I feel now.

As if I've been looking at everything the wrong way up this whole time and I didn't have a clue.

Night of Stars.

My second hand is never going to tick again: that's how slowly everything is now moving.

"C-c-celebrities?" I stutter faintly.

"Yes," Liv squeaks, hopping up and down. "All the hot models and the actorsandthepopstarsandpeople offtellyohmyGodthisissoexcitingIdon'tknowifIcaneven containmyselfanylongerand—"

"*Olivia.*" Ananya glares at her. "For God's sake. Will you *ever* be cool?" She looks back at me and smiles, except now I'm noticing for the first time it doesn't quite reach her eyes. In fact, I'm not totally sure it ever actually has. "They're all coming late, of *course*. They're *famous*. *Obviously* they're not going to get here on time. But who do you think will make it?"

Is everyone coming? Will I know them all?

I stare at Ananya blankly, then at the crowd still looking at me. All the excitement. All the sparkle. All the pretty dresses. All the lipstick and heels and eyelashes. All the *bow ties*. They're not for me at all. They think this is a party of *stars*. OF. STARS.

Oh my God.

I've done it again, haven't I.

This is *just* like the dinosaur biscuits, except I've somehow managed to turn a horrible misunderstanding into an entire evening's entertainment.

With a sickening jolt, my brain is starting to replay conversations from school all week.

Oh yes, lots of the stars are single! Most of them in fact!

Actually most stars are pretty much the same, believe it or not: some are just much bigger than others.

Of course I know the really massive ones!

I think I might vomit. I *knew* my love of astronomy would get me into trouble one day.

Quick, Harriet. Be bold.

"I've got a quiz for us," I say desperately, rushing

over to the microphone and grabbing it in my sweaty hand. "There's a handmade cake for the winning team! Umm." My knees are literally starting to tremble. "First question – what are stars primarily made of?" I clear my throat. "Anyone? Anyone at all?"

Nobody answers.

"It's hydrogen and helium!" I squeak. My voice is so high now I think I may have eaten one. "Second question – which of the following is *not* a star: a) a red giant, b) a white dwarf…"

"Oh my God," somebody says flatly. "She means stars. Actual stars. It's not a pun."

"This is *it*. This *is* the party. It's just us."

"With *jelly*." "With a *caretaker*." "And hymns." "And *first* years." "And a baby's *night-light*."

"*Such* a geek."

"It's a green dwarf!" I say loudly, except the microphone is starting to make little *thd thd thd* noises from where my hand is shaking. "Next question – what category does our sun fall int—"

"Hang on." Ananya walks forward and takes the microphone off me. "Harriet, are you saying that *none* of your celebrity friends are coming this evening? Like at *all*? Why the hell *not*?"

OK: firstly, it looks like I'm back to being *Harriet* again.

Secondly, I can't believe I've got myself into a situation where this is even a question I'm actually being asked.

"Because I don't *have* any."

There's a short silence, then several people pipe up. "What do you mean you…" "But you *said*…" "We *asked* and you told us…" "You *lied* to us."

"I didn't lie," I say in bewilderment. "You asked if I knew any models and I said yes because I do. I've met *lots*. But they're not my *friends*."

"But what about Poppy Page?"

"She hates me," I admit. The last time I saw Princess Poppy she literally asked me to leave the country. "Passionately. Like, I'm her least favourite person in the world."

"Yuka Ito?"

"The last time I was in the same place as her she fired me. So probably not." I glance around at my bits of black crepe paper. "Honestly, I'm not sure she'd have come to this even if she hadn't."

"*What about the Russian supermodels, where are the Russian supermodels, I want to meet the Russian supermodels.*"

That's Eric. Obviously.

"They're not coming." My cheeks are now bright red. "I'm so sorry. I didn't realise you thought… I didn't know... They don't like me either."

There's a long silence.

Then the students clustered closest to Ananya and Liv erupt into disappointed cries. "But she said she went to all the *parties*." "Oh my God, I broke up with my boyfriend for *this*?" "Isn't she supposed to be loaded?" "Why are we eating home-made biscuits *again*?"

"But at least *Nick's* coming, right?" Liv says, frowning. "I mean your famous supermodel *boyfriend* will be here, won't he? With his face and his hair and his hip bones and all his beautiful supermodel single friends?"

And this is exactly what happens when you don't tell the truth, even to yourself.

Everything starts to fall apart.

That's what they're all here for, isn't it.

Ananya, Liv, India, the others... They're here for Nick and beautiful Russian supermodels. For Nick's non-existent identical twin brother and famous designers and celebrities and clothes and all the glamour and glitz they think go with being a successful model.

I've been such an idiot.

They didn't look at the Tokyo photos and see a confident, inspiring girl they wanted to get to know better. They didn't see another, less geeky side to me: a brave, starry version I so badly wanted to live up to in real life.

They just saw the glittery lifestyle they thought the girl in the lake had, and they wanted a piece of it.

Which means Nat was right.

And so was Alexa.

I can see my entire new life at school teetering precariously on the edge, about to fall over with an almighty crash. For just a brief second I almost lie to keep it hanging there for a few more precious moments. *Oh, how funny! My supermodel boyfriend is just busy right now! He'll totally come to the next one!*

But I still want to believe in myself: even if nobody else does too.

Or, you know. *To.*

"No," I say as firmly as I can, lifting my chin and meeting their eyes without a flicker. "Nick is not coming to this party. He won't be coming to any of them. We've broken up."

My insides are shutting down, piece by piece.

I can feel the room slowly changing. All the warmth is gradually seeping out, along with all the laughter. They think I lied to impress them. I'm not funny any more. I'm not adorable, or cute, or interesting. I'm just back to being what I always was.

A geek who got really, really lucky.

"Well, *I don't care*," a little voice says from the back. "Harriet's still *amazing* and you're all *horrible.*" Lydia comes charging through the crowd with her elbows out, cheeks pink. "And *look.* I just found the new Jacques Levaire watch advert on YouTube so you can *bite* me, sixth formers. Harriet Manners is more successful than you will *ever* be."

And she holds her phone high in the air.

85

I am graceful. I am elegant.

I am fluid and flowing and supple: moving with the grace of a ballet dancer, the poise of a gazelle, the lightness of a gentle *Diplulmaris antarctica* jellyfish gliding through the icy water.

Effortlessly, I move through the orange sands of the Sahara with total composure and confidence. As piano music plays, the wind catches my red hair and clothes and flings them gently around me: the light glows warm on my cheeks and my eyes are full of emotion, of hope, of joy.

Frankly, I have never been more beautiful in my life.

Or glittered so hard.

"That's not Harriet," somebody says, grabbing the phone and peering at it. "That's not Harriet *at all.*"

The screen gets handed to me.

The perfect red-haired girl spins again towards the camera and grins. Her make-up is almost completely

imperceptible. Her bright green eyes are framed with pale lashes and she's flushed and natural, her freckles visible even on this tiny screen. Her dress is simple white cotton and knee length: as she laughs her hand comes up to cover her mouth and you see a bright, momentary flash of a gold watch.

It's fresh. It's modern. It's captivating.

There's no dancing. No monkeys or snakes; no camels or running or chasing. No krumping.

And it's not me at all. Not even vaguely.

No wonder it's so good.

JACQUES LEVAIRE CLASSIC TIMEPIECES flashes up at the end, and then a make-up blogger's pretty face pops up as she starts talking about how she does her hair when she's in a hurry.

"You lied *again*?" somebody says as Lydia's phone gets passed around the room and the advert plays repeatedly. "Why on *earth* would you pretend you got a modelling job you didn't get?"

"I didn't pretend," I say, blinking at them all. "I went to Morocco. I got the Levaire campaign. I *promise* I did."

Except now I'm even starting to question that myself. *Did* I? Where *was* I last week? What was the shoot *for*?

"That's kind of lame, Harriet." "Seriously, who *does* that? Are you *that* desperate for attention?" "Oh my

God, where did you get those Moroccan clothes from? I am *so* confused right now."

"I…" My mouth is opening and shutting. "I don't know what to…"

"And I just googled Nick Hidaka and found a recent interview," somebody says, holding their phone in the air too. "I *bet* she lied about going out with him as well."

A human body has enough iron in it to make a metal nail three inches long.

It feels like mine has just done exactly that.

"Please," I say quickly, leaping forward. "Don't. Don't play it. Please don't play the—"

"Funny you should say that," a familiar, twangy voice jokes and I freeze where I am: every cell in my brain suddenly turning to ice. "Dozens of dolphins follow me everywhere I go, actually. It's a bit of a problem. They're such creepers."

A faceless girl gives a little besotted laugh.

I have no idea what the question was – I'm guessing *Have You Ever Swum With Dolphins* – but at the sound of Nick's voice it suddenly feels like I'm holding the nail at arm's length and an incredibly strong magnet is starting to draw it back towards me again, point first.

"And what's Australia's favourite male model doing now he's taking a break from the cameras? We've heard you've voluntarily gone back to full-time education. We have just one question for you: *why*?"

"Because over the last year I've been reminded repeatedly just how much of a thicky I am," Nick says with a small laugh. "Seriously, though, a very special English girl inspired me. I realised how much of the world there is I still want to know about. How much I still want to do."

A huge lump suddenly rises up my throat.

"You're a mad person. Who gives up a successful career as a supermodel to go back to *school*?"

"I do," Nick says calmly. "And I am honestly loving it."

"So how's the *romantic* situation?" I can literally hear the optimism in the girl's voice. "Is this *very special* English girl still on the scene? Or should we all start sending you our CVs?"

Oh my God. No. No no no. *No no no no nonononononononono...* For just a fraction of a second the iron nail quivers, then it starts speeding towards me.

Turn it off. Turn it off turn it off turn it off turn it off turn it off turn it—

"Please," I whisper, holding my hand out towards the sound. "I don't want to hear this..."

"I don't really want to talk about it," Nick says after a short pause. "But no, we broke up. I'm just focusing on the future now."

"Awwwww," the interviewer says insincerely. "Well I'm sure there are lots of girls out there who would happily take her place."

"I don't want them to," he says simply. "She kind of broke my heart."

With a final shudder the nail I made completely out of myself glints slightly in the light.

And plunges straight into my chest.

86

There's a long silence.

The video's finally been turned off, but it doesn't really matter: I'll be hearing it for the rest of my life anyway.

She kind of broke my heart.

My brain is starting to switch off, but on the edges of my vision I can see everybody in the room now whispering at each other uncomfortably. "English girl…" "It *was* her", "Harriet dumped *him*? I did *not* see *that* coming."

Then they turn self-consciously to face me.

Another deep silence.

"Well," a voice finally says from the back of the room. "This is a bit *awkward*, isn't it?"

With one blink I refocus my eyes just enough to see Alexa, sitting at the back in one of the little plastic seats I carefully put out, wearing black jeans, a plain grey T-shirt and enormous black heels. She's the only thing in this room that isn't bouncing rays of light in every direction.

I don't know when she arrived or how long she's been sitting there.

Frankly, I no longer care.

"I think that's enough *drama* for me," Alexa says, standing up. "Girls, my parents are away for the weekend, the home cinema is set up and I've got an unlimited supply of pizza. Coming?"

There's a short pause while Ananya assesses Alexa.

Something unspoken is passing between them.

It's not *friendship*, exactly – or not my definition of the word – but it's similar. Understanding. Respect. Eleven years of shared history and experiences that aren't going anywhere.

"Yes," Ananya says finally, looking me up and down. "What a total waste of time. You were right, Lexi: Harriet's not who we thought she was. What a *geek*. Let's go."

Ananya's not a minion, I realise dully as she gives me one more icy assessment: she's Alexa's equal and always has been.

"OhmyGodthisissuchareliefI'mso*hungry*whatfilmare wegoingtowatchanddoyouthinkwecangetpepperoni because…"

Olivia, maybe not so much.

I look at Alexa emptily for a few seconds. There's a snake found in Mexico and Central America called the

405

Cantil. It has deadly venom, but instead of chasing prey it simply stays where it is and wiggles the yellow end of its tail. Birds, frogs, little mammals and lizards assume it's a worm and approach enthusiastically.

They never even see it coming.

Alexa didn't need to destroy me this time. She just had to sit back quietly and watch me destroy myself.

My nemesis gives me a little *told you so* shrug.

Then – without another word – she and the two girls I thought were my friends walk out of the room without so much as a glance over their shoulders, taking five or six other girls with them.

I look vaguely at the only one of my 'gang' left.

India's face is twisted in disgust, her top lip is curled and disdain is pretty much dripping from the tips of her fingers. "*So* disappointing," she agrees coldly, narrowing her eyes at the room.

Then she grabs a sandwich off the table, pulls the door open, shouts "*ANANYA, WAIT!*" at the top of her voice and slams it behind her.

I turn slowly towards the rest of the party.

They're now shifting awkwardly from foot to foot, trying to work out where to look. Frankly, I'm not surprised they're so uncomfortable. In 44 BC Roman conspirators threw a big gathering for Julius Caesar and then stabbed him to death.

This party is even worse than that one.

"I think maybe you should all go too," I say blankly. "Please."

I just want them out of here now.

They're not my friends, and I'm not theirs. Honestly, I don't even blame them. It's starting to hit me that I was using them just as much as they were using me. I still can't remember most of their names: I was so busy trying to fill my life with as many people as possible, I didn't really care who they all were.

And it looks like they didn't care who I was either.

There are a few guilty nods, even sympathetic glances.

But then one by one the rest of my classmates filter out of the room and into the dark.

"*We're* not going," Lydia says, staunchly folding her arms in the doorway. "*We* love you, Harriet. You've still got *us.*"

"*Yeah*," Fee adds. "We still think you're *awesome*."

But it's too late.

"Thank you," I say, gently spinning them towards the exit. "But the party's over now."

I usher them out of the door.

Then I walk back into the darkness I made, covered in stars, and sit in the middle of the empty dance floor.

You actually think that everything will be different now?

She's still Harriet Manners.

There are many survival strategies in nature.

The tortoise draws its head and limbs up inside a hard outer shell, rendering it completely protected from predators. The hedgehog has damaging prickles; the skunk ejects sulphuric compounds from its bottom. When threatened, the mother-of-pearl caterpillar launches itself backwards at thirty-nine times its walking speed, somersaulting the entire way.

But all I'm thinking about now is a sea snail.

When I was three years old, scientists discovered a *Crysomallon Squamiferum* at the bottom of the ocean: the only creature in the known world to literally build metal into its coat of armour. They found that its thick shell is made from layers of metallic sulphides, including iron pyrite.

Otherwise known as *fool's gold*.

I tried so hard.

I wanted so badly to be the glittering girl: confident, stylish, brave, inspiring. I so wanted to protect myself from my normal life. But all I was doing was covering myself in a layer of fake gold and I couldn't deceive anyone for long: just one little hole, and the world could see the real me again.

And I was pulled out and torn to pieces.

I look down at my shiny outfit, and then up at the cut-out stars. Then at the sparkle I threw all over the floor.

It was right there in the theme: I wrote it myself.

All that glitters… is not gold.

I don't have an Inner Star at all. I was the glitter and the fool, and now I'm right back to the beginning again.

Except worse, because Nat and Toby have gone too.

This time I've lost everything.

87

Tokyo – June (4 months ago)

"3,358 seconds."

We passed through tiny side streets of Tokyo, past dark wooden houses with white fabric hanging from the doorways like half-open gifts, under little archways and blue curved roofs, popping out into bustling, noisy roads and then back into the quietness again.

"3,247 seconds."

We raced past a little train station.

"2,320," I told him, as we ran over a beautiful wooden bridge stretching across a canal, painted red and stuck with long, red flags. "Nick, where on earth are you taking me?"

He laughed and turned round.

"Harriet, do you have some kind of exploding watch you haven't told me about? Because if you have, I think it's only fair I know about it. It is *seriously* going to

affect my schedule."

I grinned. "Say that again."

"Schedule."

"Again."

"Harriet Manners, don't you *dare* affect my schedule."

I pulled Nick to a stop and stood on my tiptoes so I could kiss him. "I love it when you talk itineraries to me, Lion Boy."

Nick kissed me back. Then he leant forward until I could feel his breath in my ear and whispered:

"*Timetable.*"

There are 7,000,000,000,000,000,000,000,000,000 atoms in my body, and at that precise moment every single one of them was his.

"2,228 seconds," I whispered back.

And he took my hand again and started running as I kept counting down: through the quieter streets, into the large, silver buildings of Roppongi. We ran over grey pavements, under an enormous, thirty foot bronze spider with an egg sac containing marble eggs and towards a huge, glass skyscraper.

Then we caught our breath in a lift that shot us fifty-seven floors into the air.

"At what point in our relationship," I said, leaning against the wall and panting slightly, "did we decide there would be so much running? I mean, you've met me before, right? I'm not exactly renowned for my athletic abilities."

"Well, my little geek," Nick said as the lift doors opened, "did you know that when you run you spend more time in the air than you do touching the ground? So if it helps at all, that means it's the closest we can get to flying."

Then he wiggled his eyebrows at me.

I glared at him crossly. That did help, yes. Nick was officially the only person in the world who could make me voluntarily do physical activity.

"Whatever," I said faux-grumpily. "If I really wanted to fly that badly I could just get on a trampoline and…"

I stopped talking.

While I was muttering we'd walked up tiny stairs on to a wooden deck surrounded by barriers of glass. People were scattered around us, taking photos, and in every direction was Tokyo. Stretched out and sparkling in the sunshine, leant against a backdrop of clear, bright blue.

And – far away – on the horizon, was a little cone shape.

Mount Fuji.

Nick reached out, tugged me into his side and kissed my head as I stared at it in amazement. I wanted to see

Tokyo, and he had given me all of it in one go.

"Without equal," he grinned, holding his arms out with a flourish and bowing. "Told you I could do it in the allocated time."

"Oh my God, that's so romantic. Say that again."

"Allocated," he said into my hair, "time."

"*Thank you*," I whispered, kissing the edge of his chin. Then I looked at my watch. "Although, you've still got fifty-two seconds left, according to my calculations."

"Don't need them," Nick laughed. "Actually, I didn't need any of them in the first place. I was just making you run for the sake of it."

I blink at him. "What are you talking about? This isn't your favourite bit of Tokyo?"

"Nope." He touched the end of my nose with his finger. "I was there already. My favourite bit of anywhere is you."

And then he kissed me.

Slowly, I pull my satchel out from under a table.

Gently, I touch the little coloured beads hanging in a circle round my neck: Mercury, Venus, Earth, Mars, Jupiter, Saturn, Uranus, Neptune and Pluto.

My very last gift from Nick.

Then I open my bag, tug a box from inside it and start pulling everything out carefully, as if I'm playing a very volatile game of Operation.

A Clothes Show ticket from the first time I ever met Nick under a table.

An advert torn from a magazine, depicting a boy, a white kitten and a girl, jumping in the Russian snow: the first time he ever held my hand.

The tiny toy lion he brought me when I was sick with flu, and the (unused) tissue and (unopened) packet of Lemsip that were supposed to make me better, but I kept instead.

A little postcard with a T-rex on the front that arrived a

414

few days after I said I had an inner dinosaur in Tokyo, and the letter that followed our race from the roundabout: *Told you I was faster. xx*

The folded, crumpled 1,000-yen note he gave me on the edge of Lake Motosu.

A very, very dry blue sock.

Finally – when the box has been excavated until it's all lying in front of me, like a strange archaeological dig – I get a pristine envelope out. I pull a clean, smooth piece of paper from it and unfold it gently.

And I start reading.

Dear Harriet,

You're going to be OK.

I know this, because you're Harriet Manners. You walk through this world seeing every tiny detail, but you don't see yourself. You don't see how beautiful you are, or how graceful: even in your clumsiness. You don't see how kind you are, even in your tempers. Or how brave and strong you are, even when you're scared. You never notice just how much you touch the people around you, just by being you.

So I know you're going to be OK, but I don't know if I will be. I have to go back now to a world without polar bear hairs and matching snowflakes: without knowing that otters fall asleep holding hands to stop themselves drifting apart. Without being told, at random, that duels are legal in Paraguay, or how many senses a shark has (eight) or what shape an octopus's pupil is (rectangular). I have to go back to a world that just doesn't spin the way you always spin it.

And I don't want to.

I think we've made a mistake, Harriet. I want to make this work, and I'll do whatever it takes. I'll come back to England, I'll take up modelling again, I'll travel back and forth. Whatever I have to do, I'll do it.

Just send one word and I'll come back. But if I don't hear from you again, I'll understand. And I'll do my best to move on.

Three words, three stars: Alnitak, ALnilam and Mintaka.

LionBoy xxxx

89

I stare at the box in my lap.

Oh, you thought I meant I carry the past around with me *metaphorically*?

No, I meant literally.

At the bottom of my satchel, under all my schoolbooks and fact books and dictionaries and thesauruses, so I know it's there.

I don't always tell you everything, you know.

I'm an unreliable narrator. We all are.

We don't unfold ourselves like pieces of paper for everyone to see: that's not how humans work. There are always parts of us we shut away or hide. Bits of ourselves we can't touch because they're too precious and buried too deep.

Fragments of truth we barely admit to ourselves.

Because sometimes editing our own story is the only way to get through it.

So here are the three facts you didn't know.

418

Fact 1

My letters were going abroad, but they weren't going to Australia. They were going to a little village in Brazil, so that Bunty could look after them.

"Darling," she said when I rang her in tears from my bedroom in Greenway, New York, five weeks ago. "Sometimes all you need is a good cry and an even better pen. Write it all down and send it to me, and I'll keep it safe for you."

So that's what I did.

When I couldn't hold it in any more, I pulled my heartbreak out like a splinter and sent it to my grandmother to look after. Because it helped, somehow: knowing she would protect the parts of me I couldn't hang on to any longer.

It made me lighter.

Fact 2

What happened on Brooklyn Bridge didn't stop being true, just because it hurt.

Nick and I had three choices.

a) He could carry on living a life he didn't enjoy just

to see me: doing a job he hated, putting his future on hold, flying to and fro across the world for a few grabbed moments together. I could watch him grow increasingly lost, unanchored and unhappy: divided between a real life and a girl he loved.

b) We could stay together, seven thousand miles apart, and watch as our connection slowly shattered every day: until the awkward silences lengthened, the frozen moments expanded, the distances pulled at us, until finally all we had left were memories and stars.

Or c) I could force Nick to move on.

Instead of tearing him to pieces so I could keep a few bits for myself, I could make him take all of it with him. To live wholeheartedly without me in a way that would, eventually, make him happier.

Which is – I think, from his voice on that video – what he's started doing.

Because....

Fact 3

I got Nick's letter six days before I left New York.

I've had it all along.

So he didn't reply to my letters because he didn't get

them. He doesn't know how much I miss him because I haven't told him. And he doesn't know why I broke his heart because I couldn't let him know mine was broken too.

Over the last year, Nick has made so many sacrifices for me. He has been there when I needed him, gone when I didn't: appeared and reappeared and disappeared, entirely for my sake. He has adored every bit of me, without question and without judgement.

He has given me the kind of romance some people never get in an entire lifetime.

And I'll be honest: if he'd tried one more time – one more letter, one text, one single flower – I'd have crumbled and changed my mind: it would have been impossible not to. So I guess the lonelier I got, the more I waited and hoped for it as hard as I could.

But he didn't. Instead, he grabbed happiness and started moving forward again.

Which means I finally know I made the right decision.

I may not be the girl Nick thinks I am.

Over the last month, I've been lost, scared, weak, unhappy and – at points – quite shockingly stupid. I've lost my best friends, clung to the wrong people for the wrong reasons and done a whole lot of things I'm not proud of.

But this is not one of them.

The Oxford English Dictionary says that *love* is both a noun and a verb. And – because of Nick – I know now what I didn't know a year ago.

It's not enough to say it; it's not even enough to feel it.

Love is a *doing* word: an action you have to complete continuously, every day, however much it hurts. Whatever it ends up costing you. And this time loving Nick properly means letting him go.

After all, he has saved me, over and over again.

It's my turn now to save him back.

Even if it means being on my own.

90

Suffice to say, the letter isn't clean and smooth any more.

Two teardrops have hit the page, and are now making their slow, wobbly way downward: smudging the pen like little blue snail trails.

Which doesn't really matter, to be honest.

I know every word so off by heart they might as well be engraved there.

Patiently, I wait until the tears drop off the bottom of the paper. Then I give my letter a gentle kiss, fold it in half again and put it back in my Nick Box. Followed by the yen note, the T-rex, the Lemsip and tissue, the toy lion, the advert, the ticket. I take the planets necklace off carefully and put it on top, straightening it out so it doesn't get tangled.

Then I grab the lid.

"Harriet?"

Quick as a flash, I wipe a hand across my eyes, slam the lid on top of the box and cram it back into my satchel.

423

Should have locked the front door. *Idiot.*

"Mmmm?"

"Are you OK?"

I turn with wet eyes to the doorway, and through the sparkling shine in my eyes all I can see is purple.

"Absolutely," I manage, nodding. "Fine. Superb. Coolioko. Why wouldn't I be?"

India walks across the room quietly and then sits down next to me with her hair gleaming like ink.

"First of all," she says, "because that was officially the most hideous party anyone has ever thrown in the history of parties, ever. For future generations, that party will be the one parents tell their children about to dissuade them from ever throwing parties."

I nod. To say the least. "I know."

"Second of all, because you're sitting on the floor crying into a sock."

I blink at Nick's blue sock, still in my hand.

I thought I'd put it back in the box. Apparently I'm still clutching it to my face like a toddler with a tiny, faceless teddy bear.

"Ah." Flushing, I shove it back in my satchel. "And third of all I just said *coolioko* and that's a made-up word?"

"Nope," India says, pointing at the ceiling. "Indus.

Pavo. Carina. Mensa. Volans. Chamaeleon. Reticulum. Octans. They're constellations in the southern hemisphere. You've stuck the sky on the wrong way up."

91

Authenticity.

Spiritual awareness, truth, vision.

These are just a few of the psychological qualities we associate with purple, as I discovered when I was researching my immortal duck outfit.

It's also the traditional colour of royalty.

This is because the original purple dye required 250,000 individual *purpura* shellfish – hence *purple* – to extract enough to make one single ounce. By the third century BC, Tyrian purple dye cost more than gold and wearing it was a sign that you were really worth something.

As I stare at India's bright purple hair and cool but unshakeable expression, I'm starting to realise that maybe her hair colour is perfect for her in more ways than one.

"You came back."

She grabs another sandwich from the table. "I like these," she says, stuffing it in her mouth. Then she swallows. "Obviously I came back. I only left to tell

Ananya she could walk home and then push her into a bush." She points at a pink scratch glowing on the right side of her temple and another on her upper lip. "Sadly I ended up in it too. She's always been a bit scrappy."

I blink at her. "Always?"

"Yeah. Grandad was worried she'd got in with a bad crowd, so when we moved here I promised to pry her back out again."

All known mammals have tongues.

In which case I've no idea what I've just turned into: all I can do is stare at India in total silence.

"You didn't know Ananya was my cousin?" India says, black eyebrows creasing back into essay ticks. "We've got the same *surname*, Harriet. Didn't you think that was a bit of a coincidence?"

Well, obviously *now* I think it is.

But I was far too distracted by everything else over the last fortnight to make the connection.

Actually, now I'm thinking of it, I should probably have guessed anyway. They have the same dark skin, the same icy expressions: the same subtly terrifying demeanour. And I *thought* it was weird that after only six weeks India was bossing Ananya around and calling her *Banana*.

"So you're not disappointed with *me*?"

"Don't be ridiculous," India says sharply, taking

another sandwich. "I knew you weren't still with Nick straight away: nobody stares at a desk for twenty-five seconds in silence if they're still in a happy relationship. I've hated Alexa from the beginning, and I liked you as soon as I saw you chatting to Steve and helping him pick up tissue. I knew what side I wanted to be on."

My brain makes a little clicking sound.

OK, that's enough now. India, stalking coldly to my side in the rain. Icily standing up for me in the common room. Forcing Ananya and Liv to follow her.

But all the long, cold stares of disdain...

"I know," she sighs, rolling her eyes. "I have resting mean face. It's a problem." She grimaces. "Believe it or not I'm actually quite nice."

I totally and utterly believe her.

Despite the similarities, I've just noticed the key difference between India and her cousin. When Ananya smiles, it doesn't reach her eyes: with India, it's the opposite way round.

"So I'm not a let-down at all?" I just need to check. "You haven't been conned into thinking I'm cool by my fake social status and glamorous part-time job?"

"Harriet," she sighs, standing up, "I recognise the constellations of the southern hemisphere off by heart and can classify the properties of crystal. I'm not sure *cool*

428

is on my radar." She glares towards the door. "Sadly, I'm going to have to tell Grandad I can't get Ananya away from the bad crowd. She *is* the bad crowd."

Slowly, warmth starts to spread through me: as if I'm sitting in sunshine, coated in rainbows, curled up in the middle of a hot-water bottle.

I did it.

After everything, I made a real friend. A proper one. One who likes me for the right reasons: because I throw terrible star parties and pick up loo roll and make buddies with caretakers called Steve. (I don't know where he is, by the way. His house must be *considerably* further than twenty minutes away.)

And more importantly, I like *her*.

I always have.

"Do you want to go to my house?" I say enthusiastically, standing up. "I have a game of scrabble we can play, and there's the rest of the star quiz to do and—"

"Yeah, go on then," India says, grabbing the tray of sandwiches. "That sounds cool. Can we take the lights? It'll help me focus."

She unplugs Tabby's night-light and starts heading smoothly towards the exit, hair like a chocolate bar wrapper.

Quickly, I grab my satchel and wipe my eyes on my wrist to make them as dry as possible.

Then I start following her.

"Oh I don't *think* so," an angry voice says. "Stop right there before I rip your flaming eyes right out of your sockets and use them as ping-pong balls."

"Yeah," another voice says, not quite as angrily. "Ping-pong balls. For *mice.*"

And standing in the doorway are Nat and Toby.

92

I can only see the back of India's head, but I'm pretty sure her face hasn't altered.

I guarantee it's set in exactly the same expression as always.

"That's sweet," she says flatly, eating another sandwich. "Who are you?"

"I'm your *worst nightmare*," Nat hisses at her, folding her arms. "I'm the girl who's going to tug your toenails off and turn them into earrings and then make you *wear* them. I'm the girl who's going to pull out your eyelashes and eyebrows, hair by hair, until you're totally bald."

"*Yeah*," Toby says, scowling and folding his arms too. "And then she's going to turn them into wigs. Little tiny wigs. For *hamsters*."

"Stop talking about rodents, Toby," Nat sighs. "Seriously. Rodents have no part in this threatening process at all."

"Again," India says calmly. "Who are you?"

"Toby Pilgrim," Toby says chirpily, his face clearing abruptly. He holds his hand out and I can see he's wearing a T-shirt that says I AM A, followed by a picture of a rock next to a star. "It's very nice to meet you properly, India. I believe you're in my year at school, aren't you? I've heard you're an absolute whizz at physics."

Nat rolls her eyes. "Oh my God, Toby, you're useless."

Then she turns back, all fierce again.

"So, you're the famous *India*, are you? That makes sense. Well you can just put the sandwiches down, missy. You make Harriet cry again and I swear, I will conjure accessories out of body parts you didn't even know you had."

I've been watching this entire conversation with my hand still up to one eye, frozen in shock.

I blink and then look at it. What?

"Oh no," I say quickly, stepping forward. "I'm not crying because of India. She came back to help me, actually. She's my friend."

"*Sure* she is," Nat snarls, flicking her eyes between us. "I bet she's just *lovely*. Friends of Ananya and Alexa are friends of *ours*, right?"

"Ah," India says, nodding. "Right. Gotcha. No, I hate them too if that helps. Evil witches."

"*Well* aren't you just…" Nat stops. I can see her brain

trying to fit this into her argument. "Oh. Well. OK, then," she says slightly less fiercely. Then she rallies bravely for a last stand. "And you've not come back here just to steal snacks?"

"In fairness, they're surprisingly good." India looks at the tray of sandwiches. "Want one?"

I can see Nat evaluating the situation and assessing India. I've never seen anyone not baulk at Nat's open, transcendent fury before: it's like watching a tiger growl at a unicorn. "What are they?"

"Chicken and strawberry jam."

That does it: the last ounce of fight evaporates out of my best friend. She nods and takes one.

"We invented these. They're awesome, right? Lots of protein and carbohydrates. I'm Nat. I like your hair a lot. Did you have to bleach it first?"

"Purple is the most powerful visible wavelength of electromagnetic energy," Toby says nodding.

Then he starts rushing around the room.

"Ooh, Harriet, *well done*," he adds. "This is an *excellent* party. Although what happened to the sherbet flying saucers? Or the Magic Stars and Starmix? And there's no Star Wars stuff here at all. Nat, I *told* you we should have helped her. She's missed out *loads* of important space-based puns."

I'm still staring at both of them.

What? Just… *what*?

Did the last two weeks completely not happen? Have I been imagining all of it? First the Levaire advert magicked me out of it. Now Toby's back to being Toby again and Nat appears to have forgotten we hate each other with the heat of a trillion suns.

Is this like one of those really bad television serials where I find out I've been in a coma the entire time?

Am I awake? Am I even *alive*?

"Umm, hello?" I say as Toby grabs a camera out of his bag and starts taking photos of the ceiling. "We're not talking to each other, remember? What are you both doing here?"

"Harriet," Nat says a lot more gently. "I think there's something we need to tell you."

93

I suddenly feel a bit sick.

"Oh my God," I say, sitting abruptly on a chair. "Toby and you aren't… You're not a *couple*, are you? Theo's not just a *cover*, is he?"

It would make sense: all the weird behaviour. All the sneaking around and running away.

A gross but weirdly logical kind of sense.

"A couple of what?" Toby says, taking a photo of the tablecloth. "That's not a very specific question, Harriet. You'll never get into MI5 at this rate."

Nat's still staring at me with a blank face.

Then she abruptly looks like she's going to be sick too.

"Oh my God, no. *Ugh*. What are you *thinking*? Thanks for that visual, Harriet. I'm going to have to clean my brain with a wire pad when I get home." She pauses. "But the second bit wasn't totally wrong."

I blink at her. "Theo's… not real?"

"He is real. But I've only seen him twice in the last

435

two weeks. We've only just started dating, and I'm not *desperate*."

There's a silence.

"You are making no sense at all," I tell her finally. "Then what have you been doing?"

"Toby and I have been avoiding you," Nat says flatly. "Both of us. Because I told him to."

My eyes widen slightly. *I'm not allowed to see you. I'll have to check.* It was *Nat* who was forcing Toby not to see me? Not Jasper at all?

Oops. I probably owe somebody a pretty big apology.

"But... *why*?"

Nat thinks about it for a few seconds. "Harriet, do you remember what you said in the launderette?"

"Yes. I said I had made you a customised Monopoly set and you could use a sewing machine as your placer."

The corner of her mouth twists slightly. "You said we were welded, Harriet. And then you said *I've got you and Toby anyway, so what else does a sensible girl really need*?"

I hate to say it, but for just a moment Nat temporarily transforms into me. Her voice gets slightly higher and posher, her eyes get very round and she does a little toss of her head, exactly the way I do.

I blink at her again.

Nope. Still no idea what she's talking about. "So?"

"*So,* Harriet. We already had the plan, but that just confirmed for me that it was the right thing to do. What would you have done if Toby was hanging out with you at school from the beginning and I was hanging out with you afterwards? *Honestly?*"

"I'd have hung out with Toby at school and you afterwards," I say without hesitation. "My first day sucked."

"Exactly," Nat says slowly. "190 days, Harriet. 1,330 hours is a *really* long time to stop living. You're my best friend. When you're unhappy, I'm unhappy. Not being welded was the only thing I could do."

"But…" They've both been avoiding me on purpose? To force me to make friends? "Why couldn't you just tell me that?"

"Because if you *knew* then the plan would never have worked. You'd have just buried yourself in a book again and waited it out. Like you always do."

Nat's right again. Making friends is *hard.* And I'm a big fan of both books and of being in my comfort zone.

"I watched you shut down after you came home from New York," she says more gently. "I knew that if sixth form didn't start well, you were going to just keep closing unless I did something drastic. And this time I wasn't going to be at school to stop you."

"Didn't I do *brilliantly*?" Toby says jubilantly, puffing his chest out. "I was *so* rude to you, Harriet. I really gave it some welly. You thought I didn't like you *at all*, didn't you. *Yeah*."

He holds up a hand to high-five Nat.

"Sadly I just forgot a few things, Harriet," my best friend sighs, ignoring Toby's hand and then holding up a closed fist. "I didn't know the Yuka Ito campaign would come out or factor in the impact it would have." She holds up a finger. "You see the best in everyone, indiscriminately, all of the time, and are frequently a terrible judge of character." She holds up another one.

Then she holds the final finger up and thrusts it in Toby's face.

"And Toby is an idiot who takes everything literally. I said *give her a bit of space for a couple of weeks*, not *make her feel like a pariah*, you total pillock."

Enjoy all your new friends, Harriet.

Toby was reporting back. Nat was leaving me alone because she thought I was successfully making friends.

"Exactly," she says, nodding even though I haven't said anything. "I was *so* happy you were having a party, then we argued, but tonight Mum finally remembered to give me the invitation and I realised what was probably going to happen. Toby and I ran here as fast as we could." She tilts her head to the side affectionately. "Night of Stars. You silly billy."

Scientists say we have different types of tears.

Basal tears, to protect our eyes. Reflex tears, to remove irritants. And emotional tears, that occur when our feelings get too much and our tear ducts can't handle it, erupt and spill over.

As my eyes start to fill up again, I think my body just can't fit my new burst of happiness in.

It needs to let some out, like steam out of a kettle.

My party can go sit on an anthill, frankly: I couldn't care less.

I've got my best friends back.

"I'm sorry," I say, abruptly lobbing myself at Nat and throwing my arms round her neck. "I'm so sorry for everything I said. I *do* need you. You *aren't* ruining my life or holding me back. I didn't mean *any* of it."

"I know," Nat grins into my neck. "I'm sorry too."

"Me too," Toby says, reaching into his bag. "Although, in my defence, Natalie was very much the mastermind of this plot and I was just the obedient slave with your well-being at the forefront of my mind."

"Thanks, Tobes," I say, grabbing him in an impulsive hug. "I've really, really missed you, you know. Please don't do that again."

"I won't," he says, waiting patiently for me to let go. "You don't need to worry, Harriet Manners. Toby Pilgrim Is Here, TM."

He sticks a little round green sticker on my arm.

India stands quietly for a few seconds.

Then she says, "Oh what the hell," and stiffly puts her arms round all of us. "Don't hug me back. I've eaten too many sandwiches."

"See?" Nat laughs. "My plan totally worked. New friend. KABOOM. At this rate you'll have, like, twelve by the end of the year."

There's a sound from the doorway.

"*All right there, party people, DJ Earthling is back in the…* Oh, the little minxes. They've bloomin' gone and left you, haven't they."

Steve's standing in the doorway with his grey hair sticking upwards and half a pasty in his hand. That's where he was: he obviously stopped for a snack on the way back.

He looks around, shaking his head.

"I'm telling you," he says fiercely. "They'll get their comeuppance. Just mark my words. I won't be replacing the loo roll in any of the sixth form toilets for the next week."

I grin at him.

I'm starting to realise that real friendship doesn't always turn up with a bang. It creeps in quietly, without glitz and glamour, without show or fuss.

Whether it's somebody playing CDs at your party, or giving you a few minutes in the desert to watch the stars alone; whether it's leaving a new job behind to spend three days in Morocco because your stepdaughter is sad, or spending a day arranging a gift in a shed because your daughter is heartbroken.

Whether it's doing a stranger a favour, or standing by someone in the rain, or sending flowers from thousands of miles away, or a Hug Pillow when you can't give them a hug.

Whether it's reading the letters that your granddaughter doesn't know how not to write.

And – as I stand in the Guide Hut and watch everyone start packing away my party without complaint or judgement – it suddenly hits me: I had friends all along.

I was just looking for them in the wrong places, that's all.

"Don't you worry, poppet," Steve mutters crossly as he gets a broom out and starts sweeping up the bits of glitter into a plastic pan, "you're going to be OK."

"I know," I say with a bright smile.

Because I already am.

94

My parents are suspiciously unsurprised to see us.

In fact, if I didn't know better I'd think they didn't believe my party was going to be a roaring success and were prepared for catastrophe.

Which would be offensive if it wasn't… you know.

Totally spot on.

"Hello," Annabel says smoothly as I walk back into the house with Nat, Toby and India close behind me. "Would you like some dinner?"

There are six steaming pizzas in front of her.

Either my stepmother was ready for us to come home early and magically guessed how many of us there would be, or she's recently developed the appetite of a baby blue whale crossed with one of the Mario brothers.

Or…

Or Steve was reporting back and both my parents have been driving past the Guide Hut continuously all evening, keeping tabs on everything.

Of course they have.

"Hi, Mrs Manners," Nat says, flopping herself on the floor and pulling an ecstatic Tabitha on to her lap. "This is India. Please feel free to interrogate her relentlessly before we accept her into the gang."

"So far we've already discovered lack of empathy for hamsters and no respect for authority," Toby says, grabbing a slice of pepperoni. "As you can tell from the nasal piercing and general failure to bow down to the colours of nature."

"Interrogate away," India nods coolly. "The ring just stops me picking my nose and the purple makes it easier to cross roads without being run over – nobody ever misses me standing at a crossing."

Everybody laughs as my phone beeps.

"Harriet?" Annabel says gently as I grab it out of my bag. "You had some visitors, sweetheart. They left a few things, so I've put most of them in your bedroom."

I nod and look at the message I've just received.

Hannah, Levaire hated Kevin. Went a different direction. Will pay 300 for time spent. Stephanie.

I can't help noticing we're back to *Stephanie* again, and no kisses.

The science project is coming up next term.

Maybe I should focus mine on the careful subliminal analysis of text messages and use of nicknames: I think there's potentially an entire minefield of untapped psychological investigation.

Weirdly, I don't mind as much as I probably should.

I still had an amazing trip, and that quantity of money never felt very real anyway. This feels a lot more realistic. Plus, it'll still cover everything I borrowed from Annabel, so everybody kind of wins.

I watch everyone chattering happily for a few seconds, then put my phone back in my bag, climb the stairs and push open my bedroom door.

Where I abruptly stop in amazement.

There are books *everywhere*.

Heaps of books piled on my desk, on my floor, on my bed, on the fireplace, on the windowsill. Every fact book I've handed out over the last ten days is back in my room, except with one subtle difference: there is now a tiny pink sticker on the front of each of them.

I pick one up and look at it:

FACT 1: Harriet Manners is clever.

Then another:

FACT 2: Harriet Manners is funny.

And another:

FACT 3: Harriet Manners is kind.

The final one of which says:

FACT 42: Thank you for being so nice to us, Harriet Manners. Lydia, Fee, Soph and Keira xxx

I swallow a lump – even though I'm not entirely sure they're using the word *fact* accurately and we may have to discuss it. Then I pick up a photo Annabel has propped against a mug on my desk.

It's of a little brown monkey, sitting on the stump of a tree with the Atlas Mountains behind him.

Because here's the final fact of my own that I didn't tell you:

Fact 4

The last thing Annabel and I did before we left Morocco was ask Ali to take Richard (monkey, not Dad) to a monkey sanctuary a hundred miles away.

We bought him and set him free.

Then we paid for the snakes and did the same to them.

"Harriet?" Annabel calls up the stairs. "Are you coming down? The pizza's getting cold."

I nod and put the photo down. "One minute!"

There's just one thing left I have to do.

I make a space in between all the books on my bed.

Then I sit down and pull the box out of my bag.

Tokyo – June (4 months ago)

"You could stay, you know. There are multiple octopuses in Tokyo who haven't attacked you yet, Manners. You're taking so much away from so many."

I laughed. "Did you know that an anxious octopus will sometimes literally *eat* itself, Nick? I don't think it's fair to upset any more of them: it could get messy."

Then I glanced over his shoulder at Narita airport.

Bunty was doing some kind of juggling act for a security guard, but his patience was clearly running thin and the last call for our flight back to London had already been made.

"I have to go," I said, wrapping my arms round his waist and looking up. "I'm sorry."

Nick looked down with his shortened hair all ruffled and his brown eyes narrowed.

"OK. Hold out your hand." I obediently held it out, and he slotted his fingers between mine. "What kind of table joint is this, again?"

With a flash, I suddenly remembered the first time we ever met. I was so anxious: hiding under a table at The Clothes Show, trying – as always – to escape from the real world.

Nick had been so kind. So calm.

He had understood me from the beginning.

I was just looking for unusual table joints. I thought this particular table looked very... solid. In terms of construction. And I thought I'd have a closer look. You know. From... underneath.

I looked up at my boy on the Tokyo pavement and tried to memorise every detail before I left. Every black eyelash, every dark curl: the little line in the corner of his mouth, the tiny mole on his cheek, the sharpness of his teeth.

I tried to tuck away every single piece of him somewhere safe, where I could never lose it.

"Finger joints?" I asked with a small smile.

"They're dovetail," Nick said: just like the first time. He curled his fingers round mine until they were locked together and grinned the smile that went all the way round and split me and my entire world in half. "Goodbye, Harriet Manners."

Then he leant down and kissed me until it felt like we were touching in space.

Welded permanently.

I wait for a few seconds with my eyes shut and my hand on the box, and I watch Nick's beautiful face flicker, like a bright light on a wall. It flickers and flickers, fading a little every time.

When I finally open my eyes, it's gone.

"Goodbye, Nicholas Hidaka," I say gently.

Then I smile and put the box on the floor.

I take a deep breath.

And – with all the strength I have left – I push the past under my bed.

95

Glow-worms aren't worms, they're beetles.

Koala bears aren't bears – they're marsupials – and Bombay duck is made out of dry fish. Black-eyed peas are beans, Guinea pigs are neither pigs nor from Guinea.

What I'm trying to say is: things aren't always what you think they are. You can look at something for a long, long time and still not see it properly at all.

I guess that includes me.

"Harriet?" Annabel says as I get to the bottom of the stairs. The living room has abruptly emptied, and the lights in the house have all gone off. "Did you do everything you needed to do?"

She gives me a steady look, and I know she knows.

About everything.

I've no idea *how* – magic, possibly, or hidden cameras – but she's staring at my face as if everything I have ever thought or will ever think is written there in ink.

I don't envy her: it can't be very easy reading.

"Yes," I nod. "Where is everybody?"

"In the garden, waiting for you." She pauses for a few seconds. "Harriet, I know about your list."

Of course she does. "How?"

"You left it open on your laptop just before we left for Morocco. I saw it when I was packing the suitcases."

I can feel a flush starting on my cheeks.

How embarrassing. It wasn't even grammatically *correct*.

"Harriet," Annabel says, sitting on the bottom stair and patting the bit next to her, "you're a silly billy, you know that?"

OK: that's, like, the third time I've been called that recently. Do I have another Post-it stuck on my back I'm not aware of? "I do know that, yes," I say, sitting down. "People keep telling me."

Annabel laughs.

"Harriet, you go to school even when it's hard there for you. You model, even though it scares you. Your first thought on making money was not to spend it on yourself, but to help others. You left Nat alone to be with her boyfriend when you needed her, you invited the world and its wife to your party so they didn't feel left out. You cleaned the house every time your father messed it up so

I wouldn't have to do it, and you didn't even mention it."

I open my mouth and then close it again.

Seriously. Somewhere in this house: cameras.

"I didn't realise until you were too busy today to do it," Annabel explains with a little smile. "Your father genuinely thinks he's the eponymous Shoemaker, and elves are coming in through the windows and doing it all for him."

"Oh." I shrug. Dad's mind must be a glorious place to live. "Well, you were tired. It's no biggy."

"I was, and it is." Annabel smiles again. "I'm not finished. You have a little following of fans because you remembered what it was like to be young and new, and you defend people even when they have been unkind to you."

I open my mouth again.

Oh my God: she's got them at school *too*? Is *nothing* private any more?

"What I'm saying, Harriet, is you *are* confident. You *are* brave. You have your own style, and you have always inspired everyone around you. And you know exactly who you are and stick to it when it's hard."

I can feel my cheeks getting red. She's totally memorised every line of my list and watched me working my way through it, badly.

"I do try too hard though. At literally everything."

"You really do." Annabel's mouth twitches. "It's one of my favourite things about you."

We sit in silence for a few minutes while I unsuccessfully try to swallow another lump in my throat. It's kind of annoying, sometimes: having a parent who knows everything about you.

I wouldn't give it up for anything.

Finally, Annabel stands and brushes her pinstripe suit down. "We've got a little something waiting for you in the garden. Coming?"

I nod. Then, side by side, my stepmother and I walk down the dark hallway with all the lights switched off, into a dark kitchen with the curtains inexplicably closed.

I'm just about to ask why the house has turned into the set of a horror film when my phone beeps.

Wilbur	Every other human in the world
My little doodlebug!	Hello!
Giant apple super zzz –	I'm bored of New York –
So this pigeon is homing.	So I'm coming back to UK
Visage you promptly.	See you soon.
Beer	XXXX

I grin with happiness and put my phone back in my cardi pocket. Then – with a sudden wave of gratitude so strong I nearly have to sit back down again – I impulsively grab my stepmother's hand.

"Thank you, Annabel. For being so kind to me."

She shakes her head.

"If people are kind to you, Harriet, it's because you're kind to them. If people are there for you, it's because you are there for them." She opens the kitchen door and points into the dark. "And if you don't need a list to make you a star, it's because you've always been one."

96

Outside are little patches of light.

They're waving around in the air with loud crackling sounds, spelling out huge letters with trailing lines of glitter.

H. R. T. I. R. E. T.

From the glow of the sparklers, I can see five of the people I love best, lit up and laughing.

Along with my number one dog.

"*Toby*," Nat snaps irritably, waving her firework in the air ferociously, "you're supposed to be making an A, you idiot. Not another T."

"Oh." Toby frowns. "So who's making the T?"

"Who *is* making the tea?" Dad asks. "I'll have one. Four sugars, just a drop of milk." I can't help noticing he has a big black moustache stuck on and is wearing a chef's hat.

Tabby's in her lobster pot, staring in awe at the lights.

Hugo races towards me: paws in my stomach before I've even closed the door.

"No offence, but I am *nailing* this letter *R*," India says coolly. "Seriously. Step your game up, people. It's blatantly the trickiest one."

Then I glance behind them.

In the middle of the garden is an enormous, seven-foot sculpture of a white angel with gold wings. I turn in confusion to Annabel and she winks at me knowingly: it was obviously hand-delivered while I was at my so-called party.

OK, maybe she didn't have cameras at school after all.

Slowly, I walk towards it.

It's incredibly beautiful. The face is delicately shaped, the plaster is smooth and the enormous wings have been covered in tiny gold-painted feathers and attached to the sculpture with a knot of thick white string over the shoulders.

Stuck to the left wing is a little piece of paper.

It's not an angel at all, I realise, as I turn the note over.

It's Icarus.

I was wrong and I'm sorry. Friends? Jasper x

And I can feel the light starting to shine out of me, brighter than it ever has before.

Because I know a few things about space.

I know it's big and dark and lonely. I know that all stars are moving away from each other and 99.9999 per cent of the universe is made up of nothing, including us.

But I also know that there are a lot of things about it we still don't understand.

Scientists discovered very recently that ninety per cent of the universe's light source is inexplicably missing. They can see it, they can measure it, but they don't know where it's coming from.

For just a second, I think maybe I do.

As I watch the people I love, drawing my name in the sky with glitter – as I think about the people I love and miss, all over the world – I wonder briefly if some of that light is coming from us.

If with every act of kindness, we shine a little brighter and the darkness gets a little lighter. With every type of friendship, space gets a little smaller and we get a little closer.

Making our own stars so we're never really alone.

Because however fast the universe pulls apart – however much distance there is between us – these are the ties that will hold us together.

The connections that will never break.

This is how we shine.

Acknowledgements

Thanks to my amazing editor, Ruth Alltimes, for working with me so seamlessly, valiantly and patiently, and for loving Harriet as much as I do. You have been a total champion. Thanks to Kate Shaw: my agent, my friend and my much-needed voice of reason, sense and wisdom at silly-times-o-clock. As always, I couldn't do it without you.

Thanks to the entire, incredible team at HarperCollins, who continue to work tirelessly and passionately behind the scenes as part of Team Geek: especially to Hannah, Sam, Nicola, Carla, Kate, Elorine, Georgia, Lily, Rachel and Mary. This is such a fun boat to be on, and I couldn't hope for better shipmates. Thanks also to Lizzie and Celeste, who have remained stars throughout. Your cuteness and support have been much appreciated.

As always, an infinite, heartfelt chunk of gratitude is owed to my wonderful family. Grandad, Grandma, Dad, Mum, Tig, Dan, Vero, Caro, Louise, Vincent, Judith, Lesley, Ellen, Freya, Rob, Lorraine, Mayne, Chelsea, Dixie and Handsome. It's been a rocky year, and I am so very lucky to have – and have had – you with me; I know you always will be.

Finally, to every reader who has read Harriet, loved Harriet, cheered for Harriet and worried about Harriet over the last couple of years: you are who I write for.

Thank you. xx

Some glittering reviews for the GEEK GIRL books:

"Loved *Geek Girl*. Wise, funny and true, with a proper nerd heroine you're laughing with as much as at. Almost"
James Henry, writer of Smack the Pony and Green Wing

"I would highly recommend *Geek Girl* to anyone who likes a good laugh and enjoys a one-of-a-kind story"
Mia, Guardian Children's Books website

"Smart, sassy and very funny"
Bookseller

"Brilliantly funny and fresh . . . A feel-good satisfying gem"
Books for Keeps

"There's laughter and tears in this hilarious roller-coaster story"
Julia Eccleshare, Sun

"Touching, true, and always very funny... beneath the shiny surface is a heart of solid gold"
Andrea Reece, Lovereading4kids

"I love the zany and warm-hearted way that Holly Smale writes"
Eloise Percy-Davis, age 12, Lovereading4kids

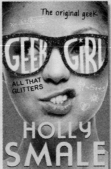

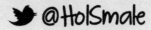